THE FIRST LADY CHATTERLEY

D H LAWRENCE

BLACKTHORN PRESS

Blackthorn Press, Blackthorn House
Middleton Rd, Pickering YO18 8AL
United Kingdom

All rights reserved. No part of this publication may be reproduced, stored in a retrieval system or transmitted, in any form or by any means, electronic, mechanical, photocopying, recording, or otherwise, without the prior permission of the Blackthorn Press.

ISBN: 9781730821462

2018

www.blackthornpress.com

INTRODUCTION

Lawrence wrote three drafts of 'Lady Chatterley's Lover' between 1926 and 1928: 'The First Lady Chatterley', 'John Thomas and Lady Jane' and the final version, 'Lady Chatterley's Lover'. All three books are published as ebooks by the Blackthorn Press.

Although all three books have the same story line of an aristocratic woman falling in love with a working class man, there are differences in their tone and sensibilities. Many critics have preferred this, the first version and Geoffrey Strickland, writing in Encounter, in 1971 concluded his article by saying, 'Why Lawrence altered the novel three times is a matter mainly for speculation. But that he altered it disastrously is, in my view, beyond question.' Strickland was of his time and for the modern reader, the last version with its more frank exploration of the sexual attraction of the two lovers is perhaps more rewarding. This, the first version, with its muted sexual scenes, lacks the reality and passion of the later versions. All three versions are now available in ebook format from the Blackthorn Press and the reader can now compare and decide.

Editor's note: Lawrence's original manuscript was not divided into chapters and this format has been maintained in this edition.

THE FIRST LADY CHATTERLEY'S LOVER

Ours is essentially a tragic age but we refuse emphatically to be tragic about it.

This was Constance Chatterley's position. The war landed her in a dreadful situation, and she was determined not to make a tragedy out of it.

She married Clifford Chatterley in 1917 when he was home on leave. They had a month of honeymoon, and he went back to France. In 1918 he was very badly wounded, brought home a wreck. She was twenty-three years old.

After two years, he was restored to comparative health. But the lower part of his body was paralysed for ever. He could wheel himself about in a wheeled chair, and he had a little motor attached to a bath chair, so that he could even make excursions in the grounds at home.

Clifford had suffered so much that the capacity for suffering had to some extent left him. He remained strange and bright and cheerful, with his ruddy, quite handsome face, and his bright, haunted blue eyes. He had so nearly lost life that what remained to him seemed to him precious. And he had been so much hurt, that something inside him had hardened and could feel no more.

Constance, his wife, was a ruddy, country-looking girl, with soft brown hair and sturdy body and a great deal of rather clumsy vitality. She had big, wondering blue eyes and a slow, soft voice, and seemed a real quiet maiden.

As a matter of fact, she was one of those very modern, brooding women who ponder all the time persistently and laboriously. She had been educated partly in Germany, in Dresden; indeed, she had been hurried home when the war broke out. And though it filled her now with bitter, heavy irony to think of it, now that

Germany, the German guns at least, had ruined her life, yet she had been most happy in Dresden. Or perhaps not happy but thrilled. She had been profoundly thrilled, by the life, by the music, and by the Germanic, abstract talk, the sort of philosophising. The endless talk about things had thrilled her soul. The philosophy students, the political economy students, the young professors, literary or ethnological, classic or scientific, how they had talked! and how she had answered them back! and how they had listened! and how she had listened to them because they listened to her!

Came the war, and she had to feel bitter about it all. But Clifford, who was an old friend and a Cambridge intellect, was by no means a narrow patriot. He fought for his country, but he sympathised entirely with the young intelligent Germans who were, like himself, caught up in the huge machine that they hated. Clifford would still read Hauptmann or Rainer Maria Rilke aloud to Constance when he was home on leave. Which pleased her very much. She felt she wanted to be 'above' the war and, at least, above the war patriotism which exasperated her so much.

But by the time the *Untergang des Abendlands* appeared, Clifford was a smashed man, and her life was smashed. She was young and remorselessly, almost crudely healthy. Under the blow she just went silent. And she remained silent, pondering, pondering with an endless unresolved vagueness.

They removed to Wragby in 1920. It was Clifford's home. His father had died, and he was now a baronet. Wragby Hall was a low, long old house, rather dismal, in a very fine park, in the midst of newly developed colliery districts. You could hear the chuff of winding engines, and the rattle of the sifting screens, and you could smell the sulphur of burning pit-hills when the wind blew in a certain direction over the park.

Constance was now Lady Chatterley, with a crippled husband, a dreary old house in a defaced countryside, and a rather inadequate income. She determined to make the best of it. She could work and read and ponder, and she was the lonely, absolute mistress of the establishment. It pleased her to manage carefully, to live within their income. It pleased her to entertain anyone, anyone who would interest Clifford. But he preferred to be alone. She went on from day to day, from day to day, in a strange plodding way. And she had a peculiar, comely beauty of her own, healthy and quiet and shy-seeming, but really withheld. And strangely isolated in herself, being unquestioned mistress in her own surroundings!

Clifford did not weigh upon her. He occupied himself reading, writing, painting, pulling himself round the fine old gardens in his chair, or slowly, softly trundling across the park into the wood in his motor chair. He gave orders to the gardeners and the wood-cutters and the gamekeeper. He watched over his small estate. Sometimes, in the autumn, he would go in his chair very slowly into the wood and wait for a shot at a pheasant. And sometimes, when he had great courage, he would take his paints and work at a small picture. He had once had a passion for painting, though he did little now. But he seemed almost happy, more happy than before his catastrophe.

Only occasionally he was anxious about Constance. She was very good to him, she loved him in her peculiar, neutral way. And he, of course, felt he could not live without her. They were true companions, as in the old days before they married.

But, of course, there was the tragedy that had fallen upon them! He could never be a husband to her. She lived with him like a married nun, a sister of Christ. It was more than that, too. For of course they had had a month of real marriage. And Clifford knew that in her nature was a heavy, craving physical desire. He knew.

He himself could not brood. The instinct of self-preservation was so strong in him, he could only contemplate the thrill and the pleasure of life or else fall into apathy. He would have days of apathy, which swallowed up what would else have been bitterness and anguish. Then the thrill of life returned. Then he could go in his motor chair into the woods and, if he remained silent, see the squirrels gathering nuts or a hedgehog nosing among dead leaves. Each time it seemed like something he had captured in the teeth of fate. He felt a peculiar triumph over doom and death, even over life itself. Only he practically never went outside the park gates. He could not bear the miners to stare at him with commiseration. He did not mind his own gardeners and wood-men and gamekeeper so much. He paid them.

Sometimes Constance would walk beside his chair into the park or the wood. Then she would sit under a tree, and the strange triumphant thrill he felt in being alive and in the midst of life would be a nervous gratification to her. He was reading Plato again and would talk to her about the dialogues, often holding her hand as he sat.

'It's awfully funny — strikes me as funny, now,' he said, 'the excitement they got out of argument, and reason, and thought. They're awfully like little boys who have just discovered that they can think and are beside themselves about it. They're so thrilled, that nothing else matters, only thinking and knowledge. I suppose, far, far back, man must in the same way have discovered sex in himself and been thrilled by that beyond all bounds — knowledge, nothing but mental knowledge! But Columbus discovering America was nothing to those early Greeks discovering that they'd got logical reasoning minds. It impresses me even now! Because, of course, my hand holding your hand seems to me as real as thought: doesn't it to you? It is as important as a piece of knowledge, don't you think? My hand holding your hand! — After all, that's life too! And it's what one couldn't do after death. If one were dead, one's spirit still might think. I still might think, and I do believe with Socrates that I should know even more fully. But I couldn't hold your hand, could I? At least not actually physically. Though perhaps, of course, there would still be some sort of connection, some sort of clasp, perhaps more vital really. Perhaps I could still keep hold of your hand, even if I were dead. What do you think?'

His big, bright, hard blue eyes were very strange, as they gazed into her face. His strong hand gripped her hand weirdly. She saw in him the triumphant thrill of conquest. He had made a weird conquest of something!

But in his thrill of triumph, she felt chilled, as if the frost of his egoism nipped her. Was he so triumphant? What about herself, and her life: her bodily life? What about her own hand that he gripped as if it were some trophy he would carry off to the other side the grave? She felt chilled and depressed, and a misery surged up in her. After all, she didn't have much to feel triumphant about — except his remarkable recovery. But if he was mutilated, what about herself? Her body had never been broken. She had not dragged herself out of the grave. On the contrary, she felt as if she were just being buried up to the waist, to keep him company. She was heavily silent and unresponsive.

A twist, a shadow, like an angry resentment went over his

'I know, dear,' he said, 'that in a sense you're the worst loser. I know how I depend on you: live on you, in a sense.'

'You know I want you to,' she murmured.

'I know! Yet there's no getting away from it, you're denied a very serious part of life. And the fact that you are denied it might work inside you, against your knowing it, and do you a lot of harm. — I want to speak of it now, so you'll know. — I don't want you to feel that you've brought me a sacrifice. I don't want you to feel like that, because I don't believe you're the right sort of woman to sacrifice that part of yourself. In fact, I married you because you were — a full-sexed woman. You did want me, before this happened, didn't you?' She murmured an assent. 'Oh, I know, and it's bitter. And I know you will go on wanting even though I'm put out of your life for ever in that respect. It's rather horrible, but we've got to make the best of it. I want to say this to you: if ever there is another man whom you really want, whom you really want to make love to you: don't let the thought of me stop you. You go ahead and live your own life. My danger is that I might be a dog in the manger to you. I don't want to be. So I tell you now. I know what happens to women who suppress their sex while they're young: there's hell to pay later. So I don't want you to do it. I wouldn't like you to make yourself cheap: and I know you won't make it any harder on me than you need. But if ever you meet a man whom you absolutely want, for your sexual life, take him. Have a lover if you have to! —'

He spoke bravely, and a little glibly. Evidently he had thought it all out. And evidently it was only hypothetical to him: an abstract man, an abstract love affair: it was easily dismissed, in his head.

She, sitting on a fallen tree holding his hand, let her head droop and said nothing. Strange feelings surged in her.

And as if the intense emotion in the air around them had attracted other life than their own, a spaniel suddenly ran out of a path and came scenting towards them, touching Constance's hand with its soft nose and lifting its head agitatedly. At the same time they heard footsteps. The gamekeeper, Parkin, came out of the cross-path on to the riding.

Constance released her husband's hold. Clifford glanced round, rousing from the apathy into which he had sunk. The gamekeeper touched his hat, and was crossing the riding to disappear into the path on the other side, making a faint sound to call his dog.

'Oh I say Parkin!' Clifford pulled himself up a bit in his chair.

'Sir Clifford!' said the man, stopping.

'Turn my chair round for me, and get me in the wheel-tracks. It's less trouble for me.'

The man came striding without a word. He was alert, smallish for a gamekeeper, and very quiet. Constance knew that some time ago his wife had gone off with a neighbouring collier, leaving him in his cottage with his little girl of five. Since that time he had lived alone and kept to himself, giving his child into the care of his mother in the village.

His gun slung over his shoulder, he took hold of the back of Sir Clifford's chair in silence. Only his quick brown eyes glanced into the face of the young wife as she stood beside the chair. Their eyes met for a second, but Constance, strangely disturbed in herself, scarcely noticed him. The man, however, silent and shut off as he was, felt the blueness and the unresolved trouble in the eyes of the young woman. But his face closed to its usual shut-off expressionless look, the mouth shut under the rather big ragged moustache.

He turned the chair carefully, and brought it into the wheel-tracks where it would go most easily.

'Na shall I wheel yer, or would yer rather manage for yerself?' he asked, in a broad local accent, but speaking gently.

'You can wheel me if you like,' said Sir Clifford.

'Ay!' said the man.

They set off in silence, each one looking straight ahead without communication. The brown dog ran, softly scenting. Last yellow leaves fluttered down.

They came to the edge of the wood and saw the open park, with the big beech trees on its slopes, sheep feeding on the grass. In the grey day the old house on the summit of the slope, among old trees, seemed timeless and utterly forsaken.

The gamekeeper stared changelessly ahead, steering the chair carefully and keeping himself obliterated. His brown moustache seemed to go fiercely in front of him. But he was vaguely thinking of my lady's blue eyes with their indescribable trouble. She was but a girl after all. Ay, the war hit the gentry hard! Sir Clifford crippled as he was, she'd neither the pleasure of a young wife with her husband nor yet children to look forward to. Ay my word, there was trouble in her young eyes, poor thing! And everybody spoke so well of her.

He thought of his own wife who had gone loose while he was away at the war. She didn't have to put up with what this young thing had! No! If she'd had more to suffer perhaps she'd not have gone off, like a trollop, with a collier who drank. But let her go and let her stay. It was good riddance. There were nice women in the world, look at this young thing, married to Sir Clifford, and quiet and soft-spoken! Ay! He wasn't the only one with troubles. This poor lass had got it worse than himself! And she was so quiet and soft-spoken, she was hardly like a lady; she was the sort of woman a man might go a long way to find nowadays. — Well, everybody must bear their own troubles and eat their own peck of dirt.

Constance came out of the cloud of her blind agitation at last, and became aware of the gamekeeper as he pushed the heavy chair in silence. The colour was red in his face, with exertion, but he held himself detached, quite out of contact. In his aloofness he had a peculiar clear-cut presence, she remembered he always stood out very distinct from his background whenever she had seen him. This distinctness, this clarity in his presence, gave her a certain impression of beauty, beauty that men rarely have. He was not handsome, with that rather big moustache. Yet he had a certain distinctness such as wild animals and birds have. She wondered if he had cared for that wife, a florid, common woman. He must have suffered from her commonness without knowing it. Now he kept himself quite alone, detached, in that stone cottage at the end of the wood. She knew nothing about him: she had just looked on him as one of the Wragby dependants. She knew he was a very sharp gamekeeper.

Sir Clifford let himself be wheeled along, apathetic. And so they came home, and Clifford rested before tea.

The days of autumn followed one another into winter. Constance took as little heed as possible. If the days would go by one after the other, unmarked, she was willing to let them. She had her duties to the house, certain responsibilities to the village. And there was always Clifford. He required her attention and occupied her feelings almost as young children would have done.

The only thing that troubled her were strange violent disturbances within herself, with which she could not reckon. She had recurrent violent dreams, of horses, of a mare which had been feeding quietly, and suddenly went mad. And she would get up in the morning with a terrible anger upon her, so that if she had not controlled herself, she could have bullied the servants cruelly and have spoken to Clifford in savage derision. On the tip of her tongue were the terrible, torturing things she wanted to say to Clifford as he sat propped up so bright and coldly alert in bed or lay so apathetic.

She never said the things. But she came nearer and nearer to saying them, and at last she was so frightened, when she got up in the morning in one of these demoniacal tempers, that she would hurry out into the park to walk herself calm. At such times her face was blank with ugly passion, and her eyes wide with fear of herself. 'I am possessed, I know I am possessed,' she would say to herself pathetically, rushing forward impelled by some savage power in her breast. She could have killed something, someone. It was a great cruelty surging in her.

And in the park, and on the edge of the wood, a reminiscence would come back on her. It was here that something, something had happened. She looked round, into the secret of the place. And it came upon her again, her dream of horses. Surely there was a group of horses, and a mare that would go mad and lash at the others with her heels and tear them with her teeth!

She stood frozen with fear. But no horses were there.

In the wood she heard the report of a gun, as if in echo of her own feelings. She walked on down the wet drive, over the wet, decaying leaves. And as she went, she heard the sound of a voice, and a child's crying. At once she listened keenly. The child was sobbing, and someone was murmuring, consoling her. She hastened forward, all her disconnected anger fastening upon the supposition that someone was hurting a child. She strode on, her face hot, her eyes shining, her body surging with haste.

Down a narrow path she saw them, a little girl in a purple coat and a moleskin cap, crying, and Parkin, the keeper, bending over her.

'Tha doesna want him to bite a' th' little bunny rabbits, does ta, an' then eat 'em? Tha doesna want him ta jump on the hen pheasants when they sittin' nestlin' down, an' bite their necks through, does ta? He wor a bad un. Look at him, and then cry for him. Look at him!'

The man's voice was strangely caressive and yet irritated, and the child would not be comforted. Constance strode up, still with blazing face and eyes, determined that some injury had been done to the child.

'What is it?' she demanded abruptly.

The man stood up and touched his cap hastily.

'Why I shot that there old torn cat, as has been havin' his own way in here for a month or two,' he said in a hard voice, pointing to the body of a great brindled cat that lay stretched out on the path. 'An' my little gel here, she thinks she must need scraight for him.' To the child, he added, 'Come on, come on, naa! My lady's lookin' at yer! Shut it up.'

He was mild enough so far with the child, but the irritable impatience was gathering in his voice, his eyes were beginning to harden. It was obvious the child was afraid of him.

Constance bent down to the little girl.

'What is it? What is it, dear? Don't cry! It was a nasty bad pussy that scratched the little bunnies and killed them. There! Don't you cry!' And she gently wiped the face of the motherless child with her handkerchief. It was obvious the little thing was afraid of the man, her father. Constance felt a resentment against him. No wonder his wife had left him. Constance felt that he did not really like his little girl.

'Were you going to have her with you all day?' She asked him.

'Mother's at the house,' he said, jerking his head in the direction of the cottage. 'She mostly comes a Sat'days, to clean up a bit.'

Constance felt he was polite under compulsion. She felt he disliked her because she was a woman.

'I should take her home then to her granny. What's your name, dear?'

The child peeped at her with dark, wilful, resentful eyes.

'Connie Parkin,' she said.

'Come then,' said Constance, smiling faintly. 'I'll take you home while Parkin — while your father does what he has to do.'

'You don't have to, my lady,' said the man.

'I'll do it,' said Constance, leading the child by the hand.

She felt the man standing, watching them go with dislike. He disliked women and despised them. He was merely stupid.

At the cottage the little old energetic woman, with smuts of black-lead on her nose, was busy polishing the fireplace. She started when the child ran in to her, and turning, she saw her ladyship.

'Why, whatever —!' she said.

'Good morning!' said Constance. 'I brought your little girl home. She was frightened when her father shot a poaching cat.'

'Did you ever! It's very kind of you, mum, I'm sure! What do you say to the lady for bringing you home, Connie?'

'Thank you!' said Connie, looking at Constance with bold dark eyes, but putting her finger self-consciously in her mouth.

'Thank you mum!' repeated the old woman to the child.

But the girl twisted and would not say it. The collier people would never say 'my lady' if they could help it. The child even balked at 'mum!' It was a sort of self-conscious clumsiness.

'I knowed there'd be ructions of some sort when he would take her off with him in the wood. He's not that easy to get on with at the best of times. Well, thank yer very much for bringin' her home, I'm sure.'

The old woman was overwhelmed by the attention, at the same time she resented being caught black-leading the grate, and with smuts on her nose.

Constance walked back to the hall, very much aware again of the cold distance between herself and the people. They were not hostile. But they were relieved when she went.

She was quite glad to get back to Clifford and her own milieu. The common people somehow made her angry. A bold-eyed child, that of Parkin's!

That evening it was very pleasant to sit in Clifford's study while he read aloud to her. At least, one's pride was soothed.

The following Saturday Clifford wished to speak to Parkin. But it had been raining too heavily for the chair to go out. In the afternoon Constance walked over with the message. She liked having some aim in her walk.

The front door of the cottage was shut, and nobody came. She walked round to the back and suddenly, in the yard, came upon Parkin washing himself. He had taken off his shirt, as the colliers do, and rolled his breeches on his hips and was ducking his head in the bowl of water. Constance retired immediately and went back into the wood, to stroll around for a time.

But in the dripping gloom of the forest, suddenly she started to tremble uncontrollably. The white torso of the man had seemed so beautiful to her, splitting the gloom. The white, firm, divine body with that silky firm skin! Never mind the man's face, with the fierce moustache and the resentful, hard eyes! Never mind his stupid personality! His body in itself was divine, cleaving through the gloom like a revelation. — Clifford even at his best had never had that silky, rippling firmness, the more than human loveliness.

It was with great difficulty she brought herself to go back to the cottage and knock at the door. She stood on the threshold and trembled inwardly. Previously, she had never even thought of him as anything but an instrument, a gamekeeper, It seemed to her almost wrong that he should have that pure body.

She heard him coming downstairs. He was dressing to go to town. She stammered as he stood before her in his clean suit and new necktie and Sunday trousers. She stammered almost uncontrollably as she delivered her message, and he listened, watching her with those hard eyes.

She did not like his face. She realised that she was weary of peoples' faces, and of their mechanical personalities, and of the monotonous, impertinent things they always thought. Could it be possible the star-like, lonely body was hidden under that ridiculous clean shirt and necktie?

'All right, my lady! I know what Sir Clifford wants. I'll see to it.' She turned away. And as she went into the gloom, she felt him watching her. He would be thinking something stupid and mean! Let him think. He was nothing. Even in spite of that hidden loveliness of body, he was nothing. She was extremely bored by common, stupid people.

Yet in her bedroom at night, she looked at her own nude body and wondered if anyone would see in it that visionary beauty she had seen for a moment in the man's. Would a man see that loveliness in her?

She slipped on her nightdress dejectedly. What was the good! What was the good of anything? Clifford, who was a nice man, was for her bodiless. And men who had beautiful bodies, had common, stupid faces she was not interested in, and common, stupid voices she never wanted to hear.

Clifford read to her nearly every evening. Sometimes he was tired. His crippled condition brought him wearinesses that in themselves were an anaesthetic. But he had a great pleasure in reading to her, all kinds of books. He loved amusing books most of all now. He was reading Hajji Baba. And Constance listened with bent head, as she sewed or embroidered. She had not bobbed her hair. The knot of soft brown hair lay silkily in her neck. And he never knew the thoughts that went on in her modest-seeming, maidenly head. He was so occupied, and gratified to have her there, and so busy, as it were, avoiding repining.

He laughed very much at Hajji Baba when that hero was so utterly repelled by seeing the naked faces of English women. Oh, if the women had only covered their faces, what fire of passion would have run through Hajji's body! But seeing all the naked indecency of their countenances, his fire was quenched.

This amused Clifford immensely. Constance lifted her head and gazed at him with her big blue eyes, so pondering and touching.

'Don't you think it is rather a pity that we never see anything of people but their faces?' she said. 'Don't you think the face is probably the worst part of most people?'

'You mean if they covered their faces and walked with their bodies naked?' he laughed. 'That's an idea! Like Renoir! He said he always tried to make the face unimportant, just merely a part of the body.'

'Yes!' she said. 'Why should we always see nothing but a face for a person. I'm sure it's wrong.'

'Perhaps,' he said. 'But I suppose the face reveals the personality,

'Mayn't there be something else beside the personality? Something which never comes out?'

He pondered this: something else beside the personality? The idea made him uneasy. He looked closely at his wife, But she was sewing so quietly.

'What would there be beside the personality?' he said.

She looked up at him with her brooding, remorseless blue eyes.

'Mightn't the body have a life of its own -- perhaps truer than the personality?'

'The body -- the stomach and heart and lungs?' he said.

But she was thinking of something else.

'Why is a torso, in sculpture, often so lovely, without a head? It has a life of its own.'

'Perhaps it does!' he assented. But he was not attending. It was dangerous ground for him, and the shrewdest instinct of self-preservation kept him off it. He began to read again.

But she had a new vague idea to ponder: the body, living a pure, untouched life of its own, apart from the face with all its complexities and frustrations and vulgarity! Faces were nearly always common. Even her own face had in it a discontent which she herself could see.

She put a thick veil over her face, like a Mohammedan woman, leaving only her eyes. And thus she stood naked before her mirror and looked at her slow, golden-skinned, silent body. It was beautiful too, and with a silent, sad, pure appeal. Her breasts were also eyes, and her navel was sad, closed, waiting lips. It all spoke in another, silent language, without the cheapness of words.

But then the mood left her again, and she entirely forgot her body. It was Christmas, and she was extremely busy. Extremely sane and sensible and busy. She could not bear even to touch with the edge of her thoughts those lunatic ideas about the body. Thank heaven she'd got over that nonsense. She had a thousand things to do.

They had some visitors for the Christmas and the New Year, mostly Clifford's friends and relatives. Everybody was very nice, and Clifford was in good form. It seemed all rather exciting and thrilling, almost at pre-war level. Clifford's aunt, Lady Eva Rolleston, was staying a few days. She had the remains of the grande dame about her, being daughter of one of the really big families. But she had rather got into disrepute, what with gambling and brandy. Still, there she was, a widow now, tall and slim and unobtrusive, a bit distraite, her blue eyes rather vacant and her fine nose a little reddened. And still she was the grande dame. She was so very simple, for one thing, and in her rather blank unobtrusiveness there was still a power of commanding deference. She sipped her brandy with a noble sang-froid, indifferent to all the comment in the world.

Constance liked her and at the same time was depressed by her. Lady Eva was somehow like a ghost, in her black clothes and her curious naïveté, which was almost girlish and winning. Yet the odd, straightforward girlishness rested upon a very hard determination never to yield one inch, essentially, to anybody on earth. A hard imperviousness and isolation, like the Matterhorn, was at the bleak centre of Lady Eva.

And she rather despised her niece Constance. The vague blue eyes would rest upon the comely young niece with strange detachment. Constance was always warmly, almost tenderly deferential to her aunt, Lady Eva. And her aunt despised her a little, but was indifferent. The daughter of the old R.A. was not of the ruling class. It was not in her to rule. Constance could run a house very well. It was in her to be obeyed. But she could not rule, she had not the ruling nature. Clifford was better that way.

Constance knew that by the grande dame in her aunt she was despised. But after all, the grande dame in Aunt Eva was only her last trick, her trump card, as it were. It was a master trump only up to a certain point. Unless you felt a little sorry for the finely made lady fallen slightly into disrepute, the 'grande-damerie', as Clifford called it, wasn't trumps at all. It was impudence.

'My dear, I think you're so wonderful, I do really,' said Lady Eva, as she sat in Constance's own sitting-room.

'Why?' asked Constance, half-candid, half-expecting a snare.

'The way you are with Clifford. I think it's wonderful, really. You must have a wonderful nature.'

'Why?' asked Constance again.

'The poor boy, crippled as he is! — not more than half a man, you might say. Of course it's the right half, for people like me. He is so witty and entertaining. But for a wife, I'm not so sure at all.'

'Oh, but Clifford is all right, I assure you,' said Constance. 'He's almost perfect as a husband.'

'Oh yes, I can see that. He takes a lot of trouble to keep you interested. Oh, he's a clever boy. No doubt, but for that accident in the war he'd be a perfect husband. But as it is, you must suffer terribly from deprivation: deprived of one side of life.'

'But I don't!' said Constance. 'I'm not deprived of anything I want. I'm not really.'

Lady Eva fetched her a vague glance.

'I'm so awfully glad if you're not,' she said. 'It would be so awful if you were. Nothing is so bad for you as to forego things in your youth, so that they come on you again when you're getting too old for them. Nothing is so bad for a woman as she gets on in life as the feeling that she's missed something: perhaps the most important thing.'

'But what is the most important thing?' asked Constance.

'That I don't know. But it's something to do with men. I was faithful to my husband. I don't say I wish I hadn't been. But I used to wish, dreadfully, I had had something else. It is a dreadful feeling, to feel you're going to die without having had what you were born for, in a way.'

'But what are we born for?' asked Constance heavily. 'It seems to me we are born for so many things.

Or perhaps we're not born for anything at all. It's just a question of making our minds up about it.'

'I don't know, I'm sure,' said Lady Eva. 'When I was young I thought I wanted reform, politics, and all that kind of thing. Well, I had that. We were in politics till we hardly knew anything else but politics, my husband and I. And of course ours was a love match — and there are the three children. Yet towards the end, when I was forty-six or so, I felt I'd lived absolutely for nothing. The one thing I'd really wanted, I'd never had it at all. And then it was too late. It's the most miserable thing a woman can feel. — I think women should experiment more. We get things into our heads, and that shuts us off from everything else. If women were more open-minded and experimented more to find out what they want, I'm sure they'd find something.'

'But what? What is there to find?' asked the puzzled Constance.

'I don't know. But we get things into our heads. I got it into my head that I wanted romantic love, and politics, something in the George Meredith line. Well, I got it. And it wasn't what I really wanted at all. Women should be awfully careful about the things they're sure they want. They're nearly always wrong, Dead Sea apples when they've got them.'

'But what do you think you might have had, that might have satisfied you?'

'I don't know exactly. But I think if I'd loved a good-looking jolly policeman for a time, I might feel better. Anyhow, that's what I think now that I wanted.'

Constance began to laugh silently.

'It seems so very simple,' she said.

'Doesn't it!' said Lady Eva. 'But I could no more have done it when I was young than fly. I could never have let a jolly young policeman have his way with me — that is, not until I'd turned him into something that was no longer a jolly young policeman. I couldn't. And now I wish I had. Doesn't it seem absurd for an old woman to be saying?'

Lady Eva was not an old woman, she was well under sixty. But she accepted her youth as over.

'It does seem rather queer,' said Constance.

'That's why I wanted to warn you. Try and get what you want in your youth. An elderly woman possessed by vain regrets is worse than possessed with devils.'

Constance looked searchingly at her aunt.

'Thank you for warning me,' she said. 'But really, I think I've got everything I want. — And women are a nuisance, don't you think? —even to themselves. I don't think it's a question of a policeman more or less, really. We should be dissatisfied by the time we reach fifty, whatever we had. I'm sure policemen's wives are dissatisfied as they grow older, worse than we are.'

'I don't know,' said Lady Eva. 'I don't think so. — But you're so much cleverer than I am.'

'I'm not clever,' said Constance. 'Only I think I've got what I want —' She tailed off rather vaguely, and Lady Eva glanced at her with remote eyes, knowing her niece was lying and hiding something. Then there was something to hide! She thought there must be.

Constance also was aware of her own lie. Why was she so barefaced? Her aunt would think all sorts of things.

The guests departed, the intimacy evaporated, and the sense that it had all been sham came down upon the lonely young couple. They had begun to live in a world apart, of their own. Then suddenly they had accepted the other, that outside world. Now they felt dejected and exhausted. They fell back in irritable exhaustion.

Clifford had a good deal of pain again and suffered in a sort of ashy silence. Constance did what she could for him. She gave her life for him for the time. If she could ever have made him better, she would not have minded.

But what was broken, was broken. And a sense of uselessness began to deaden her soul.

Her own strength and bloom began to leave her. She thought of her lie to her aunt: 'I've got what I want.' What had she got? Misery, anger and a horrible blank life ahead.

Her courage and her strength began to fail. She kept her ruddy colour, which seemed inevitable to her. But she grew thinner and thinner. The pulse in her thin neck showed she was failing.

When her sister Hilda came to see her in March there was an immediate outcry.

'Connie! Why whatever's the matter with you? You're as thin as a rail, your clothes hang on you like rags! You are ill! Whatever's the matter?'

Hilda had only one sister in the world, and no brother. Instantly she became fierce. She went in to Clifford.

'What's the matter with Connie?' she demanded of him. 'Why is she wasting away?'

'She is thinner,' he said. 'I wish you could do something for her.'

The strange egoism of his type appalled Hilda. He was such a gentleman! He had such good manners and was so extremely considerate. He tried all he could not to trouble his young wife. He bore his pains in silence, and his long hours of misery alone. He forbore to call her, tried never to disturb her, tried always to be cheerful, to make her know how indebted he was to her. He was the soul of a gentleman.

Yet he never felt Constance really as another flowing life, flowing its own stream. He idealised her, perhaps: she was a beautiful life flowering beside his own. But he never warmly felt her, not for a moment. The old, wild warmth which Hilda felt for Connie, and Connie for Hilda, was something out of his sphere: something to be suppressed.

With Hilda there came a new breath of revolt and passion into the house. Hilda had got tired of her 'devoted' husband, who pawed her and petted her but never for a moment came forth naked to her out of his amiable and would-be manly shell. So she had left him, departed bag and baggage with her two children, and was living in Scotland. She had come to spend a week with Connie.

Constance was examined by a doctor: nothing organically wrong with her. Constance was whisked off to London to a specialist, for she complained of pains at the heart. Nothing organically wrong with her: neuralgia of the nerves of the heart, brought on, like all neuralgia, by being run-down, by living off the nerves, under the pressure of the will. She needed relaxation from the state of tension into which she had fallen.

'You must come with me to Scotland, Connie.'

But Connie refused. Already Hilda had brought a nurse into the house, a quiet, well-behaved, elderly woman, to attend to Sir Clifford. Clifford had acquiesced, with a little bitterness in his willingness to do the best for Constance. And so Constance would not leave him.

A nurse being in the house, however, she took her thoughts more off him. She did not cease to care for him. She would always care for him. But the strain of anxiety on his behalf was less.

It was a curious relationship, that of the husband and wife. In some respects they were exceedingly intimate, very near to one another. When he held her hand sometimes in the silence of the evening, there would seem a great peace between them and a wonderful togetherness. They were almost like two souls free from the body and all its weariness, two souls going hand in hand along the upper road that skirts the heaven of perfection.

Then they would talk quietly together about the soul and immortality. Clifford was deeply concerned with the question of immortality. His view was the old-fashioned Platonist view: the soul of the earnest seeker after truth, after that which is essence, pure and enduring, would reach the upper levels where absolute truth, absolute justice shines in the great eternal gleam that at last satisfies the hurt heart of man.

The two horses that draw the chariot of the soul, the savage, rough-eared, unmanageable black one, and the delicate, beautiful white one, these two occupied the imagination of Clifford. 'It seems to me,' he said to her, 'that my hairy-eared savage horse got his death blow in the war, and if I struggle up to the shiny levels of heaven it will be with only one horse to my chariot.'

'I don't think you're right, dear,' she said, after she had pondered what he said. 'Think what savage tempers you still go into, though you do control them.'

'I suppose you're right. Yes! I suppose you're about right, Con. It's the black horse, sure enough. Yes, I suppose it is. Gone a bit vicious, very likely.'

He went off into a muse. He was so anxious for immortality, so anxious to feel that he would at last plunge and struggle on to that wide lane which is heaven's rampart, whence one can look down again on to earth before one turns into the full glow of the innermost heaven. He accepted the imagery of the Phaedrus myth. And he was so much afraid that with only his white horse of pure yearning, the black horse of lust dead in him, he would never come to the heights. One horse would never get him up the steep.

'Only one horse to my chariot,' his thoughts ran in bitterness.

But perhaps Constance was right. The black horse was there after all, less obvious and rampageous, maybe, but perhaps more vicious. He remembered the terrible moods that would come upon him, when he would like to destroy the world, to crush mankind to death. Yes, that was lust! That was the black horse, all right.

He was relieved. He had been so much afraid that his hairy-eared horse was dead.

And he was surprised. Did he then love the black brute of the soul, that he was ready to howl like a lost soul at the thought that the brute was dead in him?

'I should have missed my black horse if I'd thought he was dead in me, Con,' he said, looking at her with hard, shining eyes that frightened her.

'You need only remember how you feel about your uncle Everett,' said Constance calmly.

Clifford's uncle Everett was one of the old-fashioned arrogant sort, with all the tough insolence of his class superiority. Clifford couldn't stand him.

'You're a thorough-paced mystic, I'm afraid, my boy. Well well, perhaps just as well! You've got a sensible little woman for a wife.'

This sort of thing roused serpents and tigers in Clifford's soul, and he had to lie silent, for he knew it was useless.

'I'm glad my horse with the blood-shot eyes isn't dead, though,' he said meditatively to her. 'By Jove, I think he could bite off the top of Uncle Everett's cranium with one snap! — I'm glad he's not dead.'

'The gods still have a black horse and a white horse to their chariots, don't they, as they drive round the heavens?' she asked.

'By jove they do! And got 'em both in perfect running order! Only we poor mortals can't manage Blackie,' he said cheerfully.

'Don't you think it's rather cruel, the way Socrates drives his black horse — jerking him back till his mouth and tongue are full of blood, and bruising his haunches? Don't you think one could manage a horse better than that?'

Clifford looked at her keenly. She had found the taint of bullying, even in Socrates. Even Socrates was a bully! And in her heart of hearts Constance was quite determined against any sort of bullying.

'Perhaps not a vicious horse,' he said.

'But perhaps Blackie isn't so vicious. Don't you think, if one asked him what he truly wanted, he's as much right to it as the white horse or the driver? Only Socrates thinks he must only have his mouth cut and be thwarted.'

Clifford pondered this. Constance was quite good at thinking in symbols. The symbols of Plato's myths were perfectly familiar to her. She and Clifford used them as ordinary interchange. But Constance, instead of thinking Socrates perfect, was always taking another line.

'What do you mean exactly by the black horse in this case?' he asked her.

'Doesn't it mean the bodily satisfactions?' she said. 'Doesn't it mean the body straining after the goal of its own gratifications? Whether it's biting the top of Uncle Everett's head off, or anything else?'

'I suppose it does,' he said. 'But you can't say that it would be right to bite off the top of Uncle Everett's cranium, as a vicious horse might do it, can you?'

She put down her sewing, and looked at him.

'Well!' she said slowly. 'If I were you I should one day bite the top of Uncle Everett's head right off. I mean, make him look the brainless fool he is. I should do it deliberately. I should consider my black horse had a right to the bite.'

She returned to her sewing, and he, all in a flutter, pondered the new attitude to the black horse.

'You would say the black horse has a right to all his desires?' he asked.

'Well, wouldn't you? Only at the right time and in the right order. Don't you think, instead of the white horse and the driver both struggling to thwart the black one, they should say to him: Gently! Gently! Go gently, and we'll go with you! Go quietly, without overturning the chariot, and we'll drive right into the place you want.'

He looked at her shrewdly.

'Do you think it would answer?' he said.

'Why shouldn't it?' she said. 'Either the black horse has a perfect right to his own existence and his own desires and gratifications, or he shouldn't exist. And you say yourself, you feel you can't get through with a one-horse team. You are terrified if you think your black horse is dead. Yet you only want him to live so that you can thwart him.'

His spirits, which had been elated, sank again. He felt something hostile to him in this assertion.

'Don't you thwart your black horse, Con?' he said.

'I don't want to,' she replied, keeping her head lowered over her sewing. 'I don't mean to. I mean to let him run right to his goal once he finds the way.'

He felt in himself a hostility to what she was saying. Yet he replied:

'I believe you're perfectly right, dear.'

They drifted apart again. There was a strange connection, a strange intimacy between them. It was a subtle intimacy whose pure contact was in speech, in words. It was an intimacy of contest. It was as if some bright, bruised serpent of her soul crept forth to wrestle with the jealous dogs of his spirit every time the intimacy between them was broached. At the end of each talk they withdrew as if from a wrestling contest.

And for a long time she had been losing. She had felt the fight dying out of her, the power leaving her. Weakness and lassitude came over her, and she dragged around aimlessly. Her Aunt Eva had made everything seem cheap. She had felt in herself a deep indifference to Clifford's immortality and Clifford's heaven of the pure abstraction, however bright it might seem to him. His heaven was only of secondary or second-hand interest to her. And latterly it had begun to seem a certain prison: like the white-hot steel walls of a Poe story. She hated it, his heaven of pure justice and pure truth. She felt herself being insidiously, insufferably bullied by him in the name of this pure heaven of justice. She felt that Plato, exalting the heaven of pure justice, did it by committing all the time one horrible injustice. He was unjust to the black horse and unjust to the bright, bruised serpent, with remorselessly cruel injustice.

Ah yes! it was still another heaven established on bullying! A negative bullying! Clifford bullied her, not by obvious compulsion, but by insidious negation. Some part of her soul he just absolutely ignored, he killed it by not allowing its existence. As one might kill a person by withdrawing all the air from her. So Clifford was killing her. Killing that part of her soul which was her true body.

He would have done just the same if he had never been wounded in the war. Only then she would not have seen so clearly. The terrible catastrophe had made her clairvoyant.

The poor black horse of her body! He had been lying now for months as if he were dead, with his neck twisted sideways as if it had been broken by some specially vicious twist of the reins. She had felt him dead, a corpse inside her.

But now, poor beast, he was struggling to his feet again. And now she felt she must defend him, defend him from Clifford and from all the world. She must be silent and secret about him. She must hide him, she must keep him hidden.

She had, however, one ally, and this was her nurse, Mrs Bolton. Mrs Bolton was a widow. Her husband, a collier, had been killed in the mines twenty years ago, leaving her with two small children. She had worked hard, and become a nurse, and had had the post of district visiting nurse for many years. Now she had withdrawn from that work, it was too strenuous.

She had loved her husband. He was only twenty-eight when he was killed in an explosion underground. The butty ahead had called to the other men to lie down, and they had done so. But Ted Bolton was round the corner and did not hear. The explosion passed over the other men and killed him.

At the inquiry it was asserted on the masters' side that Bolton had been frightened and had started to run away instead of lying flat. That was the reason of his death, his own cowardice: or, at the best, his own funk. Therefore the compensation was not really due but would be a charity gift to the widow.

The compensation was three hundred pounds. But Ivy Bolton, the widow, was not allowed to have the money down. No, she would drink it, or otherwise waste it. She must wait in a crowd for an hour or so every Monday morning for thirty shillings a week.

But what rankled most in her was that they had said Ted was a coward, that he was running away. When she knew herself that Ted was too careless, too reckless.

She felt in her heart of hearts that they had killed her man and then insulted him. She never forgave them. But she hid it in her heart and became a very quiet woman, curiously still and dignified, curiously ladylike. She was very much respected in the district, every collier's house was open to her. They thought her a lady.

But in her own silent way she hated all the masters. All the great class of owners and bosses, she silently hated. They had been so insulting to her, so bitterly insulting to her and her dead man, with their three hundred pounds at thirty shillings a week. Thirty shillings a week! Thirty shillings a week for a little less than four years! — But never mind, she could fend for herself.

She felt sorry for Sir Clifford in his great misfortune; and in her capacity of nurse she was very gentle to him, as she would have been to her dead husband. But far in the remote, unchanging corners of her soul she disliked him. She disliked his superficial friendliness that was so polite and considerate of her, and so inhuman from her point of view. It was in this well-bred, polite, considerate treatment of her that she had learnt to recognise the cold inhumanity, the lack of heart throb, the mere curiosity, and the inward arrogance of the class-superior. She had schooled herself so well, that she herself had acquired the cool, self-assured, would-you-mind! and thank-you-so-much! manner. But underneath, her heart burned.

Something in the puzzled, lost look of Constance's eyes had gone straight to her soul. Poor child! Poor child, she had never known what it was for a man to hold her warm, real warm against his breast and comfort her with his heart! As she, Ivy Bolton, had known! That Sir Clifford didn't have a real heart to start with. He only had a lot of talk and a lot of feelings that were no good to anybody.

'You need to get out into the air! You need to get away from the house, my lady!' she would urge.

Anything, to get Constance away from Sir Clifford! Mrs Bolton used all her authority as a nurse and threw in 'my ladys' as a palliative. And she said to herself: 'She's wasting away, simply eaten up! I wish there was some nice young man to make love to her.'

But at least in the blowy March weather she persuaded Constance to walk again, to get away from the house.

'Just walk over and see the daffs in the gamekeeper's garden. They're a sight, they are really, you ought to see them!'

The gamekeeper's garden! Something stirred in Constance's soul. She had long ago reasoned herself out of any nonsense. He was just a commonplace man among millions of men. Just nothing! Just a part of the dreary nothingness!

But now something stirred in her. Even the cottage — even the cottage — it would be nice to see it. It had a certain fairy-tale atmosphere about it.

She went slowly across the park to the wood. It was a blowy day with intermittent sunshine. The trees in the park were bare, there was a rushing of wind in the wood, pale wild-flowers, in groups, bent and bobbed. Along the little paths the primroses showed their pale, happy candour. And Constance felt thrilled and happy to be in the wood, in the sound of the wind. She gathered a few violets and held them in the palm of her hand for the scent. Ah! To escape, to escape the level monotony of doom, to break through into magic once more! To pass into the life of the woods!

She went slowly across the mile of wood to the cottage. The little orchard at the back was all sparkling and shivering in a burst of sunshine with wild daffodils that grew up the slope. This was the last place where they were left. Constance sat down with her back to a young pine tree that swayed against her like an animate creature, subtly, and she watched the daffodils and caught their faintly tarry scent. And she thought again of Clifford's dictum: 'Nature is a settled routine of crude old laws. One has to go beyond nature, break beyond. And that is one's destiny that makes one break beyond the settled, arbitrary laws of nature.' She herself saw it differently. She couldn't feel the laws of nature so arbitrary. It was the laws of man that bothered her. She couldn't feel anything very arbitrary about the tossing daffodils, dipping now in shade. If only one could be simpler and more natural! If only one could be really simple! Men were so complicated and full of laws.

The cottage below her was closed and silent. There came a faint waft of smoke from the chimney. But there was no movement about the place. It was a little stone house with a grey slate roof, at the foot of the slope where the daffodils grew. Constance liked to look at it. But she had no desire to go indoors and be intimate with it. The house where the keeper's wife had lived, she who had run away with a collier because she hated the loneliness and the taciturnity of her husband! The cottage with the kettle and the teapot always on the hob! No, Constance had no desire at all to feel its homeliness and its tight intimacy. She wanted to stay outside.

She turned away, to go home. The afternoon was fading. It must be past four o'clock, and it would be mean of her not to be there at tea-time, to drink a cup of tea with Clifford.

She went across to the spring riding, the broad green way that passed by the little icy spring where Robin Hood used to drink. Forget-me-nots and new-mown hay were going to make a foam in that riding in May. But they were not here yet. Only a few primroses, and dead leaves still, and a wind roaring in the oak twigs overhead.

She heard a light tapping on the right, and wondered if it were the woodpecker. No, it was a hammer. She remembered the little hut and the small clearing where the keeper had built a straw shelter for the pheasants. It was here he gave the birds their corn in the bad weather. A cock pheasant ran across in front of her with a squawk, the hammering ceased. The keeper was listening.

She went off down the narrow path to the hidden place where the hut was. The yellow dog came running towards her. She saw the keeper rise suspiciously, looking cautiously and suspiciously through the trees. He was always on the watch, on the alert for poachers, trespassers, enemies. His life one silent conflict with the encroaching colliery population: and himself always alone.

He was in his shirt-sleeves, having been hammering at a chicken coop. He was preparing for the setting of the pheasants' eggs. He touched his cap and waited for her to come near.

'I wondered what the hammering was!' she said. 'Will you set eggs under hens this year?'

'Yes my lady! We did well wi' pheasants last year, so we maun do better this year if we can.'

Clifford sold his pheasants to the market, and made a decent sum by it.

Constance went into the small hut. It had a work bench and tools, traps of various sorts, a corn-bin, tar and tar-brushes, and a few skins pegged out. The man had knelt down to his work again, as if oblivious of her. She looked at him as he knelt there hammering.

He was as aloof as ever, with that guarded, hostile look in all his bearing. His face was not bad looking, if it had not been so hostile in expression. The moustache stuck out fiercely from under a rather short nose. He was a man nearing forty. And had nothing to do with anybody, except fiercely and vengefully to watch for poachers.

He had been beaten up twice, very severely handled by poaching colliers, forced to remain in bed with his injuries. But he had had his revenge and got three men into prison. He was feared and disliked in the district, a sort of black man of the woods to the children. When they ventured in a few yards into the hazel copse for primroses or nuts, their hearts beat fast. And never did they go far enough to let Parkin get between them and the hedge. For if he cornered them and seized them, he frightened them unspeakably, taking their names and their fathers' names, so that for weeks whenever they saw the policeman in their street they turned pale, thinking he was coming with a summons.

Constance knew him for what he was, the terror of children, the object of hatred of the poaching colliers, whose whippet dogs he shot and buried in gloating secret if he caught them in the wood; and to the wife who had left him a perpetual source of rage. And yet she, Constance, liked him. She liked him physically, she liked the way he bent over his hammering, she liked his silent, even his vengeful isolation in himself. She liked him because he was at war with everybody.

He was at war, really, with Clifford and herself, as much as with the poaching world. It was with difficulty he was courteous. And he spoke, both to her and Clifford, with the broadest accent. He did it deliberately, as many of the local people did nowadays, as an intangible kind of insult to the mincing-mouthed gentry: a defiance, a sort of contempt. He was an excellent keeper because he looked on the wood as his domain, and because he was practically never interfered with. But he resented even Constance's walking about the woods when the birds were sitting, and he hated Clifford's motor chair. Fortunately that could only come down the big drive.

Now, as she sat on a block at the door of the hut and watched him putting the coop together, she could tell he wanted her to go. He wanted to be alone. He could only live with a certain space round him, and the trees. The presence of any other human being was a clog on him, made him irritable, nasty.

But Constance did not want to go away. For some unexplained reason his mere physical presence was grateful to her. She had no desire to talk to him: in fact, she knew quite well she did not want to hear the things he would have to say. If he had anything to say, which was doubtful! But she liked to be there. She liked to see him stooping, doing the rough carpentry. It made her feel she was working too.

He looked round at her at last, stealthily, quickly: then looked away again. She took no notice. She did not even speak. Only she still sat there on the block of wood, leaning her arms on her knees, her face in a muse. And he went on with his work till it was finished.

Then he placed the coop beside the others, returned, picked up the tools. He hesitated. He had never really faced her since she had sat down, always had moved with averted cheek. But now he came towards the hut, still not looking at her. He passed her and went through the door. He had not looked at her.

She rose and stood in the doorway of the hut, facing him.

'It's very pleasant here,' she said.

He looked up at her quickly, suspiciously.

'D'yer think so?'

'I do! When will you set the hens?'

'When I've got the eggs.'

He turned and took his coat. She watched him button it over his breast. But he never looked at her, only he resented her watching him, with her blue, vague, wondering eyes.

'I shall come and sit here sometimes,' she said. 'I like this place, and I want the hens to be used to me.'

'Ay!' he said. And he set his cap and picked up a couple of mole-traps, to depart. She stood a little aside as he came out of the door, and he brushed against her. But he said nothing. She stood while he locked the door of the hut.

'I suppose you're going to your tea now?' she said.

'Ay! Just about! When I've set these traps.'

He spoke to her coldly, almost contemptuously, as if to a pestering child whom he wanted to be rid of. She was rather amused. She still stood by the closed door of the hut without moving to depart. He hesitated. Then very swiftly he touched his cap and muttered:

'Well, I'll be off!'

He ducked forward, and was striding to the path.

'Good evening!' she said. 'I'm going too.'

She started after him towards the path. He turned swiftly and touched his cap again as she went by. Then, at a distance, he followed her down the narrow path and on to the spring riding where he turned away in the opposite direction.

But as he was turning again, into another side-path, he looked back after her. She, glancing back after him, saw him do so. He disappeared in the trees, and she slowly plodded her way home, smiling to herself.

'After all!' she said to herself. 'He's amusing!'

She was late for tea.

'I'm so sorry,' she said. 'It was so lovely in the wood. I watched Parkin getting the chicken coops ready. It's really spring.'

She laid down her little bunch of wild daffodils, a few primroses and violets, and a few silvery specks of willow catkins.

'I must go out there tomorrow. The ground will be dry enough for the chair,' he said.

'Do!' she cried. 'You will love it.'

The following afternoon they went together into the woods, and she was quite happy, apparently, bringing him different flowers and leaf buds.

'"Thou still unravished bride of quietness," 'he said, looking with emotion at the wind-flowers and violets in his hand. 'Spring flowers always make me think of that,' he said, 'far more than a Grecian urn. Don't they you?'

'Yes!' she said, vaguely. Then she added, 'But why ravished? It's such a violent word! If bees come, or little insects, I don't think they feel ravished, do you? I mean the flowers.'

'Maybe not,' he said. 'They're quaint, aren't they? — The nodding violet! — Do you know, I don't think we should care half so much for flowers if it weren't for the lovely things poets have said about them.'

She stopped suddenly. Was it true? It was only half true. The things the poets said had indeed opened doors, strange little doors to the flowers, through which one could go. But once passed through the poet's gate, the flowers were more flowerily unspoken than ever.

She was not in a mood for literary allusions, and Clifford's way of making abstract love to her in words and suggestions, she found today irksome. 'Not that! Not that!' she said to herself almost without knowing she said it.

They stayed their hour among the trees. The sky was grey and chilly. It seemed a little uncomfortable, and the time dragged. They were both glad to go home and be apart for a time. She felt she must be alone sometimes.

The next day it rained in showers, so she could go alone to the woods. She wandered very silently, watching for the pheasants. And at last, as it began to rain again, she drifted to the hut. All was locked and deserted. She sat on the block under the little porch and watched the rain and listened to the soughing of the wind. It was so lovely to be quite alone, and quite still in the wood, watching the rain, listening to the noises of the wind and trees, inhabiting the eternal shadow of the forest.

As the rain slacked off, the brown dog came running silently to her, putting its paw on her knees. The keeper came after, touching his cap.

'It's so lovely to be out of doors and alone in the wood,' she said to him as she rose and made way for him to unlock the hut.

'Ay!' he said, as if she had spoken unintelligibly. She seated herself in silence again, rather sorry he had come to disturb her. Today she did not want him. She had been so happy watching the rain making ghosts among the oak trees in the fullness of solitude.

Still, she did not mind him. He busied himself quietly in the shed. At least he would not talk to her, nor make literary allusions.

'Are there two keys to this hut?' she asked. 'Could I have one? I should like to be able to come here if it rained, and sit and watch the rain.'

The man looked at her curiously in the eyes, to find out what she was after. He had reddish brown eyes with a small, hard bead of a pupil.

'There's only one key,' he said.

'Couldn't you have another made?' she said.

He would not answer, but bent stooping among some pieces of wood, sorting out one that would fit. And still he did not answer. This was direct opposition. But Constance was not going to be frustrated.

'Couldn't you have another one made?' she repeated, and there was danger in her voice now. She would not be affronted.

The man turned to her, and heaved a sigh of anger as he said:

'Yi, we could!' Then he looked her in the eye again, as he added:

''Appen Sir Clifford 'ud build you another little hut like, sort of summer house for yer. There used to be one, I believe, down against the spring.'

'No!' she said shortly. 'I want to be able to come and sit here and watch the little pheasants when they hatch out.'

He was assiduously measuring a bit of wood and did not answer, did not even seem to hear. This annoyed her.

'So you'll get another key made, will you?' she said.

He turned away, bent down over the wood again, and said with his back to her: 'I have to be here me-sen, a good bit, now t'bods is startin' layin'.'

'What of that?' she said sharply. 'I shan't interfere with you.'

He still kept averted from her.

"'Appen as t'bods won't want strangers round,' he said.

'I don't consider myself a stranger,' she said. 'Don't say any more. But I want a key so that I can come and sit here when I wish. When can I have it?'

He kept his face averted and answered not a syllable. But she could see he was blenched with anger. He must have his own way, or he went into a devastating temper.

'When do you think you can give me a key?' she insisted quietly.

He turned to her slowly and said in a voice of hate: 'How many bosses am I reckoned to have here?'

'Good gracious!' she exclaimed. 'This is ridiculous!' Then she mastered her own hasty rage. 'But don't be angry,' she said. 'Nurse says I must be out of doors and away from the house because I fret when I'm indoors. — And when I'm here, and I feel you're somewhere about I feel safe. That's all! You see, everything isn't easy for me either.'

Which was perfectly true. The tears rose to her eyes, and she turned hastily away and walked from the hut and down the path, suddenly sobbing bitterly into her scarf because of the strain on her heart. She walked hurriedly away, out of the wood and into the park.

And it was several days before she went into the wood again. She felt queer and still and wanted to avoid any contact. To Clifford she was very kind, but she did not really feel him, was not really aware of him.

She went to the wood one evening after tea when the blackbirds were whistling in the yellow light. Still she did not go to the hut. She went down to the spring, which bubbled in a little well, clear as crystal and very cold. It was true, there had once been a hut or a shed on the bank above. She sat down in the stillness; and heard the pheasants calling as they flew for the keeper's corn before going to roost.

But this place by the spring seemed chill and sad, as if there were ghosts. A thicket of larch stretched away uphill, and that too was gloomy. And on the grassy banks was that silence and woe of places which had lived long ago and lost their life. So many men in the free past of the forest must have camped and drunk here, for the well was famous. — No, it was sad.

She rose and turned sadly home while the blackbirds whistled their last wild cries. There was a great rustling of birds in the evening. How lovely and how sad it was! She went slowly in the ebb of life.

The brown dog came running after her. She turned. Parkin was following her, saluting.

'I browt yer that there key, my lady!' he said.

'Oh thank you!' she said dimly. Then, as she took it: 'Was it a lot of trouble?'

'How, trouble! It worna no trouble.'

In a queer, explosive way, the words burst out of him. He wanted now to reassure her. But he was like an explosion.

'Thank you then!' she said.

After this she would go often after tea, as the evenings lengthened, and walk in the wood and sometimes sit in the hut. In the little clearing by the hut the coops were put out in a circle, and hens were sitting on the pheasants' eggs. Towards sundown the pheasants would come running furtively for the bit of corn the keeper had scattered, the cocks steering horizontal in all their brave plumage.

And Constance would sit very still, watching. And the keeper would come and go quietly, almost benevolently. He had accepted her presence and accepted himself as her male guardian angel of the woods. He never interfered with her and rarely spoke to her. But when she did not come for almost a week, he watched her when she returned. And it was a long time before he brought himself to say:

'You wasn't poorly, was you?'

'No! Nurse has been away for a week, so I stayed with Sir Clifford.'

'Ah see!'

She was delighted when the pheasant chicks began to run out on to the grass. They were so tiny and odd. She had to help to feed them. They would stand, with their tiny tremble of life, in her hand and peck from her palm.

She looked up at the keeper, and her blue eyes were bright and moist and wonderful.

'Aren't young things lovely!' she said, breathless. 'New young things!'

'Ay! T' little baby bods!'

He spoke almost condescendingly but understandingly. And his red-brown eyes had widened and looked strangely into hers.

She remained crouched among the busy, tiny little birds, and she was crying. She felt a great abandon upon her. And he, trying to go away from her, was spellbound. He could not go away from that soft, crouching female figure. In spite of himself, he went and stood by her, looking down at her.

'Y' aren't cryin' are yer?' he asked in a bewildered voice.

She nodded blindly, still crouched down upon herself, her hair falling. He looked down upon her folded figure, and almost without knowing what he did, crouched down beside her, knees wide apart, and laid his hand softly on her back. She continued to cry, breathing heavily. And the touch of her soft, bowed back, breathing heavily with abandoned weeping, filled him with such boundless desire for her that he rose and bent over her, lifting her in his arms. All that could ever be that was desirable, she was to him then. And she, lifted up, for one moment saw the brilliant, unseeing dilation of his eyes. Then he was clasping her body against his. And she was thinking to herself: 'Yes! I will yield to him! Yes! I will yield to him.'

Afterwards, he was gloomy and did not speak a word. He avoided her. Even when she was leaving, and she softly said: 'Good night!' and looked to meet his eyes, he would not look at her. And that was the only word spoken between them.

But the next day she came again. He was not there. He appeared as late as possible, to shut up the coops. Darkness was coming on, the chicks were all hidden under the hens, asleep, the wood was falling into silence. Like a ghost he came, very late, through the drizzling rain. And like a ghost he saw her sitting waiting in the porch of the hut. And he shuddered with desire. But he quietly closed up the coops and gave no sign even that he had seen her.

She still waited. Perhaps he would go away without seeing her; pretending never to see her!

But no! He hung a long while round the coops, the darkness gathered. Then at last he came slowly towards her.

'You're late!' she breathed softly.

'Ay! Ah meant ter be!'

She paused.

'Didn't you want me to be here?' she almost whispered.

He looked at her, and the flashing dilation of his eyes belied his set face. He was in the torment of passion, almost brutal now. She went home alone in the dark, feeling a little bruised.

But the next day she went again in the evening. And he was there. He came up to her and looked at her almost maliciously.

'Don't you feel you've lowered yourself with the likes of me?' he asked brutally.

She gazed, hurt and wondering, into his eyes. And at once his eyes did that strange thing she had never seen in any other person, darkened and dilated and seemed to give off quivering lights, very lovely. And she put her hand up and touched his face.

'Not when I touch you,' she said. 'When I touch you, you are only lovely to me. — But one never knows what a man will think afterwards.'

'D'yer like ter touch me, though?' he asked, in a soft, doubtful voice.

'You're lovely to touch! You're lovely to touch!' she moaned.

'Ter thee am I? Like thee ter me?' he said, in the full slow tones of the dialect, with such a soft, warm flooding of truth. He had forgotten her difference for the moment.

She began to cry, and wept uncontrollably. He seemed stupefied with dismay.

'Never mind!' she whispered shakily as the tears ran into her mouth. 'It's happiness, really.'

And that time, for the first time in her life, passion came to life in her. Suddenly, in the deeps of her body wonderful rippling thrills broke out where before there had been nothingness; and rousing strange, like peals of bells ringing of themselves in her body, more and more rapturously, the new clamour filled her up, and she heard and did not hear her own short wild cries as the rolling of the magnificent thrills grew more and more tremendous, then suddenly started to ebb away in a richness like the after-humming of great bells.

And then she lay lapped in a new womb, a new throbbing of life all round her. And she loved the man, loved him with all the depths of her body and her body's splendid soul. While he with a wet mouth softly, strayingly, unconsciously kissed her. And suddenly she clung to his body again in the last surge of gratitude that lifted her as on a wave to him.

She wanted never again to leave him, never, never.

And when she did leave him to go home it was not really going from him. His warmth remained upon her and stayed in her. And he went in the wonderful semi-consciousness, or super-consciousness of passion, across the wood, and she was with him as the air of night was with him.

She was home in time for dinner. She did not notice Clifford watching her. Her face was soft and glowing, and her blue eyes were open like the night. But for him they were not open.

After dinner she asked him to read to her, and he chose Racine. She heard his voice going on and on, speaking the French in the grand manner. And when he made comments to her, or asked her opinion, she looked up at him with those glowing eyes and said:

'Yes! It's very splendid, just the sound of it.' He, thrilled in his turn, read on. And Constance drooped over her sewing, hearing the throaty sound of the French as if it were the wind in the chimneys. She did not hear one syllable of the actual Racine.

She was filled, herself, with an unspeakable pleasure, a pleasure which has no contact with speech. She felt herself filled with new blood, as if the blood of the man had swept into her veins like a strong, fresh, rousing wind, changing her whole self. All her self felt alive, and in motion, like the woods in spring. She could not but feel that a new breath had swept into her body from the man, and that she was like a forest soughing with a new, soft wind, soughing and moving unspoken into bud. All her body felt like the dark interlacing of the boughs of an oak wood, softly humming in a wind, and humming inaudibly with the myriad, myriad unfolding of buds. Meanwhile the birds had their heads laid on their shoulders and slept with delight in the vast interlaced intricacy of the forest of her body.

From the man, from the body of the man, the pure wind had swept in on her. 'Because I was willing,' she said in a muse. And like the calling of the last bird awake, in the infinite soughing and the vibrating hum of her body, the call repeated itself: 'Because I was willing!'

She thought for a moment of the man. Where was he? But her mind could not roam. The best part of him was most utterably within her, identified with her. She did not need anything more. To be alone, rocked in the breeze that had swept into her from him, that was what she wanted. Not to have to bear any further touch, any less essential contact.

And meanwhile the voice of the other man, Sir Clifford, went on and on, clapping and gurgling with strange sound. Not for one second did she really hear what he said. But it sounded to her like the uncouth cries and howls of barbarous, disconnected savages dancing round a fire somewhere outside of the wood. Clifford was a smeared and painted savage howling in an utterly unintelligible gibberish somewhere on the outskirts of her consciousness. She, deep within the sacred and sensitive wood, was filled with the pure communication of the other man, a communication delicate as the inspiration of the gods.

When the reading was ended she looked at Clifford, and his peculiar naked face, with the rapacious eyes of the men of our civilisation, made her shudder. It was the face of a most dangerous beast, domesticated but utterly crude, inwardly insensitive.

And with the swift instinct of self-preservation, the deepest of all the automatic instincts, she smiled to this cultured gentleman, to her softly throbbing blood a dangerous domesticated savage, and said to him:

'Thank you so much, dear! You do read Racine beautifully.'

'There's something in it, you know,' he said. 'The feeling may be a bit stereotyped, but then I begin to think all our feelings are, really. They run very much to pattern. Only we've tried to put new curves and flourishes in them, like the art nouveau, mostly in very bad taste. I can't help feeling that Hamlet is in bad taste. Orestes or Phèdre are much deeper down to the bedrock of the same sort of feelings, without so much contortion.'

'Yes!' she said slowly. 'I'm sure you're right. I'm sure that's true.'

She didn't know whether she meant anything, or whether he meant anything. Only her instinct was not to thwart him or to frighten him, but to reassure him in himself. He was another kind of creature, domesticated and dangerous.

So she helped him as usual and kissed him goodnight, as if he had been some strange idol which she must propitiate. 'Mein Abgott!' she said to herself, as she saw herself quietly kissing. 'My idol! My once-god! Mein Abgott!' she murmured to herself as he held her gently in his arms before she retired.

And there were tigers in her heart, creatures of the old jungle of the soul, ready to spring at his face. But she soothed them down. She would not be angry with him. He was the god that had fallen and become an idol. She could still make offerings to the idol in respect of its old godhead. She could be gentle to him and even grateful to him to the end. He was an image of her old household gods, her teraphim.

So she went upstairs. The nurse slept downstairs in the next room to his. Mrs Bolton had insisted on this. For he was often awake in the night, and it soothed him for someone to come in and speak to him.

He was curious: so thoughtful of everything, so thoughtful for everybody, he was finally limited entirely to himself. No breath entered him from any other living being or creature or thing. He was as it were cut off from the breathing contact of the living universe. He loved a beautiful landscape, a beautiful flower. Most of all he loved art, pictures, books. Because here his mind and critical appreciation could play freely. He could get real aesthetic pleasure from books and pictures, something that thrilled his nerves and gave him a feeling of pride, of conquest, of overweening. But it only carried him further away from any deep bodily interchange and left him, as it were, high and dry, as a man who has already died to everything except nervous appreciation or irritation.

It was as if he had already lost his body and was nothing but a network of nerves. Except that since he had been so fatally wounded, and his life had been so nearly destroyed, he had a secret, crude will to live. The will to live was the deepest thing in him, and all he cherished now were those things that would keep him alive, actually physically alive.

For this reason his health was important to him beyond anything else: and his food mattered to him because it would keep him alive. He watched like a lynx to see he was well nourished, and ate rather too much. He pulled himself round the garden in his chair that worked by a lever, never relenting in taking sufficient exercise to keep him fit. He knew that Constance sheltered him and kept his life flowing. He could depend on her. And so he clung to her with his will and was wary not to overtax her.

He was indeed remarkably well, a new sort of man. The upper part of his body seemed to broaden and fill out, became almost massive, hulking. And his once long pale face also filled out and broadened, became ruddy and full of a new will, the will to live. The features were still sensitive and critical, the light-blue English eyes were bright and over-intelligent. But there was in it all something secret and assertive, the peculiar assertion of the will to live, the right to exist, in the crippled man, that betrayed him and gave him a hard, almost impudent expression.

He was remarkably healthy, considering. The only thing that troubled him was that he could not sleep much, he was awake a great deal during the night. And this filled him with a nervous terror of his own extinction.

Then he would waken Mrs Bolton, and she would bring him food, or make him weak coffee, or play a game of cards or draughts or even chess with him. He taught her chess, and she was proud learning it, being a quick, intelligent woman. She wanted to be able to do all the things the gentry did, so that there was no more mystery in them for her. Then she would be through with them.

So Clifford had a new interest, teaching the elderly woman to play chess with him, even for his own wicked amusement teaching her French. She learned slowly, but surely.

This left Constance much more free. Mrs Bolton was glad to be good to Sir Clifford and to take from him what teaching he could give her in the acquirements of the gentlefolks. But she would never discuss the miners with him. He had developed into a keen business man. A large shareholder in the neighbouring collieries, his interest was in the pits. And he thought and schemed and studied and had long conversations with the colliery manager and the mining engineer and with the members of the company. And a great deal of his will power and intelligence went to the running of these two collieries from which he drew most of his income. He made sacrifices in his income and capital to have the pits modernised in their working. And now the bread that he had cast upon the waters was beginning to return to him. He watched the colliery returns with an interest and an intensity that never slackened, as if he would force the pits to pay and to pay well.

All of which Ivy Bolton knew. But in these matters she was entirely dumb. She attended Sir Clifford faithfully and gave him some of her life. But she never forgot that she was in the enemy camp. And she was quite ruthless in her attempts to release Constance from the grip of her husband, quite calm, quite cool, quite unscrupulous. She almost willed that the young woman should find a lover in another man.

Therefore, womanlike, she watched Constance's face and almost by instinct knew that something was in the wind. This evening particularly she had wondered, seeing Constance come home with that fresh new face, so lovely! The widow's heart yearned with the old passion of love, which had been cut off so cruelly in her. She yearned now even to know of it, to be sure.

She wondered where Constance could go for love. There was nowhere, no one possible. She went so often to the wood at evening. There was the gamekeeper, Parkin. Impossible! A disagreeable cruel fellow. No woman would think of him.

And yet! Woman-like, she knew he was a man by nature passionate. She knew by the mere turn of his nose and that fierce, wicked little pupil to his eye. That he had turned hateful, she also knew. But womanlike, she was aware that passionate men can be most hateful and most loveable.

Still, she thought he was impossible.

Sir Clifford slept badly that night. Parkin, on the other hand, after coming back to the hut where she had been, and sitting there in silence, his hands folded between his knees, gazing out into the night at the stars that seemed slippery between the boughs of the oaks and seemed, somehow, like the body of the woman; after gazing a long time motionless and thoughtless into the night, as if all the night were woman to him: at last lay down on the straw in the hut, and wrapped in a soldier's blanket, slept immovable.

It was still dark night when he awoke. He looked up at the stars. It would be four o'clock. He sighed for the woman: straightened his corduroy clothing: and with his prowling quietness, fully awake, went softly out into the wood, taking his gun.

He walked softly, stealthily, fully awake, eyes dilated on the darkness. But still the night was all woman to him. He made his silent, alert round of the wood in the moonless night that was heavy and chill.

And then at last, as the first pale uneasiness appeared in the east, he hesitated. He should go home to the cottage now and knock up a fire, and eat. But the other limitless yearning was on him, and he turned and slowly walked across the wood again, slowly into the park, while the dawn and grey clouds rose up together to make a grey day.

The world lay grey in the motionless dawn as he crossed the park slowly. He was going towards the house. It stood on a knoll of the park, quite naked to the park, in front. All gardens were behind. Only the drive swept round in a loop to the steps between a few big old trees. But across the drive was only the rough grass of the park.

Mrs Bolton had been praying for dawn. Sir Clifford had been so long awake. With the coming of day he would go to sleep again. She drew the curtains of his bedroom and turned off the light. Then she went across, through the partition doors, to the windows of his study, which opened on the front. If she let in all the daylight, and he was sure it was day, he would sleep. And she would snatch a few hours before the nine o'clock breakfast.

As she silently drew back the curtains, she saw a man standing motionless in the middle of the drive, a little way from the house, gazing at the house. In the greyness of dawn, of the clouded daylight, she could see it was the gamekeeper, with his gun in his hand. There was nothing remarkable about his being there on the watch.

But, motionless as he was, she watched him. And there was something in the stillness, almost boyishness, of his figure in the big-skirted coat that betrayed a man a little dazed with love. It was also slightly ridiculous, like a love-sick dog standing eternally outside the house of his inamorata.

She smiled a little to herself, grimly, and said to herself, 'I should never have thought it! Fancy!' And she gave a little clicking of mock distress with her tongue against her palate in consideration of Sir Clifford's young wife, Lady Chatterley, carrying on with her husband's gamekeeper. 'You'd have thought she'd have looked a bit higher.'

Nevertheless, Mrs Bolton triumphed. Why she triumphed, she did not know, but she triumphed. Furthermore, she was determined to be really in the secret. And further than that, she was determined that nobody else should be in the secret. She would keep Constance safe. She would never, never let anything get round to Sir Clifford, not if she could help it. A gamekeeper! Not very different, as far as that goes, from her own dead man who was forever young, only twenty-eight. Well, my lady wasn't so very different from Ivy Bolton when all was said and done! And she hoped that Parkin fellow would be decent. That was the chief danger! If that Parkin fellow would be decent. — Anyhow he seemed to be a good lover!

The nurse glanced through to the other room, at the great shoulder of Sir Clifford hulked to sleep under the bedclothes. 'You shall never know, if I can help it,' she said. And she went silently to her own room.

And when in the village the women pitied Lady Chatterley as a nun-wife, Nurse Bolton replied, 'Oh, don't you make any mistake. I made that judgment myself and had to take it back. Sir Clifford's all of a man, I can tell you: though you'd never believe it. You never would. But they hope for a child! Oh yes! And I shouldn't be surprised.'

She enjoyed saying this. She felt another triumph.

The day was showery. Constance still had a desire to be alone. She busied herself all the morning in the house and in the afternoon was driven to the small town in the motor car Clifford had bought. The country was looking its most dismal in the rain, the spring not yet burst through. The car ploughed uphill through Tevershall village, a long, dark-red straggle of small dwellings with glistening black slate roofs like lids: and poky shops with stacks of soap, or turnips and pink rhubarb, or huddled drapery; and Wesleyan Chapel, then Methodist Chapel, then Congregational Chapel, then Christadelphians or whatever they were: but all alike dreary and ugly to a degree. And at the top of the hill the old church and old stone cottages of the previous agricultural village, before the mining had started.

Tevershall was the home village for Wragby Hall, but both Clifford and Constance avoided it completely. It was a village that catered absolutely for the miners and consisted of miners: and it did not like the Chatterleys. The only thing to do was to leave it alone. So the inmates of the hall left it alone, scarcely setting foot in the two straggling miles of ugliness. And yet, thought Constance, in one of those dwellings he was brought up, and his old mother lives in one of them with his child! And he belongs there.

She sighed. It was the hopeless, dismal ugliness that so depressed her. She had been used to Sussex, and a lovely old house in a fold of the downs. She could never get used to this awful colliery region of the north Midlands. And yet she liked it too: it gave her a certain feeling of blind virility, a certain blind, pathetic forcefulness of life. If only it could realise how ugly it was and change a bit.

The car mounted the hill and ran on towards Stacks Gate. Away to the left, hanging over the rolling country, she could see the shadow of Bolsover Castle, powerful-looking. But beyond and below it was a pinkish plastering of newish dwellings, and plumes of black smoke, plumes of white steam rose in the damp April air from the collieries.

A great new hotel, red and gilt and splendid, the Coningsby Hotel, stood at the road-crossing. Further on a few yards, was Stacks Gate itself, fourteen rows of new, spick and span pink dwellings, set down as it were by hazard in the dismayed fields. And beyond them, the big new colliery, sending up huge feathers of steam, a rich colliery with all the modern contrivances for by-products. Here, indeed, there was not a chapel, not a church, not even any real shop. Only the great proud colliery like a noble activity of the devil, at one end, and the huge hotel at the other. The hotel was in fact merely a miner's pub, but it had all the modern adaptations for by-products, just like the colliery.

And the people had filled in; even since Constance had been at Wragby Stacks Gate had been created, and the human element had flowed into it out of nowhere, even in her few short years of married life.

The car ran to a high place again, and away in the distance Constance saw the looming of the great Elizabethan house, Hardwick, noble above its great park. But already they were turning, dipping between old, blackish-red miners' cottages that lined the road and led down to the old town of Uthwaite, whose twisted spire pricked up in the valley, beyond great 'works', collieries and foundries.

Uthwaite was a little knot of an old, old country town crouching in a valley below the big, open, rolling country where the castles and great houses had once dominated like lions. Now, however, a tangle of railway lines ran into the town nakedly, and everywhere the collieries and foundries and 'works' steamed and smoked, obscuring the little town. Around its old crooked streets hordes of oldish, blackish-red miners' dwellings crowded, lining the big new highroads. And in the wide region where the castles and the stately homes hung couchant, smoke waved against steam, and patch after patch showed the new mining settlements upon the repeated slopes of the open country. One meaning blotted out another, and though the great houses still loomed, the stately homes of England, they were mostly empty, just shells. The handsome old Georgian hall at Fritchley was just being pulled down. It was too big, like a great handsome derelict.

Constance felt that the old world was doomed. Even Wragby, she felt, was doomed, The great landowners when they opened the collieries doomed their own ancestral halls. One thing pushes out another.

For a long time Constance had rebelled against this awful ugly Midlands and northern world. It was unbearable. Yet even in her short time she had seen it grow. Now Fritchley Hall was being broken up, and Shipley was to come down next year: Shipley, such a pleasant 1760 stucco house, with its suave round bays and its beautiful rooms panelled and delicately painted! Even King Edward had liked it, liked to stay there, because it had such an atmosphere. And Squire Manby, as the people called him, how he had loved his home and the great, proud beeches that stood apart around it!

The squire died: his heirs inherited the wealth that had come from the mines. But the collieries were almost on the doorstep. The park had a right of way through it, and gangs of colliers lounged and sauntered by the lake, looking out of work. The old, proud squire did not mind.

'The colliers have made my income,' he would say. 'They are as ornamental to the park as deer.' He said this to King Edward.

'I agree with you,' said the king. 'If there were coal under the lawn at Sandringham I would open a mine there and think it fine landscape gardening.'

But that was the last generation: even the last but one.

Now at Shipley the grand beeches were already gone, and the park looked queer and bald. The hall was to be broken up. Rows of dwellings would be erected. The present Manbys had a house in town, a lodge in Scotland, and a villa near Nice. They detested Shipley.

Constance knew it all. She knew the Manbys, she knew all the county. Everybody had very carefully called, very kindly and warmly offered her — what? Not friendship exactly. Acquaintance! The Duke and Duchess of Coningsby, the chief family in the county, were really attentive. Poor Clifford! That was it! 'That poor young Sir Clifford Chatterley!' Oh but people were kind, when they were sorry for you.

Kind! Was it kindness? She thought of Parkin and the soft dilation of passion in his eyes, with those quick, quivering lights. That peculiar naked softness of passion that flashed with such strange lightnings. Kindness? She began to feel that many of the great old words had lost their meaning, like flowers that have withered yet leave the husks standing. Kindness? — 'Oh yes, people make a point of being kind to Constance and me.' This was what Clifford said to Lady Eva. But what did it mean? — make a point of being kind?

Constance brushed her thoughts away, for the car had stopped at the back of the old church at Uthwaite, in the curving narrow street. She got down to the pavement. The policeman saluted and held up the traffic for her.

Here, at least, in the old core of this town she was my lady! She crossed the road to the old druggist's shop.

She spent some time, shopping and chatting a little. Even she had a cup of tea in the clean, awkward little tea-shop. It was nice to be on one's own again, even for an hour. Like being in London again, going to the Academy School of Drawing and popping into tea-shops and restaurants.

As she went home in the car, the rain started again. She looked out of the windows. No! She would not go and see Parkin tonight. Not tonight! — But thinking of him and the beauty she had seen in him, in his body, in his naked, dilated passion; some quick of loveliness apart from his uncouthness and commonness, something tender and fragile, yet really him, and beautiful as an open crocus flower; thinking of this, a tenderness came over her, a wistfulness, for this disfigured countryside, and the disfigured, strange, almost wraithlike populace. Perhaps there was a wild, tender quirk of passion in many of them, something generous and unsheathed. Yet at the same time, they were so crude, so limited, so inflexibly ugly.

'If one could have a sense of life-beauty with them,' she said to herself, thinking of Parkin: 'The beauty of a live thing! If one could waken them to that! Not art and aesthetics, which somehow is always snobbery! Look! He is beautiful. Even his face when it suddenly softens and goes fresh like a flower! I shall tell him so. I shall tell him. They are so terribly cut off from their own beauty, these people. — And yet I feel they've got it, somewhere: even when they look so ugly. But they've got something tender in them that might blossom out in generations into a lovely life. It only needs developing. — Oh, how wrong our education is! How wicked we are to them, really!'

'I had tea already in Uthwaite,' she said to Clifford.

'Did you, dear? In Miss Bentley's tea-shop? And how was the assiduous Miss Bentley?'

'Just the same,' she said.

Miss Bentley was an old maid, dark and with a rather large nose, who served her teas with a careful intensity with which one might administer a sacrament.

'It's very fine,' said Clifford, 'mashing the tea with as much soul as dear Miss Bentley puts into it. But that Ceylon tea is hardly worth it. She should have been a ministrant in some temple of virginity. Did she ask after me?'

'Oh yes!' And Constance imitated Miss Bentley's hushed murmur, 'May I ask how Sir Clifford is, my lady?'

Clifford laughed. 'Did you tell her I was blooming?'

'Yes! I said you were wonderfully well. And if she came to Tevershall she was to come up to Wragby to see you.'

'The deuce you did! What a pretty fool I should look, with Miss Bentley almost kissing my hand! I know she would if she dared. —Well, and what did she say to that?'

'She blushed. Yes, she blushed and lowered her eyes for a moment. She looked quite a young thing. She must have been pretty too. And then she said she didn't think she would dare to presume.'

'Dare to presume!' he laughed. 'She is an absurd old thing. Do you think she has a special feeling about me?'

'I think she has: you are the preux chevalier of her imagination.'

'I suppose that kind of thing is what made preux chevalier;' he said.

'Of course! The men lived up to it.'

'Did they, I wonder! At least it was a pretty bluff.'

They had a quiet happy evening together. It was raining and very dark out of doors. She thought of the other man. Then, when lamps were lit, didn't think of him any more.

'Look here, Con!' said Clifford as he filled his pipe after coffee. 'Do you really care a bean whether you're immortal or not?'

She looked up at him. He was in good form, and he looked well.

'It's not one of my problems, I think,' she said.

'Ha!' he drawled. 'No, I don't believe it is. — I fancy it is one of mine. Do you mean you really don't care whether you're immortal or whether you aren't?'

'I don't know quite what sort of immortality you are thinking of.'

'Oh! — Yes you do! — Whether your soul, or your self, or your essential you, call it what you like, will reach a state where it is — well — perfect, if you like. And being perfect, it has a life eternal of its own.'

She put her sewing aside to attend to him seriously.

'Well!' she hesitated. 'I don't really feel very interested in a sort of long-drawn-out immortality, I must confess.'

'But when you come to die? — And we all must.'

'I know. But when I come to die —' she frowned. 'I think I shall have enough faith — to — to be glad — and just to leave it to the Lord.'

'Ah! So you don't really care what becomes of you afterwards?'

'Not very much. Whatever it is brought me into being will carry me out again in its arms, as it were. A baby before it's born knows it will be born and leaves it at that. But it doesn't even know what being born is, or consists in, or anything. And the same with me about dying. I know I'll die and be carried away. Where, how, when, why, I've no idea, and I don't know how to make any idea of it. So I leave it as an unborn baby leaves it.'

'Plato's ideas, and heaven, and those things, mean nothing to you?'

'Pictures! They make pictures. But they're like a picture gallery. I'm an onlooker, I'm not in the picture. If I try to put myself into the picture, it's only a strain on me. — No! With heaven and Plato's ideas and all those things, I feel as I do in the National Gallery, or in the Uffizi. I'm looking at something rather lovely, or very lovely, but the world is outside, and my life is in the world.'

He puffed at his pipe.

'Do you mean to say,' he cried, 'that nothing means any more to you than anything else? — Than Miss Bentley, for example?'

'Miss Bentley fussing about a butter-knife to the butter doesn't interest me. But when she blushed and looked like a shy girl for a minute — that interests me as much as Plato or as much as Titian.'

'Does it really?' he asked in amazement. 'Why?'

There was a silence. She did not know what to say. But she felt she had to have something out with Clifford: establish her own sort of immortality, perhaps; not always be commandeered by his.

'Immortality can't be anything we know. It can only be something we feel,' she said.

'And we can't feel it because it doesn't happen to us till we're dead!' he said.

'Why?' — she paused, dazed. 'I think that's silly,' she said. 'If I don't feel I'm immortal now what's the good of fussing about it later on? The first time I ever really felt a Titian picture — I used to think his nude women silly and boring — but when I one day suddenly felt in all my body the soft glowing loveliness, loveliness of the flesh — then I said to myself, quite distinct and alone — "that is the immortality of the flesh."'

'Titian's art, you mean,' he said.

'No! I don't. Titian's art only revealed to me what I've been able to see ever since in people: the immortality of the flesh. I saw it in Miss Bentley when she blushed.'

'But not when she was bringing a butter-knife?'
'No.'
'Why not then?'
'Because she was fussing.'
'Well, but —!' he laughed. 'Her flesh was the same.'
'No!' she said. 'It changes.'
'Do you ever see the immortality of the flesh in me?' he asked.
'Sometimes.'
'When, for instance? Now?'
'No, not now.'
'Why not?'
'You look tough.'
'Only when I look tender, then? — Not when I look tough?' he mocked.
'When there is a certain tenderness on you, and you look as if you didn't turn the wind, if you know what I mean.'
'And when do I look like that?'
'Sometimes. Sometimes when you are a bit sad, and you're not thinking. Or when you're feeling rather pleased because you know you are better. Or when you're suddenly really angry.'

He was silent for a long time. Then he said bitterly: 'When I look at my dead legs I don't see much immortality of the flesh, I assure you.'

There was almost a cynicism in his tone, something that frightened her. And a voice inside her warned her: 'Don't go any further.' She had a sudden dread of him, as of something perhaps fiendish.

'Clifford,' she said suddenly, looking up at him. 'You know I am fond of you. And I want always to be fond of you. Never mind what has happened to your legs. You are you.'

'I am I!' he repeated. 'I am I! And when I am out of the body, perhaps I shall be a real thing. Till then I'm not.'

'Yes you are! Think what a great part of life you are, even to me!'

'And what I'm not, even to you,' he said.

'Never mind that,' she said.

'I mind it,' he said. 'Titian's women! The immortality of the flesh! Do you think I don't know what you mean, even if you don't know yourself? — I hope you'll find a man to love you and give you babies — the immortality of the flesh you're after.'

'Would you mind if I had a child, Clifford?'

He looked up at her suddenly.

'If you had whose child?' he said.

'I don't know. Would you mind if I had a child by a man?'

'Couldn't you promise it would be by the Holy Ghost?' he said satirically.

'Perhaps!' she murmured. 'The Holy Ghost!' There was a pause.

'Why?' he said. 'Do you think you're going to have a child?'

'No!' she murmured. 'Not yet.'

'Not yet! How not yet?'

'Would you mind if I did have a child?' she repeated.

'Whose child, I ask.'

'But need you ask? Isn't it the Holy Ghost, if one looks at it that way?'

'It's no good my looking at it that way. All I see is some man or other who probably was never in the war and so —'

There was a pause.

'But why need you ask which man?' she said softly.

'Haven't I the right?'

'Have you?'

There was another dead pause.

'No by God!' he said suddenly. 'Probably I haven't. Probably I've no right to a wife at all: a wife in name and appearance. No, I've no right. I've no right to you. You can go to what man you like.'

'No but listen, Clifford! I love you. You've taught me so...

(Pages 87 — 90 of the original manuscript missing)

'I shall go to Nottingham this afternoon, to the dentist,' she said. 'I suspect one of my teeth.'

'Will you?' he replied in a peculiar tone.

A dull red colour came into her cheek. He was pretending to let her know by his tone that all kinds of things might lie behind this visit to the dentist.

'I got an appointment for three o'clock,' she said, 'so I shall have to be off.'

'You'll be home for dinner?'

'Oh yes!'

'Oh! You will!'

His pretended surprise was an insult. The colour again came to her cheek. But she departed.

She was growing angry herself. She had tried to be simple with him and take him at his word. And, it seemed, she had just stirred a nest of vipers. She sat in the car, rather stiff and aware of nothing. It was almost a shock to her when the chauffeur opened the door and asked her where she would care to go. She was in town, in the market place. The hour and a half had gone by without her knowing, she had been so tense and involved.

She saw her dentist, drank tea, made a few purchases, and set off home. She was amazed at the hard cold anger that filled her at the thought of Clifford. What a subtle, cruel tyranny he had exerted over her all the time! He had absorbed her life and had sought to absorb her will, her very thoughts were never to be free of him. How cold he was, really! What a cold determination there was in him, coldly to subjugate her! Yes, a subtle, cold determination to have her subjugated. Perhaps he wasn't aware of it even himself. Perhaps it was instinct, cold and serpentlike: to have her insidiously mastered.

She realised now why her sister Hilda disliked him so. Constance had said: 'Hilda, you seem to hate Clifford.' To which her sister had replied: 'No I don't. But I dislike him, he is distasteful to my pride.' It had seemed a funny thing to say. And there had been a note of cold despising in Hilda's voice. — It had puzzled Constance. She had not imagined anyone could coldly despise Clifford. He was fine, and rather noble.

But suddenly she saw the cold, limited egoism in him: his cold will acting like the will of some non-human thing under all his fair and gentlemanly tolerance. Suddenly she saw the cold coils of the serpent that had been closing around her, and she recoiled in revulsion. 'No!' she said aloud. 'You shan't do that.' — And a new, severe, hurt look came into her face.

The other man? Would he be the same? — A subtle, insidious bully? She knew his wife had said he was a bully. Was he another of them?

She thought of Parkin, of his fixed, aggressive face. Yes, probably he too would be a bully; but much more openly. With him it would be a clash of wills and perhaps a certain brutality. Violent, ugly, malevolent he would be if he were opposed, like a thing at bay.

But he would never be cold. He would snarl and bite and be beastly: but not this pure, almost spiritual coldness of Clifford's, that slowly edged itself to its own ends like a serpent, and slowly coiled the folds of its invisible will around one. It was so subtle, so invidious, and somehow so pure. It always seemed pure and white and irreproachable. That was so awful! The white irreproachable purity of the will, that would subjugate her ultimately into nothingness. — Yes, in time she would become just a half-animate automaton worked entirely from Clifford's will, coming as he willed, going as he willed, thinking only the thoughts he released in her mind, feeling only the feelings he allowed to come forth. And all the time he would appear so selfless, so considerate, so utterly quiet and unassuming. He would seem to leave her absolute liberty. Never would he utter a command, never would he say You must! You shall not! I do not allow it! Never! He would always seem to leave her entirely mistress of her choice. And all the time he would subtly have stolen all choice from her, she could only choose as he willed.

For he himself was absolute in all his universe and she was only a thing to be made use of. His immortality, his heaven of the pure truth, the pure ideal, the pure light, it was only himself in his own oneness exalted to an absolute and everything but himself fused away. No room for her, no room for anything. If she were there in the final white glare of his heaven, she would have to be so fused down that she was gone, gone entirely, become a pure part of him in his final transfiguration.

She shuddered with pure revulsion, and sheer rebellion. 'Never!' she said. And again: 'Never!'

She felt the thing was unrighteous and unholy. She now understood Hilda better, and Hilda's revolt, and Hilda's apparent peace, being alone. — For Hilda's husband in a clumsy way had been the same. Hilda must subserve his immortality. She must melt her mere mortality into his immortality.

Ugh! How gruesome! How repulsive, this white abomination of tyranny! In this respect at least, the gamekeeper was better. He had no preconceived immortality, no sense of his own absoluteness. He might make a woman cook his dinner and mend his clothes, but he would not all the time be sucking her soul away, like a white stoat at her throat. No! He might bully in the obvious way and even hit his wife in the face. But after all, that was not so bad. It was open warfare. Open warfare, open warfare, if there must be war!

And of course, there would only be spells of warfare. After all, when the keeper's eyes dilated and became full of soft, flashing lightning, she felt so real, so real. She had yielded something to him. That was true. But not to his bullying. Only to his sudden real desire. And yielding, she had come so much more alive, so much more herself.

Bullying was bad. All kinds of bullying were bad. That she decided in herself, absolutely. But far worse than physical bullying, which might hit you with a clenched fist, was this silent, fair, pure bullying of the spirit. That, no, never! It made one lose one's very soul.

For a time she felt she would leave Clifford and go away with the keeper: buy some little farm in Scotland, and there live with him. She had enough money of her own. And Hilda would help. They might even all live together.

But then something inside her said: No! — No, she must not take him away from his own surroundings. She must not try to make of him, even in the mildest form, a gentleman. It would only start a confusion. No! She must not even try to make him develop along those lines, the lines of educated consciousness. She must leave him to his own way. His instinct was against education. His instinct made him refuse to speak King's English, even to her. He stuck to the clumsy vernacular in a sort of defiance.

She sighed wearily. Apparently it was impossible to have a whole man in any man. Her two men were two halves. And she did not want to forfeit either half, to forego either man. Yet neither would she be bullied by either of them in his halfness.

No! If Clifford forced her to it, she would leave him. But it would mean leaving the other man too. She could not, and would not take him along. It would be too humiliating for both. She would go alone, to Hilda. It would be best to be alone, as Hilda found it.

She arrived home tired and heavy, and almost blank of feeling altogether. She had not the energy to notice whether Clifford were amiable or unamiable, or if she noticed she was not able to feel anything in response.

As a matter of fact, he seemed remote, affecting the snows of Everest. Which was all to the good. Let him wear the snows of Everest on his loftiness for ever, so long as it kept him detached, without encroaching on her.

They passed a short, silent evening, reading. She only pretended to read. Her brain felt like a piece of cork. And she had no feelings whatsoever, except the abysmal lethargy of nullity, corklike and insentient. So that as early as possible she rose to go to bed.

'Good night Clifford!'

'Good night Con! Sleep well!'

His voice so perfectly pleasant and kindly as ever. She wanted to say to him: 'Do drop it! I am not taken in.' — But of course, she did nothing so vulgar. She softly closed the door, with well-bred attention.

The next morning he was the same, but a little wan, a touch of the small boy in his solemnity. Constance felt nothing much — what was the use of feeling anything? Only she hated this nullity which came over her emotions when they had been wound up too tight. She felt an absolute nausea at the thought of any more struggles of will between herself and Clifford, or between herself and anybody else. Ah! just to be alone, and not forced into tension ! — Why couldn't Clifford be as good as his word? Had he only said that he wanted her to bring no sacrifice, just in order to throw another cold coil of his power around her? Well, she had taken him at his word, so now he could either uncoil or coil upon himself alone.

It was raining again, and no escape from the house. During the course of the morning, as she was passing Clifford's study, she heard the sound of men's voices and went in. It was the gamekeeper asking for certain instructions, and Clifford, very alert and competent, giving them.

Parkin turned and met her eyes as she entered. In his red-brown eyes with the small pupils there was question and a sort of fear, an animal anxiety. He could read nothing in her wide blue eyes.

'Good morning!' she said quietly.

'Good morning my lady!' he replied, saluting hastily.

'How are the young pheasants?' she asked.

'Ay! my lady! — doin' nicely,' he said.

'I want to come and see them again soon.'

'Ay! Come then! Ay!' — He hesitated, then turned again to Sir Clifford. 'Well, I s'll get summonses for the two of 'em then, that's what you mean?'

'That's what I mean,' said Sir Clifford.

'All right! Then I'll go down to Clipstone about it?'

'Who are you taking out summons against?' asked Constance.

'Two Stacks Gate colliers — third time they've been caught, and poaching rabbits out of season,' said Sir Clifford. He seemed to have brisked up, taking action against somebody.

'Where were they poaching?' she asked, turning to the game-keeper.

He gave a sweep of the arm.

'On the south side — in the park. I catched 'em wi' six snares an' two rabbits.'

'When?' she asked.

'This mornin', just come daybreak. I was waitin' for 'em, so I had my nephew Jack there an' a',' he said loudly.

He too seemed to have been on the warpath. He stared down at Constance with his small-pupilled eyes like some animal that hunts. And in him she could read no expression now, for the peculiar animal anxiety had gone. Only his small eyes were searching for something in her, as an animal might search the human face, missing all human contact.

'Isn't it a pity to prosecute,' she said slowly, turning to Clifford. Not that she really cared.

'Isn't it a pity to poach rabbits, or anything else,' said Clifford, 'in breeding season?'

'Horrid! And I do dislike those snares,' she said.

'We s'll 'ave 'em all ower t'wood if we dunna lay hold when we 'n got 'em,' said Parkin, with a certain hard satisfaction.

'You're quite right, Parkin! You step down to Clipstone,' said Sir Clifford.

'Ay!' said Parkin. And saluting, he departed with a tread of heavy boots.

'That man does love laying his fellow-men by the heels,' said Clifford, smiling.

'Horrid!' she said.

'Very useful in a gamekeeper,' he said contentedly.

'I suppose all men are gamekeepers one way or another: something is game to them,' she said bitterly. And she too left the room.

From the front window she could see Parkin striding down the drive, determined to draw blood. The skirts of his big coat flapped, his brown dog ran at his heels. He was once more going to take the world by the nose. It would make him more unpopular: the whole mining population resented the summoning of poachers intensely. But it seemed to give him satisfaction. He strode with a grand sort of stride, baggy coat-tails flapping. The son of man goes forth to war! She smiled to herself grimly.

Nevertheless, she liked the cool way he had met her in Clifford's presence. He wouldn't have roused suspicion, not if the whole of Scotland Yard had been present. Yet he had been afraid something was wrong. She had seen it in his eyes. Perhaps he had been afraid lest she had given him away. Then he was at once reassured again and no more concerned than his own little brown dog. Amusing, too, the way he had come up, right into the lion's den, to find out.

At luncheon Clifford seemed in quite a good humour. He went out in his chair in the afternoon, the weather having cleared up, and she walked across the park and through the fields to be alone. She was still rather angry. And of course, she was in suspense, not knowing what Clifford would finally say.

She had waited now for two days for his reply. This evening she would approach him again. And if he tried to put anything over her she would depart the next day to Scotland, to Hilda.

Having passed Marehay Farm, she turned, taking the footpath that went uphill through a corner of the wood, through the thick fir plantation called the Warren. It was very unlikely indeed that Parkin would be anywhere about: his game did not lie in this direction even if he were back from his errand in the village.

Having climbed the rail fence into the wood, she hastened along on the disused path between the dense fir trees. She always disliked this shut-in density of youngish, bristling trees. She always hurried through to get to the open park. There was something sinister and very lonely about the place.

A bird broke out, startled. And as she turned the bend, nearly through this isolated place, a man stepped out of the dense wall of the firs. Her heart stood still: but it was only Parkin.

What a savage instinct the man had! She had hoped to escape him!

He stood motionless while she came slowly up. Then he touched his cap, still waiting till she was quite near. She mumbled a sort of greeting.

'Ah was wonderin' if there was ow't amiss, like!' he said in a constrained voice, his eyes on her flushed, perplexed, weary face.

'Nothing particular,' she said, pushing her hair aside fretfully. 'I told Sir Clifford there was a man I liked, and I might have a child by him.'

He was staring in her face with that keen, animal look of search. She met his eyes for a second, and for a second she turned all molten, beyond herself.

'Yer didn't say who it was?' he asked.

'No, I didn't.'

'Didn't 'e ask yer?'

'Yes.'

'Yer didn't tell him, like?'

His quick, smallish, brilliant eyes were moving on her face in a dazzling way.

'No!'

He waited. And she could tell it was with a great effort he refrained from coming towards her. There was a powerful force that drew his breast strings to hers as by a strong magnetism. She could feel it.

'What then?' he asked, short.

She looked up at him helplessly. And in the instant he was to her and had his arms around her, and she was lying against his breast, where she had to be.

'Tha wor na slivin' past me, wor ta?' he asked, in a low, crooning, pained voice that had triumph in it too.

She did not answer. She turned molten again, in strong waves, as if, surge after surge, she was losing her solidity and her consciousness and becoming a pure molten flux. She looked in his face as her consciousness left her mind, and she saw only the curious concentrated dazzle of his eyes.

He took her aside, among the dense trees, and in the thicket her short, almost whimpering cries of passion, purely unconscious, sounded in his soul in a sort of ecstasy of triumph.

But when she came to herself she would not stay with him. 'I must go,' she whispered. 'I must go.' But not just yet. Then her voice became more her own. 'I must go,' she said in a low tone. And he rose and helped her with simple decency.

Even as she stood gathering herself together she thought of the cunning of the man. There was a low pile of fir boughs on the ground, and he had flung his coat over them.

He had expected it then! And she had been taken so utterly off her guard!

Silently, with dropped head, he was pulling on his coat.

'Am I all right?' she asked.

He looked at her, and brushed dry fir needles from her coat behind, and took them from her hair.

'Ay!' he said.

'I must be quick,' she said.

There was a pause.

'What did yer tell 'im, then?' he asked, in a low voice.

'Oh!' she felt very vague, and not very much interested about it all now. 'What I told him? — Why I said — I said I would never tell him who. And I said he'd have to promise not to ask me or bother me or I'd go away.'

'Where?'

'To Scotland, to my sister.'

'By yourself?'

'Yes!'

Their eyes met for a moment. He looked away into the trees.

'What did you tell him for?' he asked.

'Well! — It came out. And if I were to have a child — it would be legally his — it wouldn't be fair.'

He did not answer for some moments. Then he looked at her.

'You think, as 'appen you might have a child, like?' he said.

'Yes. Don't you think?'

Her eyes met his for a moment, and she saw the passion still in his reddish-brown glance.

'Yer wouldn't mind, then?' he said a little awkwardly.

'I? — I should like it — for myself. — But I must go. — If ever he even suspects about you I shall go right away.'

'What for?'

'I can't live with you. And I couldn't live with him if he had thoughts about you.'

He was silent for what seemed a long time.

'Then we'd best stop as we are, like: if we can manage?' he said rather sadly, perplexedly.

'Why yes!' she said, a little impatiently.

He turned to accompany her.

'Don't come with me,' she said shortly.

'Nobbut ter th' road,' he said, hurt.

They crackled through the dead boughs without speaking till they came to the path.

'Yer wouldn't fret, like, if yer went away somewhere an' niver seed me again?' he asked.

She glanced up at him and saw the pondering in his eyes. 'I should mind,' she said. 'But what else could I do?'

He looked at her for a long time.

'Should you mind?' she asked him.

'Me! Ay! —' He seemed to think. 'Ay!' he said again, as if with far-reaching thoughts.

'Well!' she said, a little impatiently. 'You've got a wife and I've got a husband — so we have to take what we can get — and — and make the best of it.'

'Ay!' he said slowly. 'Ay! — But —' he hesitated. 'I should like yer ter lie a night wi' me — Ah should!'

'Goodbye!' she said, to get away from the peculiar hypnotising spell of his fox-red eyes. 'I shall come to the hut.'

'If I'm not there,' he said, 'yer might chop a bit o' wood so's I s'll hear, yer know. I s'll hear.'

She went on, and he turned into the trees whence they had come.

She ran into the park, running with impatience, as if running away from something. She recognised the power that passion had assumed over her. She felt strange, different from herself. It was all very well entering on these voyages of new and passionate adventure, but they carried you away from yourself. They did not leave you where you were, nor what you were. No, she was aware of a strange woman inside herself, a woman wakened up and imperious. She was running now to get home to tea, but she was running also to get away from this new thing that had come upon her. She was running to escape from the woman inside herself, the woman who felt so fierce and so tender at the same time, so soft and boundless and gentle, but also so remorseless, like the sea.

All her life Constance had been known for her quiet good sense. She had seemed to be the one really reasonable woman on earth. Now she knew this was gone. She had burst out as if from a chrysalis shell, and she had emerged a new creature, in feeling at least. Why did nobody ever prepare one for these metamorphoses? Why was one never told that the great facts of life, and the great danger, was this starting of the whole being, body and soul and mind, in a new flux that would change one away from the old self as a landscape is transfigured by earthquake and lava floods, or by spring and the coming of summer.

She had been so sensible up to now. And now she felt everything was leaving her. She had thought to appreciate this other man just as a body, as one might appreciate the Greek marbles, for example. And now instead of Greek marble he was a volcano to her. Or he turned her into a volcano.

She was frightened. One thing she clearly saw: that human nature under all its dead surface of habit is, like the earth, volcanic and will inevitably start to upheave one day, when the pressure from within is too great or there is a call from the outside; just the one mysterious call that is the Open Sesame.

It had happened to her with this man, this mere gamekeeper. Even that very morning she had seen him striding down the drive in his baggy coat to go to the police station, and she had smiled at his importance and his hurry. She could still see him objectively as something ridiculous and apart from herself. And now — she groaned in spirit — she could not detach herself from him, her independent existence was suddenly gone.

Her first words when she got home and saw Clifford were:

'I'm so hot! I hurried home. I went over to Marehay to see if the rabbits were doing as much damage as Allcock says. I met him, and he showed me. But I shouldn't be surprised if they weren't our rabbits at all. There's a warren in his little spinney, you know.'

And even as she was saying it she felt so unspeakably bored, bored by the look on Clifford's face, bored by the house, bored by her own words, that she could have cried. She was crazy to be with the keeper, to be near him, near his body: even having tea with him in his little cottage. Only, only to be near him!

Yet here she was gasping out about Marehay and rabbits and damages to Clifford. Why wasn't she calm? Why wasn't she balanced, her old self, her famous poise. Why couldn't she recover her well-known poise. Suppose Clifford noticed something!

The keeper — he was just a common man. She had seen him so this morning. She insisted on it. Yet all her body cried with a thousand tongues: No! No! He is unique! Poor Constance groaned in spirit. It is just race-urge which transfigures him for me, she told herself, using one of the H. G. Wells catchwords which she so despised. Her body laughed aloud. Race-urge! Well why not? Transfigures! Yes, a transfiguration! Ha ha! A transfiguration! A man suffused with the brightness of God. Ha ha! How's that? Most men had lumps of clay in them that no fire could transfuse. Her keeper had a certain fineness and purity of flesh. He was always bodily nearer to God than most men, than Clifford.

'And what do you think happened to me!' said Clifford, with arch importance.

'What?' said Constance.

'Miss Bentley actually called — sent in her card!' he cried it out in triumph.

'Never!' she cried, her eyes glowing. Clifford was utterly uninterested in her and her tale of rabbits. And she, she had torn herself away from the other one for nothing.

Clifford seemed in a perfectly good humour, as if there had never been any strain between them. She listened to him in perfect acquiescence: all about old Miss Bentley in a short and modish dress of tearose yellow. Some far corner of her critical feminine mind was interested. But her dynamic self was so bored, so bored, screaming with boredom.

She fled at last upstairs and sat down in a low chair by her window. What could she do? How could she recover her poise? — How lovely he was, really! How he had pounced on her! How humble she ought to feel, how grateful to him, for feeling this straight unerring passion for her! How lovely it was to be near him! How lovely he was. If only she were near him now, just even to smell the corduroy of his coat. So common, an old corduroy coat! Made stripes on one's face if one leaned against it. How ashamed she ought to be! — a gamekeeper, in her husband's employ! But his body! — the unspeakable pleasure of being near him. 'Ay!' she imitated in her mind the broad sounds of the vernacular. 'Ay! Ah should!' And she laughed a little, she liked it so much. It amused her down to her very toes.

But she could never live with him. No, no! Impossible! She was not a working man's wife. It would be a false situation. He would probably begin speaking King's English — and that would be the first step to his undoing. No no! He must never be uplifted. He must never be brought one stride nearer to Clifford. He must remain a gamekeeper, absolutely.

And herself? It would be absurd for her to become a gamekeeper's wife. Her piano, her paints, her books — leave them all behind? But even if she did, she wouldn't be able to leave her thoughts behind, and all she had acquired, the whole run of her mind.

'When the hounds of spring are on winter's traces —
'

He was one of the hounds of spring: a Plutonic hound. Pluto, not Plato. And she was an escaping Persephone, Proserpine. Well, she'd rather be married to Pluto than Plato. She'd rather be caught by the wild hound of Pluto than by the speculative spaniel of Plato.

This amused her very much. She was so pleased with her own wit.

But at the same time, she was sad. The keeper would never know the difference between Pluto and Plato, not if he lived another hundred years. That was the whole Plutonic point: you didn't even want to know. But she herself wanted to know: she would always want to know. She would always want to read Swinburne again sometimes: she would always want sometimes to play a bit of Mozart to herself: she would always want to go to see a collection of Cézanne or Renoir or Van Gogh, if she were able: she would have to go to the Uffizi gallery again before very long: she wished she could go tomorrow to hear Kovantchina again or to see a Russian ballet: she would love an evening of sheer talk as she used to have it in Chelsea: or if she could sit in a Bier-Halle again in Heidelberg or Munich, and hear student songs and philosophise: and she would always like to be able to glance at The Times Literary Supplement to see if there might be some thrilling book.

She couldn't do any of these things in a gamekeeper's cottage. Or if she could it would somehow be false and wrong. Clifford could share it all with her. But Parkin — the very name seemed ridiculous to her — she wondered what his Christian name was — probably Bob or Billy — and she didn't want to think of him as Bob or Billy — she didn't want that sort of contact with him.

No, she would just be an anomaly in a gamekeeper's cottage. Besides, he had a wife. — She was on the alert at once. He must get divorced from that wife.

Constance had a small income of her own. She could take a little farm, and he could be a farmer. Then she could have her own rooms and her own life and still live with him.

But no! The meal times! The inability to converse! She knew she would have to have conversation. And when Hilda came, and at meals they talked all beyond him, and somehow he looked small, a cipher at his own table! No, no, it wouldn't do, she could never live with him as his wife.

She had almost recovered her poise in her effort to be reasonable. Of two things she was convinced: that she would never try to 'elevate' him, to bring him towards her own level of life: and that she could no more abandon her own way of life than he could his. Therefore — oh bitter conclusion! — it was useless to try and bring their two ways of life together.

Then why their two bodies? Why this passion, which meant more than the rest of her life to her? — Ah, if she could be in the cottage with him now, just lighting the lamp! Perhaps they would have — she tried to think of something really common — bloaters, yes, bloaters for supper, grilled bloaters. The house simply reeked of grilled bloaters. And he sat with his elbows on the table, in his shirt-sleeves, and picked bits of bloater bones away with his fingers. And drops of tea hung on his fierce moustache. And he said:

'These 'ere bloaters is that salty, they nowt but brine. Pour us another cup o' tea, leass.'

And he would nudge his cup towards her. And she would rise obediently to get the brown teapot from the hob, to pour him his cup-a-tea.

She would never be able to imitate his speech. You couldn't even spell it. He didn't say 'these' but 'thaese', like the Italian paesano. And not 'nowt' but 'neôwt', a sound impossible to write.

She gave it up. Culturally, he was another race.

But she laughed to herself at the picture of the bloaters and the cup-a-tea. She would still love him, because of the loveliness of his flesh-and-blood being. Even the smell of bloaters in his hair wouldn't make him anything but physically attractive. She would love to sleep with him. He wouldn't even wear pyjamas. Probably he slept in his day shirt. But curiously, nothing would make him physically unattractive.

But if they lived together they would humiliate one another. She, because she was in another world of culture than his. And he, because his state of nature would ignore so much of her; and he had no goal, no onwards in his life. He was static. It was that that she could not bear. He was static.

Even Clifford, poor Clifford, yearned and reached for that precious immortality of his, when he would be identified with the pure ideal. In a vague way Constance sympathised with him. It was better than reaching for nothing at all. But it was always a disembodied ideal. A weariness.

She sighed and felt weary. Then she cheered up, thinking at least she could have the keeper's children, like a fresh fountain of life. And perhaps her children would be able to discover a new immortality in which the disembodied ideal had some sort of a body again.

She really agreed with Clifford: you had to have an immortality of some sort. She was somehow not interested in the long-drawn-out kind, as she called it, the immortality after death. It bored her to be immortal merely when she was dead. It was more imminent, really. One was perhaps more immortal when one never thought about it. Surely the keeper was immortal when he stepped out of the trees! Surely he was something else than commonplace, he had his immortality upon him. It wasn't his business to think about it. But somebody should think about it.

She really wanted to ask Clifford about it.

He was very amiable at dinner.

'I wondered why you didn't come down,' he said. 'You were a long time upstairs.'

'I was thinking about things,' she said.

'I guessed as much. I nearly sent Nurse up with a penny for them. — What did you think?'

'Oh, it was all vague.'

'I've been thinking too,' he said, simply and pleasantly. 'Does the physical side of sex really matter to you, Con?'

'I'm afraid it does,' she said demurely, smiling to herself at the way he put it.

'Do you feel, really, you couldn't do without it?' he said.

'I'm afraid I do feel rather like that,' she admitted.

'And is there a particular man you care about, physically, enough to have children by him?'

'Yes,' she said: still amused by the way he put it.

'Then,' he said, 'I think you're quite right, there's nothing to do but for you to go ahead, and for me to keep my mind off it altogether. The man's a decent man, I suppose. And if it's a wise man who knows his own father, my so-called children will have to be unwise. — Or shall you tell them later?'

'I haven't got any yet,' she smiled.

'Quite! But let's be premature. Promise me that you'll never tell them I'm not their father; and I know you'll try not to damage your own name or make me look ridiculous, but promise me, and I promise to leave you carte blanche and to keep my mind a blank in that direction.'

She was rather breathless. She sat awhile, dazed.

'Do you really mean it? — You won't try ever to find out things?'

'About you and your physical love affairs I will not ever try to find out anything: I wish to know absolutely nothing. And I accept your children for mine. — But promise me what I asked.'

She still pondered, as if there might be a trap.

'It's awfully good of you. I promise you as far as one can promise those things. — I'll never let the children know you are not their father — if there are children. — And I will be careful —'

She ended rather vaguely.

'That's all then,' he said. 'I suppose you wouldn't like it made legal? — Ask old Morley to draw up a mutual document to the effect?'

He smiled wryly. But she did not speak.

'Are you sure you don't mind awfully?' she said at last. 'I should feel so bad if you minded much.'

'All right then!' he replied. 'I'll only mind a little. The great catastrophe happened. This is only one of the consequent difficulties.—You're sure you'd not rather depart altogether with Mr X?'

She looked him slowly in the face.

'No!' she said. 'I don't want that.'

'Just for the breeding season, as it were,' he said — and she wondered for a moment, wildly, if he knew. — 'I suppose it's natural, and it's no use trying to go against nature. The war should have taught us that. — All right, my dear, breed! It's nature's law. I hope my heir will have a father worthy of a future baronet: but I trust your taste. —It's all awfully like an H. G. Wells novel, where prize specimen human males are raised on a sort of antiseptic stud farm, and led round to the passive females at the proper season — about May, I suppose, about now. But it's the consequences of the war, so we'll say no more.'

There was a dead silence between them.

'You wouldn't rather I went away and left you?' she asked dully.

'My dear child, don't you see it's myself I curse, really, for putting you in this predicament. I admire your grit. Go ahead! I look forward to my son and heir.'

'Supposing there weren't one?' she said.

He spread his hands and lifted his shoulders.

'A la guerre comme à la guerre,' he said, with keen irony, 'et depuis la guerre comme depuis —'

She felt depressed. It was so plucky of him, but not very human. Perhaps she was even a little disappointed.

'You're awfully good, Clifford!' she said. 'And you know I'll stick to you, don't you? — If you want me to.'

'My dear girl, what would my life be if you left me? I'm getting off cheap, in deferred payments, really. — I've thought it out and have come to the conclusion that wisdom is justified of all her children. You will surely be justified of yours. Go ahead and produce that son and heir.'

She didn't quite know what he meant, and doubted if he knew himself. And she felt he needn't be so glib about son and heir. But she admired him, and she really wanted to stick to him.

The trouble was, he seemed to her now so boring. There was no wonder in him.

The world looked different to her. It had come alive. She used to see it aesthetically. Now it had come alive, and was — she didn't know what to say — portentous. She shivered to think of her other world, the cardboard aesthetic and automatic world where she had lived with Clifford. To see the trees bulging and urging like ships at anchor on a tide: to feel the world full of its own strange, ceaseless life! — She caught her breath, fearing to lose it again, fearing lest she might die down to the original machine-measured hours. Now the clock mattered so little. The soft, full surge of the day had no minutes to it.

'I must be very careful,' she said to herself, 'not to lose my touch with him. It is he who connects me up with real life. And that is what I really want. It's not so much the passion itself — it's this, that all the stage setting of the world has come real, it lives with me, and I'm not on a stage with actors and dummies any more. Oh, let me pray never to fall back into that bored deadness! — After all,

I'm like the woman who touched Jesus. You touch the living body, and the flow starts in you, the dead dries up. Oh, if I can only keep in touch all my life, all my life. They say passion dries up, and love dies out. I hope it won't be so. I hope I never need lose touch again, not even when I die.'

The problem haunted her. The new soft flowing of life all around her that was the kingdom of life itself, must it die out? Must she, later on, fall back into the periodic excitement and boredom, interest and depression, feeling of creation and feeling of emptiness, which had been her life up to now? It all seemed to her so dried up, so dead: even the excitement and the fervid interest and the very creativity. It seemed somehow mechanical, like sparks out of a machine.

But was it possible? Was it possible that one could stay in the soft flow of life without falling back into the old dreariness? That one's life could be all the time like a little river running between rocks and sedges and under bridges, and never dried up? She felt sure that in the past people had suffered and known sorrow and pain and fear: but they hadn't been inwardly bored, and outwardly mechanically active.

She thought of the people round her: the servants, for example, and Mrs Bolton. Did Mrs Bolton have a real source in life? Or was she dried up in her soul?

No, it seemed she had a source. Yet her husband had been dead so long.

'Is it long since your husband was killed, Mrs Bolton? — Very many years?'

The nurse sat very still. Her face was rather long, and pale with a healthy pallor. But she had fine grey eyes, very searching. She looked at Constance.

'Twenty-three years, my lady, since they brought him home,' she said. And her mouth closed firmly.

Constance felt her heart lurch. My God! If they brought home the dead body of one's own man, which had been the living body on earth to you!

'How awful!' she said breathless, her eyes awe-stricken.

She had known the fact all along. But she had never realised till now that a man could be, in his body, the living clue to all the world to a woman.

'I don't know how you lived through it,' she said.

'No! I didn't know myself. — But I made up my mind when I looked at him before they closed the coffin: I'll never forget you, lad! I believe you'd never have left me. And I'll never leave you! — And I haven't.'

Constance looked stealthily at the nurse. A colour had come into her cheeks, a flush of the youth and the fire of the young wife.

'Was he good looking?' Constance asked softly.

'No! — Not what you might call particularly good looking. But — he looked to me like no other man did before or since: though I've had far better offers, as you may say, than him. But no! I never forgot him. And I never forgot his face neither as he lay there dead. He'd got a red moustache, though his hair was so nice and fair. And his mouth looked as if it would say something to me if it but could. It did. His lips were shut, you know, but like life: as if they was just goin' to speak to me. An' I waited for it. Yes, I did. — But I knew what he wanted to say —'

'What?' whispered Constance, her eyes full of tears.

'Ivy!' said the other woman, and her face began to quiver. But she gathered herself together, and became stern and remote. 'He just wanted to say my name. — And I've heard him saying it ever since. I have! — I promised never to leave him. — An' I never have left thee, lad, have I?' she ended, speaking with strange, quiet fierceness to the dead.

And Constance felt another presence in the air, something male and reassuring. Not a spirit. But as if there were present in the house the man whose very existence is a reassurance to a woman.

'And then they said he was a coward, running away because he was frightened!' said the woman, stilt speaking with indignation into the void, as if to the man himself.

'Who said it?' asked Constance.

'The masters! — And those that were for them, on the inquiry.'

There was silence between the two women.

'And you never felt he really went away from you?' asked Constance.

'Never!' emphatically declared the other woman. 'Never! I lost him. But he's never left me. I miss him, God knows. But I've never been apart from him. And the heart makes up for a lot.'

Constance was pondering. The heart! Did the heart rule, after all, once it was awakened? How strange, the awakening of the heart! She thought she had loved Clifford. And she had loved him. But, she knew it now, not with her heart. Her heart had never wakened to him, and left to him, never would have wakened. No, not if he had never been to the war at all. — His terrible accident, his paralysis or whatever it was, was really symbolical in him. He was always paralysed, in some part of him. That part in a man which can wake a woman's heart once and for all was always dead in him. As it is dead in thousands of men like him. All the women who have men like him live with unawakened hearts. Perhaps many of them prefer it. An awakened heart is a strange other self, and a great responsibility.

'Is it your heart which never forgets him?' she asked of the nurse.

Mrs Bolton gave her a quick look.

'That's how it feels. Once a wife, in your heart, always a wife, I say. That is, if you've got a heart. Many hasn't. And many don't believe in it. But having a man goes to the heart with very few, as far as I can see. With me it did and does, and will now while I live.'

Constance was thinking: Will it with me the same? And it seemed a strange bondage. But also a relief. She quivered a little in her heart: it was so unbelievable that she should never again be free of that man, the keeper. Unless, of course, with her pride she determined to make her heart cold. She could do that. But the penalty was too great. Better put up with anything than have only a cold heart. She knew it too well.

'And are men the same?' she asked: the old, old question.

'I don't know so much about men,' the nurse said. 'I've not had much to do with them. But it seems to me they must be very much the same, only they don't think about it as much as women do. And of course, a good-hearted man, if a woman makes an appeal to him, she can get almost anything out of him. I find among the colliers, if one woman's got into a man's heart, any other woman can get pretty well what she likes out of him, if she's only a bit appealing, on the right string. I know I could coax most of them into almost anything. It's only with the hard ones, and these sneering young ones that are coming up today, that you can do nothing. But they're mostly good-hearted, good-hearted to a woman, even if they're a bit common sometimes.'

'Do you think working people are more good-hearted than the others?' asked Constance.

'Well —' the woman hesitated. 'You mean the gentry?'

'Yes.'

'Well! — They aren't half so nice in their ways. But it seems to me, they're more good-hearted. Mind you, I know them better. And I've done a good deal for them, even if it is my duty. So if they're not good-hearted with me, who will they be? — And of course, I don't know the gentry in the same way. How could I?'

'No!' said Constance, looking with wide, vague eyes at the other woman. She was wondering if he was good-hearted. She knew he was. But she wanted this woman's verdict too.

'And I suppose, even those that seem disagreeable have good hearts underneath,' she said.

'Often they have. Why the good-hearted ones, they often take things harder than the others, and then they're like a bear with a sore nose. You have to handle them a bit gently.'

She spoke with a motherly kind of toleration, as if she were the old mother to a thousand men.

'Like our gamekeeper,' said Constance. 'He seems always to be wanting to summon somebody. But I suppose he's not so bad underneath?'

The wily nurse knew her ground at once.

'Why his wife,' she said, 'was one of these florid sort of women, on the loose side, and that may have turned him. Anyhow his old mother sticks up for him. "They can say what they like about our Oliver, if .they leave him alone he's no harm to anybody: but them as meddles with him knows it." — She's a bit of a tanger herself, she is: and likes her glass of beer. But I get on all right with her. "Eh, Nurse, you're one o' them downy birds, you are! It's not often you give a squawk."'

The nurse laughed to herself.

'What does she mean?' asked Constance.

'She means they won't get much out of me. And they won't. Oh, she's a bit rough, but she's all right. The father was one of those easygoing men who drank too much, so she brought the boys up, and she brought them up rough. "Oh, get out o' th' house, gret lorrapin' nuisances!" — She drove them out of the house: she was too clean and tidy to have sons about. She made life a regular battle, and now none of them can live with their wives. She's proud of it. "Never a woman as can live with 'em! So what has their mother had to put up with!" — But she made them like it.'

'And do they drink?' asked Constance.

'No, not to speak of. Their father cured them that way. But it's a word and a blow with them all. — Though I don't know much about Oliver — the keeper here. He lives all to himself, and it seems to suit him better than the mine.'

'Is he much disliked?' asked Constance.

'Oh, they hate him. You see, they used to be allowed to poach rabbits while Sir Clifford was at the war and Parkin was a Tommy. So there's been nothing but battle royals since he's been back in the cottage. Oh, I've heard them vow and declare they'd lay him out, more than once. But they won't. They know he's doing his duty. I always tell them so. — But they mortally hate him, even the women. He's so hateful if he catches the children getting a few bluebells!'

'Yes!' murmured Constance.

'But Sir Clifford says he's a marvellous keeper, and I can well believe it. There's two sides to everything. It's just which side you're on.'

'I think he's really a nice man,' said Constance suddenly, a little flush in her cheeks.

'Oh, yes! I often say, the nastiest are the nicest, if you know how to handle them. But there's not many as sticks up for the keeper: except his old mother, and she says he's ruined because his father would never give him a leathering. It's always the father's fault, to hear her talk. But in my opinion the fault's hers if it's anybody's. And anyhow as she says, he harms nobody if they don't meddle with him and his rabbits. But you'll see a different side to him, maybe: you and Sir Clifford.'

'He seems a nice man, to me,' said Constance quietly.

'Ay, well! — He doesn't like me, I've scolded him more than once, and he's unforgiving.'

'But how old is he? Are you so much older?'

'I'm fifty. Yes! I was a year younger than Ted. Fifty! And I never seem to myself any older than twenty-seven; and him twenty-eight. Yes, he's never got any older than twenty-eight, as you may say. — But I'm fifty by reckoning. — So I suppose Oliver Parkin, he'll be about thirty-six or seven. He'd be a lad of thirteen or fourteen when I first began nursing, and his father was ill, and died with hardening of the liver —'

'Perhaps,' said Constance, 'they hurt his pride when he was a boy.'

'Perhaps they did. But he was a defiant little demon, you could have killed him and he wouldn't budge an inch. I believe he liked his drunken father. "Oliver, ma duckie, shall ter go ter th' Three Tunns for me," I can hear him wheedling. "It'll ma'e thee bad!" the lad would say. "Eh, ma lad, it'll 'appen ma'e me a little better." And that boy would find threepence somewhere for a pint, while his mother was slaving taking in washing. If she caught him she'd drink the beer herself. My, the battle royals! She's as hard as whit-leather, and she'd get hold of his hand that held the can, and he'd fight and call her all the names and try to spill the beer. But there'd be a drop for her to drink. And then he'd call her such names and just disappear, gone for a day or two. — There was never much love lost between that woman and her sons. But she slaved for them —'

'How many sons were there?'

'Three others. This one was next to the youngest. The youngest, Albert, he is more steady. He lives with his mother and Oliver's little girl.'

'Don't you think Parkin likes his little girl?'

'It seems to be in the family not to care for your children. — But she's like her mother, on the brazen side.'

There was a pause.

'You must know so many people,' said Constance.

'Oh, among the colliers! I know most of them. I don't know much about Oliver Parkin, because since he became keeper I've hardly seen anything of him. He was cheeky to me when he was a boy: but what could you expect? And you never know. He may have a good heart, if ever anybody could get there. But it would take a different sort of woman from most. With most women he'd just put their backs up. But of course he'd show a different side up at the house here.'

Constance paused, wondering if the woman suspected anything. She was a queer creature, with her dead young husband in her heart, and her endless intimacy with the mining population, and her odd histrionic power of making people real. She was an actress in a curious way. Her real heart contained only her dead husband. To the rest she was a sort of actress. And secret as the grave, where she wanted to be.

'It isn't much of a life for a woman,' said Constance, 'if her heart never wakes, is it?'

'It isn't, my lady! And a woman who has a heart in her will wash away if it isn't wakened: or else go queer in some other way. Oh, I know! There's many that have no real hearts. I know them. But those that have, blessed be the man to her whose heart needed wakening and he wakes it. Be he who he may! If you've got a heart you don't want to live for money and things, you leave all that to those with poor little hearts. That's why the wealthy, for all their niceness, have no hearts when you come to the bottom of them.'

'But perhaps you don't know them,' murmured Constance.

'No, perhaps I don't. Perhaps I don't want to. My own man meant more to me than all the wealth and the wealthy ever could, and they said he was a coward. — But never mind! And if a wealthy man won't go to your heart, a poor one may. And then, let him be what he will, he's done more for you than the others. It just depends what you're willing to abide by.'

'Yes!' said Constance, rising.

'And no matter what our station in life, we have our thoughts, and we make our judgments. And nobody can ever stop it.'

'Why should they try?' said Constance, trying to get away.

'And if there's something in you, my lady, makes one say more than one should it's because you're a woman, and a true woman, and a body's heart burns for you and not against you.'

'I know you wouldn't do anything against me,' said Constance.

'Neither shall anyone else, if I can help it,' said the nurse, her eyes flashing. Then she went to the door and departed without another word.

Constance was a little afraid of her. She seemed a bit mad.

And for the first time in her life Constance felt a quiver of dread, a fear, as it were, of far-off revolution. She knew a good deal about the terrible revolution in Russia, and the convulsive class hatred which had wreaked itself without expending itself there. But Russia was Russia, romantic and awful and anyhow incomprehensible. England was another matter. 'We are not divided, all one body we —' She had always felt that this was true, underneath, they were all one body. She had never in her life felt the smallest fear, class fear, of her countrymen.

Now a strange twinge, like a premonitory twinge of travail pain in a woman who has so far borne no children, went through her. She felt a twinge of indefinite and awful dread, a dread of her own fellow-men and women, a special class fear. For a long time she would not believe where the strange twinge of fear-anguish came from. But at last, she had to admit, it was from her contact with the lower class.

She had touched them, in actual passionate contact. And out of the touch came a twinge of wild, unknown fear. Perhaps they were her destroyers, the destroyers of her and her class! Perhaps even now the keeper was gloating over a certain subtle destruction of her. She remembered the infinite subtle malice of his voice when he said: 'Don't you feel you've lowered yourself, with the likes of me?' — Did he feel that somewhere she had lowered herself with him? And did he gloat over it? And Mrs Bolton? There was something sinister in her friendliness. Was she too gloating over a fall?

This thought caused a tremendous revulsion in Constance's soul and threw her back towards Clifford. He and she were on one side in the division. All her class loyalty returned upon her. The flow started again between her and her husband.

And in the fear of the new danger, she walked to the wood to speak to the keeper. He was there at the hut because it was after tea, her time. He saluted as she approached. What was he thinking? Was he triumphing again over the fallen 'my lady'? Was he thinking, 'Here she comes, my lady, my strumpet'?

'I mustn't stay,' were her first words to him. 'I have to be back at once. — Are you all right?'

'Ay, I'm all right!' he said.

'Clifford,' she began — then hesitated. Should she continue to say 'Sir Clifford' to this man? No, it was too late. 'Clifford knows I am not faithful to him — I told you.'

'Ay!'

'Well! I don't think he suspects who it is.'

'No!' he said, utterly without meaning.

(Pages 137 – 138 of the original manuscript missing)

The keeper thought about it, but his mind resolved nothing.

'So you can go on like you have been doing?' he asked.

'I don't ever want anybody to know about us — about you and me,' she said. 'You don't, do you?'

'I shan't tell anybody,' he said, laconic.

There was a long pause.

'What makes yer come to a feller like me?' he asked at length, getting a question off his mind. 'Cause yer think yer can take it or leave it as you like?'

She too pondered. Why had she come to this man?

'I don't know!' she said slowly. 'But once I saw you washing at the back of your cottage, and I thought you were beautiful.'

'Me!' he said with a grinning, mocking incredulity.

'I thought your body was beautiful,' she said. 'And — and I wanted you — I don't know why.'

'My body was beautiful!' he reiterated, still grinning.

'Yes!' she said. 'I still think it is. There is something beautiful in you. I should be glad to have your children.'

He had turned his face aside and was staring through the little window, silent. Then he looked round at her, and there was a queer little smile on his face: even now, as if he'd been insulted.

'That's a rum un,' he said, 'as I should be — bewtiful, as you ca' it — to one like you, who knows all the tip-top young fellers, eh?'

'I don't mean handsome,' she said.

'Handsome is as handsome does, 'appen!' he said irrelevantly but grimly. Then he added: 'But you don't take me serious, do you?'

'In what way, serious?'

'Not like you would one of your own sort?'

'Why not?'

'You'd niver marry me — not if you was free as the wind — you'd niver marry me,' he said, in a certain contempt for their relationship.

She was silent for a long time. Then she said:

'You'd never want me to, would you?'

It was his turn to ponder.

'If you wasn't above me, I should. Ay! You're above me, though, an' I'd non want ter marry a woman a lot above me.'

She held her peace for a time. At length she asked him:

'Are you sorry we've come together — as much as we have?'

He did not reply at once. He had to think it out.

'No, I'm not sorry, so to speak. Eh no! I should like to go on an' let rip. It's not that. But what do you think of me? You look down on me.'

'No!' she said. 'I'm grateful to you.'

'Ay!' he retorted. ''Appen so! An' for the times I've had wi' you, I am. It's been extra. Oh ay! But not thinkin' o' that. — Why, yer don't think anything of me, how could you!'

She was puzzled what to say. Already he had a grievance.

'Well —' she said, 'If you don't want me —'

He turned and looked at her, smiling almost frighteningly.

'You come when you like, an' you go when you like,' he said, 'an' you take no count of me. But what about me, when I wait and watch across th' park, an' you never come? An' I say to myself: "She wants none o' thee tonight, lad! Go whoam an' hang thy gun up!" — Ay, I'll wait! Yi, an' I'll go home, an' wait again th' next day. But I know right enough. You think nothing of me. You look down on me. Only you enjoy a bit o' cunt wi' me. But you look down on me, cunt an' all.'

How strange he was! More alien than a foreigner, as if he belonged to a bygone race of men! What language was he speaking?

'Listen!' she said. 'And don't be unjust. Listen! I love you. Just the woman I am, I love you, and I want to sleep with you in your cottage. I want you to tell me my body is beautiful to you. I want to be your wife, really. — But can't you understand, can't you see, there's Clifford. I can't leave him in the lurch! He understands that I need you. Can't you understand that I need him?'

He looked at her with a peculiar glare.

'What if you told him you'd been wi' Oliver Parkin, th' gamekeeper, carryin' on wi' him? What would he say?'

'I don't know. I shall never tell him in any case.'

'I bet you won't. No, an' I's warrant you won't! Eh!'

She sank into profound dejection. She could feel the mockery, the scepticism, the jeering in the fellow's voice. The radical hostility in him, and the contempt he felt for the sex relation with her! Because he wasn't her class equal he felt a contempt for his very love or passion, whatever it was, that he felt for her.

'Well!' she said at last, rising slowly, and turning to the door. 'We'd better say goodbye! I am grateful to you for what you've given me. I am! You've been good to me.

— But we'd better say goodbye! — And forget it. I'll just be as I was before — before this spring.'

He threw back his shoulders with a sudden heave.

'Eh!' he said. 'Don't say as I've been good to you. You've gen me more than I've gave you.'

He looked into her eyes, that were blue and miserable and heavy with reproach, and his face twisted with passion as if he were going to cry. It had suddenly come over him again, the blind, overwhelming desire to touch her, to lay his hands on her body.

She saw his hands lift involuntarily towards her.

'No!' she said, shrinking away. 'No! You hate me really. I must go. I mustn't come any more.'

She opened the door wide and looked at the silvery evening with bluebells rich blue under the twilight of boughs. And as she hesitated, wondering at the uncanny beauty that was out there, he put his arm round her waist.

'Wait a bit!' he whispered. 'Dunna go!'

His powerful hand was on her, pressing into the softness of her body.

'I must go,' she said, trying to writhe away.

'Hark!' he said. 'Hark!' And he caught her in both his arms. 'Hark! Dunna go! Dunna go! Ah dunna want thee ter go! Dunna go an' leave me for good! Say tha'lt come back. Say tha'lt allers come back — here i' th' wood. Say I s'll allers ha'e thee here i' th' wood, for allers! Say summat as'll keep! Say as summat'll keep — summat.'

'What shall I say?' she murmured.

'As tha'll — tha'll niver break off — say as tha'll niver break it off, atween us!'

'What's between us I'll never break off,' she said. He drew back, looking at her doubtfully.

'Never!' she repeated.

He let her go, suddenly, and turned to the workbench, taking up a hammer and some nails.

'Let's nail it in,' he said, taking her by the arm and leading her out into the lovely twilight that was blue with hyacinths and pale with new leaves. He took her across to a big oak tree that spread its budding boughs over the clearing.

'Shall yer drive yer nail inter th' oak tree wi' mine, for good an' a'?' he asked her.

'Yes!' she said uneasily.

He took a large nail and with a few heavy blows drove it deep into the trunk of the tree. Then he gave another nail to her.

'Nail it in aside of mine,' he said.

She drove in her nail close beside his, and he put the hammer in his pocket.

'Tha's done it,' he said.

'Yes!' she replied. 'But I've got to go now.'

'Shall yer come soon again?' he asked.

'Yes.'

'An' shall yer stop a night i' the cottage wi' me?'

She paused before she replied:

'Soon I will. We'll arrange, shall we?'

'Shall yer though?'

He watched her as she turned to go.

'Don't come with me,' she said, meeting his eyes. He said nothing but stood still, watching her go. There was a watchful, unyielding look in those red-brown eyes of his, which made her know she would not have everything her own way, even here.

The evening was very lovely, the after-glow of sunset clearer almost than the sun among the knotted twigs of the oaks overhead. On the riding tall forget-me-nots were myriad tiny stars in a Milky Way, fluffing always up. She hurried past them, feeling that they were laughing at her: each its own tiny speck of a laugh. Because she would be late for dinner. Late for dinner! Late for dinner! called the wild birds.

Clifford had come to the top of the steps in his wheel-chair, and sat there watching the west. It was a brilliant May evening, full of the wild, uncanny disturbance of an English spring.

She waved her hand quickly to him when she saw him, and he waved back. She pulled off her hat as she came up the steps. Her hair was wild, her face soft, her eyes large and dilated.

'The wood is so lovely!' she said. 'Why must one always hurry home?'

'Did you feel you had to hurry home?' he said.

She paused and looked into his face, and her heart smote her.

'Only because it was lovely,' she said. 'I wanted to come home as soon as the sun went. But then I was rather far. — Why didn't you come and meet me?'

'I!' he said. 'Only a real lover should come to meet you on an evening like this.'

She put her hand quickly on his hand that lay on the wheel of the chair.

'No, I was thinking of you,' she said.

'You are so beautiful,' he said. 'You are like a flower: and rather like a dryad, but without any sharpness. I wish I had met you on my feet in the wood. Did you feel it a twilight wasted?'

'I? Why? No, it was lovely: a world to myself! Except I spoke a few words to Parkin.'

'Did he intrude on your nymph's career?'

'No, he was only there. — Aren't you hungry? I am. Shall I just wash my hands and come to dinner as I am?'

'Do, darling! —' He caught her hand suddenly. 'Are you happy?' he asked in a low voice.

She was arrested at once.

'I — I never thought about it,' she said. 'Why do you ask?'

'Because you look so beautiful,' he said, still in a low tone, secretly. 'You look so adorable. I couldn't bear it if you were unhappy.'

She bent and kissed him quickly on the brow.

'My love!' she said to him, tender as a mother.

'Yes!' he said. 'Perhaps it had better have swept me away altogether. I feel like the Artful Dodger who has dodged death and wishes now he hadn't.'

'Oh don't!' she said. And she squeezed his hand.

'I want to cry and howl,' he said pathetically.

She stopped again and kissed him.

'You shall cry and howl if you wish,' she said very softly. 'I will hold your head against me. You cry if you wish, my dear, my poor dear!'

'There!' he said suddenly. 'I'm all right again. It's May — for oh! it is not always May! — Alas no! It's often must! — Wash your hands, darling, and I'll go in.' He began to wheel his chair across the hall with his hands. At dinner he was quite gay. But afterwards in his room with her he was sad again.

'I honestly think I should have died,' he said. 'They should have let me die.'

'Clifford! don't!' she said, coming over and holding his head against her body. 'But why, dear? Because something is lost it hadn't better be all lost, had it?'

He felt the soft, slow, healthy breathing of her warm body against which she pressed his face.

'Would you mind, truly, darling, if I were safely across the Styx?' he asked.

'Why ask such things?' she said, pressing his head closer into her. 'You know how glad I am that you like life.'

'I ask such things,' he said, 'because there's no reason for me to live if nobody else wants me to live. And I felt, when I saw the sun set, and you didn't come, that you'd be better off if I were dead, and perhaps you knew it.'

She slackened her hold on his head.

'That's cruel of you, Clifford,' she said, in a low, serious voice. 'I shouldn't be better off if you were dead. I should be worse off. I don't want you to die. I need you in my life. — And still for all that, it's cruel to make me responsible for your living. You want to live yourself? You've got a great desire to live, haven't you?'

'Oh darling!' he replied. 'I felt such an agony of uselessness this evening while all the birds in the world whistled their good male music. I felt an agony: useless! useless! useless! only an obstruction to life!'

She looked at him. His blue eyes were wide and fixed. He was letting off his agony on her.

'But Clifford!' She sat down and slowly began to cry. Once she had begun, she sobbed blindly, and he could not soothe her. But curiously enough, underneath it all she was rather happy.

'Darling! My own darling!' he repeated. 'I am a brute! I am an undeserving brute and a lamentable Hamletising swine. Darling! If only you'd kick me! Or smack my face! for I deserve it. — But don't, my dear girl, don't cry, for I can't bear it. You're far, far, far too good to me. Con, my darling Con, please, please don't cry. For my miserable sake, once more, don't cry, darling! Don't, for my selfish miserable sake! — I am not worthy of you, my poor girl, genuinely I'm not.'

But she wept in a burst flood of distress. And underneath she was rather happy. She wept in her old and very sincere grief for Clifford. And underneath she was rather happy because she had knocked her nail in beside the other man's nail and had promised to go to his cottage to spend a night with him.

The grief, too, seemed older, shallower, less radical than the other, the adventurous sort of happiness.

When she had wept all her tears away they passed a quiet, tender evening together. She was happy then with Clifford, when he was quietly, almost wistfully straying and musing, talking fitfully. They talked about everything, people, books, ideas, art, and all in a quiet illuminative way, without emphasis or repudiation, just straying on in harmony.

'Yes, I agree with you,' he said to her. 'Immortality is a sort of fourth dimension, it's always there, only we lose the sense of it. I do agree with you, it's not a long-drawn-out thing. Only we lose something inside us which feels our immortality and so doesn't bother about it. — Now tonight, talking quietly with you, I've had the feeling of immortality. And what else should I want? — We share our immortality in common, you and I, don't you think?'

'Yes,' she said slowly. 'We share an immortality in common. — But there are lots of immortalities, even. I felt another one when I was coming home through the forget-me-nots, and they seemed like little stars of laughter all laughing. — But I do think you and I share an immortality, and that's why it hurts me so when you say you don't want to live. It hurts my half of the immortality, that does.'

'What a fool I am! What an ungrateful brute!' he swore softly. 'I've got life, and I've got you, and then I whine! — Smack my face another time.'

'Shall I?' she said, smiling and kissing him goodnight. She knew he had been quite happy after his outburst. And she laughed to herself.

'Shall we go together into the wood?' he said next morning, when another lovely day had come.

'Yes!' she said. 'Now?'

She and Mrs Bolton helped him into his motor-chair. His legs were absolutely helpless: they had to be lifted into place, one at a time. But he had great strength in his arms, to pull himself up. Constance hardly felt the shock any more of lifting those long, inert legs and covering them up with a rug. She had steeled herself. And now she reminded herself, when her pity was likely to give her a twist of anguish, that he had always believed in the mortality of the body and the immortality of the spirit. He ought not to mind so terribly: and perhaps, truly, he did not. Perhaps in a way it was a relief, an escape for him, his crippled condition. It was really easier to be only half a man.

If men had believed in the immortality of the body they would never have made that war, or any such war.

When Clifford was seated in his chair, at the back door, he slowly started off to the light puffing of his little motor round the house to the front, to the drive, where Constance was waiting for him under the great beech tree at the turn of the loop. He came slowly and proudly along in his low three-wheeled chair that puffed so mildly as it bore him forward. And as he came near her he glanced round at the long façade of the low old brown-stone house, and said:

'"Stone walls do not a prison make, Nor iron bars a cage" — not since man has invented motor traction, do they? See how I can leave the house. Do you think the soul looks back on the body as I look back on the old place?'

'The soul doesn't go out for a ride in a bath chair,' she said.

'Maybe not!' he laughed. 'But perhaps it's something similar — our mental flights and spiritual excursions. — I think we must have some repairs done to the old place in the autumn — or next spring. Don't you think I might spend a few hundreds on it?'

'Yes! I do! If there isn't a coal strike.'

'Quiet! What do the beggars want to strike for, really? They'll only drive us back to some sort of slavery again, that's all they'll do.'

'Drive who back?' she said.

'Oh, all of us! We, typifying the governing classes, shall in the end be forced to institute a mild form of slavery to keep the working class at work. There's no other real alternative except anarchy.'

'But would they let you? Would the working people let you?' she asked.

'Oh, we should have to do it quietly, while they weren't looking. But we shall do it: have to.'

'But why?'

'Why? It's obvious. To keep the mines working and the whole machine running. To let it stop means starvation and raving anarchy. The change to Communism means the stopping of a big part of the machine, inevitably. Which, in our tight little island, means anarchy. Nothing to be done then but to slip the light-weight shackles on in time. What else is there to be done?'

They had come to the brow of the park and were looking out over the rolling slopes, with their separate, beautiful trees, away to the outer morning, where could be seen the colliery sending its usual white plumes and black plumes, and the dark glisten of the slate roofs of the miners' dwellings: and topping it all, the old square tower of the church, of brown stone like Wragby House, away on the opposite hill. The dwellings, in curious overlapping steps of slate roofs, mounted up to the church and its bunch of trees.

There was something phantasmal in the view.

'Do you think there must be a war between the classes?' she asked him.

'No! But I think the few must govern the many.'

'You don't think there might really be a mutual agreement?'

He slowly shook his head.

'No!' he said. 'Between the haves and the have-nots there will never be a permanent mutual agreement: except in so far as a tug-of-war is a mutual agreement. One side pulls the other side into extinction: or what is much better, a mild, benevolent form of slavery.'

'Don't you think men are anything except haves and have-nots. Are you, for example, just a have?'

'As far as the coal question goes, I am. It's all right, so long as you don't raise the question. But once you've raised the question, there you are! — You're at opposite ends of the rope, and you'll pull till you pull your guts out — or pull the other party down on to his face.'

'But it needn't be so.'

'I don't know about needn't. It is.'

'But if you didn't hang on to your own end of the rope? — if you didn't hang on to your possessions?' she said.

He looked round at the house, at the park.

'Poor old Wragby!' he said. 'I'd feel like a captain who abandons his ship to the enemy.'

'But are they the enemy — the miners?'

'When you see them skulking in the park, trespassing, trying to poach, don't they seem like the enemy to you?'

'Yes! But — need one let even Wragby come between oneself and — and — and the people?'

'Aren't you jolly well thankful that Wragby does stand between you and Tevershall village? How would you like to live in Bonfoot's Row, for example — or any of the other rows of miners' dwellings?'

'I shouldn't. — But the miners see no reason why they shouldn't live in Wragby.'

'Oh yes they do!' he said slowly. 'They see every reason but one — and that is an abstraction, not a reason at all.'

'What is?'

'Their equality of man, or whatever they call it. They know themselves that equality is all bunk. They know themselves the difference between a gentleman and a collier. And you've got to emphasise the difference and drive the fact home. Oh, property is at the root of all religion. Even The Times Literary Supplement says that the ownership of property has become a religious question. And they're jolly well right. I own Wragby in so far as man does own earthly property. Wragby stands to me for what is decent and dignified and, if you like, godly in man. Pull Wragby down or turn it into a school for colliers' kids, and you've pulled so much human dignity and decency and even godliness down into the muck. I believe it, religiously. Wragby is a ship that still sails on in the voyage of discovery of new human possibilities. It sails ahead, and the miners' dwellings wash along, the dirty little craft, in the wake. — Do you think any miner's dwelling would have had a piano, for example — the old example — if Wragby hadn't helped to bring pianos into being three hundred years ago? So it goes on.'

Constance suddenly saw that this was true. Suddenly she knew really why she didn't want to bear children in a miner's dwelling, or bring them up in a gamekeeper's cottage. They would only be born into the great flotilla of dirty little craft which by themselves were making for nowhere and had no direction, meant nothing. Only the proud ships like Wragby led the way into unknown seas. It was true. There would never be more than a few, comparatively few leaders and onward seekers. And these would always be 'gentry'. And they must always have ultimate control over property. Must! Otherwise there would be no proud ships to dare the unknown seas, all would be a flat-bottomed squalor of nowhere-goers. It was not the giving up of property that would help mankind. She agreed with Clifford. Perhaps, on the contrary, it was a religious duty for a man to fight to keep his property today. She felt that to fight was more honorable than shoddily to let slide, to be bullied into yielding up.

'But Clifford,' she said, 'do you really feel that the gentry are leading on in a voyage of discovery? If they are, why is there a tug-of-war?'

'The tug-of-war is part of the great experiment. The property question has still to be finally settled.'

'You mean settled to remain just as it is?'

He was quiet for a time.

'Perhaps!' he said. 'Or at least, fight for every inch that is yielded. It's a question that's got to be fought out, you can't argue it out or shake hands and agree. It's a passionate question. I'm for sticking to every inch of Wragby, and of my rights to coal royalties and so on. The colliers can show me no better title. — If they'd turn Wragby into a day-school for kids, I should call it a degradation, a move in life on the downward scale. You must have the higher type of life.'

'Yes!' she said. 'I know! And I do believe it. — But isn't there anything else? — You see, Wragby isn't mine to fight for. I've no ancestral halls. So it leaves me rather untouched.'

'Does it?' he said sarcastically. 'It wouldn't if you had children —' he paused for a moment or two — 'do you think you might have children?' he asked, looking at her with strange bright eyes.

'It is possible,' she said, flushing darkly.

'Well! I hope you may, if only to carry on this fight. By gad, it's a big fight, and I'd like to help to train up a lad to hang on to Wragby. It's the thing in our future — the fight for property, the right to own property, or to continue to own it.' He looked round again at the old silent house that crouched its rather sad brown length in the May sunshine. 'Imagine having to fight for the right to continue to own Wragby!' he said. 'Give me a son, Connie! It's all I ask of you.'

She did not answer, but turned away, and he started his chair cautiously on the downslope of the path across the park. His face was gleaming with fight, as white clouds gleamed in the sky.

Give him a son to fight for Wragby! Only that! And the physical son of a gamekeeper, at that, and the grandson of a collier! Nay, it was too preposterous and cruel.

She followed the chair slowly along the red gravelled path in which the weeds were sadly encroaching, between the tasselled trees and the open spaces of grass where cottony young cowslips were coming forth from their cotton wool, between tufts of grass. And the funny, fluffy tenderness of the immature flowers stirred her strangely. That! That! That! That peculiar downy sensitiveness and that vulnerability of young things, which uncurl and come out into the world with such incredible daring, considering how the world is crowded and they are so soft and easily squashed! That! That kind of courage, and that kind of strength! That! That! That! That was what she wanted. Something so delicately sensitive and so softly daring, opening an eye on heaven.

Oh, why didn't Clifford have some delicate, delicate soft physical feeling for the colliers, to wake a response in them? But he was so tough. He was so much more tough and insentient, really, than the ugly mute colliers. He was tough and clever, clever and tough, and with no soft, frail tendrils of perception and true intelligence reaching out on the air. She felt, if she had been a man, she could have found the clue to this gruesome business of class war, which she felt had really started. But she was only a woman, she could only sympathise with a particular man, not with a whole villageful or a whole class.

They came to the wood, and she opened the gate. In front stretched the open cleft of the riding between the silent grey trees. The chair pugged slowly in, slowly crushing its way over the forget-me-nots and the creepingjinny and the woodruff. Clifford steered as far as possible clear of the flowers. But like foam after a storm, they were flung out right in the way.

'You are right, my dear!' he said. 'It is amazingly lovely.'

They were passing the hazel copse, where among the many many brown chords of hazel stems, in hiding, tufts of tall fierce bluebells stood, and big, grey-green leaves spread themselves on the shadowy earth. A woodpecker darted away. Dead hazel catkins lay on the damp green leaves of the riding. The chair moved slowly ahead.

Till they passed the hazel thickets and at a cross-path came to the open oak-wood, which sloped uphill in a beautiful free slope. This hill had been cleared of undergrowth, and many trees had been cut during the war, so that it was rather sparse in cover, open to the light. And the bluebells made sheets and patches of living purplish blue in the clarity, and between the wreckage of stumps and old wood-chips, spaces on the earth of sheer blue, with only young trees rising around.

Clifford had to keep his chair going till he got to the top of the hill, for fear he might get stuck. Constance followed behind. If out of the cold, grim earth things came so tender and in a perfect glow of blueness that seemed somehow to chime, why need man be so tough, only tough, like the great sinews in a piece of boiled beef. Why? Why? Why, while one was alive, why be merely tough? Even the oak trees had the softest little brownish hands, feeling at the air, touching the soft air. The grey bark was hard and tough. But every twig ended in the softest little unfurling paw. Why not? Why not? One must fight the winter; but even then the tender little paws are only gloved. They shut up, but they don't lose their sensitiveness.

Clifford at the top of the hill sat and looked down at the green interlacing of boughs and the heavenly sweeps of blueness that lit up all the green, downhill, downhill, below.

'Yes!' he said. 'It's very fine, a marvellous colour in itself. But it's absolutely no good to paint.'

That too was probably quite true. So many things were true in a composite world.

To the left, in the thick old forest, ran the path that led down to the keeper's hut. Thank heaven it was too narrow and uneven for the chair.

'Shall we go down to the spring?' said Clifford.

'Let us!' said Constance.

And the chair began slowly to advance down the gentle slope till it came to the great sheets of bluebells and rode through them. A strange ship! A strange vessel surging through scented blue seas! The last pinnace left on the unknown oceans, steering to the last discoveries! Quiet and content, like the captain at the immortal wheel, Clifford sat in an old black hat and slowly, cautiously steered. And Constance, one of the mere boats, came slowly in his wake in a grey knitted dress, down the long gentle slope. And the chair softly curved out of sight as the riding swung round in the dip below.

And the keeper came striding rapidly from behind. She heard the drop of his feet, and turned.

'I thought,' he said with a faint smile, 'you was going to be my wife in the wood, an' his —' he jerked his head in the direction of the vanished chair — 'in a' t' rest o' th' world.'

His red-brown eyes looked annoyed, yet somehow, yes, they were like the as yet unfolded brown oak leaves, soft and aware.

'I mean to be,' she said, looking up at him. 'But Clifford wanted to see the bluebells.'

He was silent and uneasy. Then came the low question that burned him before he could get it out:

'When shall you come?'

She was just a little afraid. Yet a voice beyond her control spoke out of her.

'Tonight,' she said.

She saw the flash of his eyes, and turned aside.

'Ay, tonight!' he said in a low, strangled voice, 'to th' house, no? I mean th' cottage?'

'Yes.'

'Am I to wait for yer inside park gate?'

'Yes. Some time after ten.'

'After ten.'

From below there came the sound of Clifford's 'coo-ee!' among the trees.

'Coo-ee!' called Constance, back to him. It was their old call to one another.

'He mun shout for me if 'e wants me,' said the keeper softly.

Constance nodded, looked the man in the eyes for a moment — she was his wife in the wood — and hurried downhill after Clifford, calling.

The keeper turned away with a certain quickness of impatience.

Constance found Clifford already at the spring, a little way up the opposite dark hill, where the larch-wood bristled with a burnt appearance all round, and great leaves of the burdock shoved out into the riding. It was ghostly and sinister as ever.

Only the spring was pretty. It bubbled up in a little, brilliantly clear well that had pebbles on the bottom which wavered and danced. Bits of eyebright and cinquefoil flowered among the grass on the bank. Then the water ran rapidly downhill in a tiny ditch.

'Will you drink?' asked Constance.

'Yes! Will you?'

'Yes.'

There was a little enamel cup hanging on a tree. She took it and filled it for him as he sat in his chair.

'Shall we wish?' he said as he took the cup.

'Yes, let us.'

'Let me see — what shall I wish for?' he asked.

'You mustn't tell!' she said.

They heard the distant tapping of a woodpecker, then the cry of a cock pheasant. It was very still, though a soft wind was blowing, and more clouds were moving in the sky.

'The water is so cold!' he said, sipping. 'One might wish extravagant things. I expect men and women have wished the most extraordinary things at this well.'

He drank slowly, in silence, and handed her the cup.

'Have you wished?' she said.

'I have.'

'You mustn't tell me,' she said.

'No! You wish too.'

She stooped at the spring, rinsed her cup, and filled it. And she thought to herself: 'I won't wish. I might be meddling with my real destiny.' So she drank slowly, gasping a little at the coldness.

'Have you wished?' he said.

'Yes,' she gasped, taking no heed of what she said.

She gathered a bit of woodruff, and watched a mole rising to the surface, swimming out of the earth with its pink little hands and blind face.

'Do you see the mole?' she said.

'Yes! I wonder Parkin hasn't had him. — What a life, eh, burrowing and wriggling your way down in that yellow earth! Unpleasant little beasts!'

'He seems to see with the pink tip of his nose,' she said. 'Do you think he smells, or what does he do, waving his nose-end in the air?'

'He looks like an orator,' he said.

She gave him the woodruff to smell.

'Such a fashionable old-fashioned scent,' he said.

The larches too were putting out tiny green brushes, out of their twiggy dreariness. Constance glanced up at the sky that seemed so disconnected.

'I wonder if it will rain?'

They started slowly back, the motor-chair faintly puffing. Clifford steered carefully over the damp, grassy, uneven riding. And so they came to the bottom of the dip and turned to the long slope ahead, where bluebells spread in the light among their trees.

'Will she get up, do you think?' she asked.

'We will try. I hope so.'

'If not,' she said, 'you must call Parkin.'

The chair tugged slowly, unevenly up through the tall strong hyacinths that lit up a blueness around. More and more slowly it struggled. Then it stopped.

'Call!' she said.

'Let's try again.' He did not want to call the man. The chair made funny convulsive noises and struggled a little further. A dog gave a short bark. The keeper's spaniel came running up, wagging its tail to Constance, very friendly, but shying away from the chair.

Parkin came striding down the slope. He saluted as he came close, then stood at ease in front of the chair, looking down at the little motor.

'I'm afraid she won't get me up again,' said Sir Clifford.

'Looks like it, doesna' it?' said the keeper, pushing back his cap and gazing down at the chair. Then he stooped, touching the engine under the wheels. He tapped the little tank.

'Got enough petrol?' he asked.

'Oh, I think so,' said Clifford.

Parkin leaned his gun against a tree, and kneeled down to the little engine, touching various screws, and poking intently.

Then he stood up, his feet apart.

'Try her again, sir!' he said.

Clifford obediently tried his engine again.

'There's a bit o' dust or something choking her,' said the keeper. 'Run her a bit hard, like.'

Clifford ran his engine faster. It stuttered and spluttered, then ran free.

'There!' said the keeper. 'Sounds as if she's come clear.'

Clifford in silence started the chair. It crept slowly forward as if it had not enough life to get up.

'Am I to give her a push?' said the keeper. ''Elp her a bit?'

'She ought to do it,' said Clifford. 'Wait a bit.'

Constance and the keeper followed the chair, inch by inch. She was wondering at the curious freemasonry of men when a machine was in question. Parkin was a different man — a soldier. Yet he treated Clifford so freely, good-humouredly. Clifford was the officer, Parkin the Tommy.

The chair, as if dying of heart disease, came to an end amid a particularly fine patch of bluebells like a derelict in shallow water.

'She'll hardly do it! She's hardly got power enough,' said the keeper.

'She ought to manage it — it's not steep,' Clifford persisted.

'Ay, ought! She ought — but she won't. You'd best let me push you, sir.'

'Wait a bit,' said Clifford.

And he began to run his engine fast: then he put her into gear with a jerk.

'Nay!' said the keeper. 'You'll rip her guts out.'

The chair charged in a wild swerve sideways to the trees.

'Clifford!' cried Constance, rushing forward. The keeper jumped and grasped the chair by the rail behind. But Clifford, putting on all his pressure, had steered into the riding, and with a strange buzzing noise the chair was fighting at the hill. Parkin pushed her from behind, and she went smoothly forward, as if pacified.

'She's doing it all right,' said Clifford, looking round in triumph, only to see Parkin's red face over his shoulder.

'Are you pushing?'

'Ay, a bit.'

'Don't then! I asked you not.'

'Why —' Parkin began, slackening.

'Let go!' said Clifford; 'she's got to make it.'

'Ay — got to!' said the keeper.

And he released the chair: which immediately seemed to choke. Clifford, seated a prisoner, fought with his machine. Strange noises came out of the poor thing, and strange, pathetic lurches took place. But she refused to budge.

'Curse her!' said Clifford, violently shutting off, white with anger.

Parkin silently took the chair and gave it a gentle shove up the hill, among the shattered bluebells. Clifford glanced round, yellow with anger.

'Will you get off there?' he cried. 'Wait till you're asked.'

Parkin stepped smartly aside, automatic as a soldier forming fours. But once apart from the chair, he stood with his feet wide in the peculiar lounge of a man who does not stand at attention.

The chair began slowly to move backwards.

'Clifford, your brake's not on!' cried Constance, rushing in to the rescue.

Clifford violently tugged at a light lever. The chair stopped.

'It's obvious I'm at everybody's mercy,' he said satirically.

There was a solemn pause, Clifford in the chair yellow with anger, Constance standing at a loss, the keeper standing at ease, save for the slight mocking tilt of his eyelids, and the keeper's dog sitting behind his master, alert, eyeing the chair with greater suspicion and dislike. A cock pheasant bolted across the road absurdly. Everything was absurd. But the tableau vivant remained motionless.

'I'm sorry I lost my temper, Con,' said Clifford at length.

'Oh, I don't mind,' said Constance.

'Parkin, do you mind wheeling me? I beg your pardon for the way I spoke to you.'

'The pesterin' things 'ud make anybody get their rag out,' said the keeper.

Even then it was not so easy to get the chair started, for the brake was jammed. They poked and pulled. The keeper sweated. At length he took off his coat, lifted the back of the chair bodily up and with a sudden jerk loosened the wheels, unconscious of everything save his effort. Clifford, tilted perilously, looked round in irritation and saw the red face of the keeper, the veins in the neck swollen.

'For God's sake —!' he exclaimed. But at that moment Parkin put the chair down, and it moved, under his control, slowly backwards.

'She's loose,' he gasped.

Then he looked round.

'If you'd give me that bit of a log!' he said to Constance, pointing. She brought him the piece of tree root, and he scotched the chair. He put on his coat, wiped his face with a red handkerchief and strode for his gun.

'Are yer all right then?' he said quite gently to Sir Clifford when he had hold of the chair again.

'Quite all right, thanks.'

'Shall we be movin', like?'

'Do let's get out of here.'

And the keeper put his weight behind the heavy chair. It was not easy, the thing was heavy. He scotched with his foot, and took his coat off again. Then, sweating, he pushed slowly up the incline. When he paused to breathe, his chest heaving, Clifford said:

'I'm awfully sorry to be so much trouble.'

'Don't you mind about me — it's a warm day, like.'

Curious the two men were, so polite, so careful of one another, walking round one another. Constance had had visions of friendship between the two men: she could unite them in understanding and friendship. Now she saw that she might as well try to unite fire and water. There was a categorical opposition between them. Each made the other feel a fool, and each resented it in his own way.

All the way home Parkin did not speak, and he did not even look at Constance. He wheeled in silence, his gun slung across his shoulders — he had put on his coat at the park gate — and his dog at his heels. Clifford made a little conversation to his wife about his Aunt Eva, about a new chemical by-product at the mines.

When they came to the house Parkin helped Sir Clifford into his house chair gently enough, then went away without ever looking at Constance.

'Do have a meal and some beer in the kitchen — and thanks awfully!' said Sir Clifford, whose conscience smote him because of his temper.

The man saluted and was gone.

'He's quite a good sort, Parkin,' said Clifford at luncheon. 'You know that as soon as a man handles you. But he's something of a fool— and rather on the insolent side.'

'Do you think he's insolent?' said Constance.

'Dunna yer think so yersen, like?' said Clifford, mocking the vernacular.

'It only seemed to me his way.'

'Exactly! He thinks he's a whole hill o' beans, himself — as the Americans say — and we're a pair of hand-fed cockatoos. He's no real respect for us. None of them have nowadays. Not even Mrs Bolton, nice as she is. They know we're lenient and on the whole good to them. They respect what we've got, all right, but they don't respect what we are.'

'And ought they to?' she asked naïvely, also looking a much bigger fool than she was. Clifford spread his hands and lifted his shoulders.

'And do we respect them for what they are?' she said. 'Don't we only respect them for what they do for us?'

'What are they, apart from what they do for us, after all? After all, what is Parkin apart from keeping the game. Why should I take him seriously?'

'No reason at all. You don't anyhow. — But I suppose he thinks: What are we apart from what we've got!'

'Apart from what we've got, we keep life going — we renovate the mines, we find employment for him and all the likes of him — we make it possible for all the Parkins of this world to exist. If they don't know it they must be taught.'

'Perhaps they will never believe it.'

'Then they'll have to. After all, what is Parkin apart from a pheasant and a gun? You wouldn't raise a shout about his immortal soul, would you? — He's just so much live human meat, no more.'

'Do you think so?' she said. 'You don't think there's any life-mystery in him?'

He pulled up short.

'Oh, as to life-mystery!' he said. 'That remains mysterious. He's just a half-tame animal with a certain animal niceness and a certain half-tame nastiness.'

Constance left it at that.

She had promised to spend the night in the keeper's cottage: let her remember that. — 'Just a half-tamed animal with a certain animal niceness and a certain half-tame nastiness.' Poor Clifford! It was rather sour grapes, perhaps. Well! 'A half-tame animal, with a certain animal niceness'! What more was she herself? And Clifford wasn't even that.

She was going. She spent the afternoon thinking about it. She would have to steal out like a thief in the night. But what the eye doesn't see the heart doesn't grieve. And she had no patience with a heart which grieved merely because the eye told it to. Prying, restless, insatiable, indecent eyes of other people, they saw far too much, and swamped the heart in their miserable visions. The heart can feel what it has to feel, in the dark as well as in the light: perhaps better. She herself wanted to pry into nobody's secrets. Her own were enough for her.

Therefore she made her plans slowly and calmly, without fear. She felt she did her duty to Clifford. The rest was her own. But she would avoid messes as far as possible.

And she was in no burning hurry to be gone. It was a responsibility, going to that other man. He too was insisting already that she should be his wife, even if only while she was in the wood. A circumscribed area in which she was to be his wife. His cottage being her 'home' within the wood area.

Always responsibility! Men were like that. He had one wife. What did he want another for, even if only in the wood? If they were nice, they were serious. And if they were not serious, they were not nice. Men!

In the evening she played cards with Clifford. She did not like difficult games, so they played bezique. She was quite happy playing with him. But at ten o'clock she left off and kissed him goodnight.

She had thought it out calmly enough. She went to bed, lay down and pressed her hollow in the bed, and lay awhile still. Then she got up, took off her pyjamas and flung them on the bed as she did in the morning. She slipped on a batiste nightdress, over that her woolen dress, over that a dark, thin mackintosh. Her hair she plaited and twisted under a dark hat, and on her feet she had rubber-soled shoes. It was done in a moment.

She looked round her room. It looked exactly as it did in the morning when she got up. If the maid came in early, before she was home, she would conclude that her mistress had done as she often did: gone for a stroll before breakfast. No one would be surprised to see Constance coming home through the park at half-past seven.

Then she listened. Clifford had ears like a lynx. She went softly down the long corridor and down the service stairs, through the leather door, so into the kitchen. The servants were in bed: she had ascertained that before going upstairs herself. By the light of her flashtorch she unfastened the kitchen door and went out, closing it softly behind her. Tonight it would have to stay unlocked.

She spoke a quiet word to the dog, and in another minute was out of the yard and crossing the garden at the back. So, she came to the park, for she had unlocked the garden door in the afternoon.

The night was warm, half-dark, with clouds and a gleam of a biggish star through murk of clouds. The big foundry at Cross Gate made a glare on the low clouds, and this gave back an uncanny lustre into the night, so that once she was accustomed to the dazing unreality, she could dimly see her way. In the vague sky she saw a black place that was rain. And the soft wind blew the edges of fine rain at her. But it was not much.

She went quietly and soberly alone in the night and came at last to the big gate at the wood. She saw nobody. She opened it quietly, and was closing it behind her, when she started. He was there.

'You've come then,' he said in a low tone.

'Obviously,' she murmured secretly, in reply.

'You wanted to, did you?'

'Yes! Or I shouldn't have come.'

They went forward. It was much darker in the wood, and she stumbled.

'Shall yer have my arm?'

She bumped into him. So she took his arm, and he pressed it to his side. She could feel the thud of his heart. And they went in silence, feeling strange to one another, yet magnetised together.

It was a long way through the wood. But he went with that tramping certainty she knew in him, and he supported her.

'There are so many strange noises,' she whispered.

'Eh?'

'There are so many strange sounds in the wood.'

'Ay! It's the trees creakin' an' rubbin' together.'

At length they saw a dim light. It was the cottage.

'Did you leave a light?' she asked.

'I allers do at night,' he said, 'whether I'm out or in.'

He quietly unlocked the door, and she entered. He fastened the door behind her, and turned up the lamp. There was a low fire in the fireplace, and on the table plates and glasses.

'Shall y'eat a bit?' he asked.

He had hung up his coat and his gun and his coat, and was in his shirt-sleeves. His eyes were flashing and changing, and he was rather pale. She sat down on the sofa in the small, cosy room. He sat down in his Windsor arm-chair, and began to unfasten his leather gaiters and take off his heavy boots. The dog in the scullery was rather noisily lapping something.

She looked round. The varnished dresser stood on glass supports and had on it various cottage ornaments. Over it hung an enlarged photograph of a young, fairish man with a rather thin, sticking-out moustache and square shoulders, and a woman, dark and with frizzed hair, wearing a black satin blouse and a big lace collarette. She looked common.

'Do you ever see your wife?' she asked.

'Eh?'

He had placed his boots and leggings at the side of the white hearth, and was in grey worsted stockings. He glanced up quickly, and followed her glance to the enlarged photograph.

'My wife! No! She's livin' wi' somebody else.'

'Don't you want to see her?'

'No.'

'Why not?'

He glanced at her quickly. Their eyes met, and from his a spark flew.

'I dunna want to. — Should we go up then? Shanna ter take thy things off?'

'Yes. Upstairs!' she said.

He lit a candle, blew out the lamp, and she followed him to the stairs.

'Shut stairfoot door,' he said, 'for t' dog.'

Balanced on one stair, she carefully closed the stairfoot door behind her. The steep stairs creaked as he went up in stocking feet, and she followed. Probably the other woman had followed him like this.

On the tiny landing were two doors, one open. She followed him into the crowded small bedroom. The big iron bedstead was pushed against the wall, the bed covered with a white quilt. A yellow chest of drawers was against the opposite wall, and by the window, under the slope of the roof, a dressing table with a swivel mirror stood penned down. The room was colourless and ordinary.

'Do you always sleep here?' she asked.

'Me? Ay! I sleep in this bed.'

She took off her hat and mackintosh and hung them on the nail behind the door. Then she sat down on the edge of the bed and slowly pulled off her shoes.

'Did you never like your wife?' she asked him.

He had been standing motionless by the door. He gave a writhing movement of repudiation.

'Dunna talk about her. It's not what ter's come for, is it?' He looked at her strangely, anxiously.

'No!' she said. 'Only I had to think about her.'

'Eh!' he said.' 'Er's not a nice woman, an' 'er niver was.'

'But you liked her once?'

'Eh! I liked what I had of her — for a bit. An' then I didn't like 'er — an' don't. It's enough.'

She slowly pulled off her stockings and garters, while he still stood there against the door, motionless and inscrutable. Then she slipped her dress over her head, and stood in her thin, delicate white nightgown. She laid her dress and stockings over the bed-rail. And he still had not moved.

'Shall yer sleep agen t'wa'?'

She got quietly into bed.

And then, only then, he sat down heavily on the edge of the bed and untied his tape garters and pulled off his stockings. He stood up to push off his cord breeches, and she saw his feet white and clean but gnarled out of shape by clumsy heavy boots.

He stood in his shirt — she had known he wouldn't change it — and looked at her.

'I canna believe as yer really want me,' he said, looking down at her with dark, glowing eyes. He was a mature man, not a boy.

She smiled at him faintly. And the last thing she saw was his face as he bent near the candle and blew out the light with a quick breath. His face, lit up intensely like that, had something — it seemed so ridiculous — of the pure masculine angel about it. She smiled again, in the dark room, as he touched her. She realised how he had recoiled from all women after that common wife of his: and how his desire fought against his recoil and mistrust; his old dislike of the hard, unloving woman he had known in his mother also fighting furiously against his intense desire of a mature, lonely man for a woman to believe in with his body. A woman with a gentle, warm soul and a warm, soft desirous body! that was the burning flicker of his hope. But the ache of experience drew back and resisted, told him not to want her.

She had understood a good deal, looking at the 'enlargement' of a bold woman in a black satin blouse, and that young man with the square shoulders and defiant eyes.

'There then!' she thought, as she softly stroked his male, live body. 'I won't deceive you in my heart, at least.'

Because, when he did break away from his cramping mistrust, his was such a clean passion.

He slept with her right breast cupped in his left hand, for she had her back to him. And she knew that at first he must have slept with his wife like that, because his hand came like a child's, and gathered her breast and held it as in a cup. If she moved his hand it came back while he slept, by instinct, and found her breast and held it softly enclosed. And it was as if he balanced the whole of her gently in the hollow of his hand, as if she were no more than a dove nestling, all nestled in the strong palm of his hand.

She lay perfectly still, yet not asleep. All her body was asleep under the heavy arm laid across her. Only her mind, like a small star of consciousness, shone faintly and wondered. His arm lay across her, her breast was balanced in his hand, she was encircled and enclosed by him even while he slept.

So this was what it was to be a wife! How implicitly he made a wife of her even if he had got her only for this one night! The curious united circle of the man and the woman! It was a kind of prison too.

No, not a prison! If one thought in that way it was really a prison to have a body at all. If one wanted to be so tremendously free one must evaporate into nothingness. That hard little freedom of a separate, completely separated individual, that was worse than a prison. It was just a nail through one's heart.

She didn't want to escape him since he didn't want to let her go. Curious how he made a circle round her! No, she did not want to escape him. Never! Never! She wanted to feel the circle more inevitably and absolutely around her.

Slipping round under his arm, she clung to him and kissed him on the face, on the shut eyes, waking him again to her passion, his mind still dead asleep. And then she too slept. The star of her consciousness set, she disappeared this time entirely under the heavy arch of his arm, her breast slipped back again into the palm of his hand as if into a socket.

It was dawn when she awoke with a slight start, utterly unaware of where she was. That strange low window. She turned round. He was already awake, and he looked at her. Strange, the red-brown eyes, wide open, looking at her so near. She felt immediately drawn to his breast.

'Is it day?' she said, laying her head on his breast, suddenly.

'Ay! It's about five.'

She heard the resonance of his voice, and opened his shirt, to lay her ear over his heart. Thud! Thud! So deep! She softly kissed the man's breast-nipple. He had drawn her close and with infinite delicate pleasure was stroking the full, soft, voluptuous curve of her loins. She did not know which was his hand and which was her body, it was like a full bright flame, sheer loveliness. Everything in her fused down in passion, nothing but that.

Then afterwards, she became aware of the sounds of the wood, birds calling, and the noise of a train in the cutting.

'Is it a fine day?' she said.

He got out of bed and drew the curtains of the low window, stooping to look out. So he must stoop and look out each dawn. What a lonely man he was, really! And rather absurd in a shirt with a tail to it.

'Yes!' he said, when he had scrutinised closely. 'It's fine.'

She lifted her head. She had heard the whimpering of a dog downstairs.

'It's Flossie!' he said. 'She thinks I'm late.'

'What time?'

He looked at his watch on the chair.

'Just after six.'

'It doesn't matter if I'm not home so very early — I shall just say I went for a walk,' she told him. 'I often do before breakfast.'

'Do you?' he said, sitting down on the bed.

She felt lazy and voluptuous. He looked at her.

'Should I get your breakfast?' he asked.

He was restless now, to be up. She sighed.

'No!' she said. 'I shall have to be home for breakfast.'

'What time shall you start?'

'I shall have to be home by about eight at the latest.'

'I'll make a cup o' tea.'

'Will you?'

He pulled on his stockings and breeches with a certain alacrity, and turned to go.

'Kiss me!' she said, holding out her white, soft arms to him. He bent to kiss her, and she pulled his head to her breast, kissing his hair and ears. He put his arms round her, felt the silky weight of her, the hollow yielding of her flexible waist, the weight of her hips. And the desire for her came over him again completely.

She laughed to herself after a while, feeling his weight motionless upon her. She loved it so. And she thought: 'And the grasshopper shall be a burden, and desire shall fail—' Was it from the Bible? How awful if desire should fail! How gratefully she loved him, that his desire did not fail.

It was he who lay still now, clasping her, and she who knew she must go.

'I must go,' she said.

'Ay!' he said, unheeding. And she left him, as motionless he lay upon her, clasping her.

'I must go!' she softly admonished.

And without a word he got up and out of bed, and sat with his back to her, pulling his breeches back again round his waist. He got up looking round at her. She was sitting up in bed, curiously childlike and innocent.

'Do you feel I'm your wife in the wood?' she asked, pleased.

'My wife onywheer!' he said. 'I've niver 'ad no wife, I niver knowed what a woman wor like afore. Did thee?'

'No, I never really had a man either.'

'No?' he looked at her searchingly.

'No! — Less than you've had a woman.'

'Ah well!' he said. 'It's summat!'

And he opened the door and went downstairs.

When she came down he was dressed in boots and leggings, and was starting a fire. She had her hat on, was carrying her light waterproof. He rose at once and reached for his coat and gun.

'Don't bother to come with me!' she said.

'Yi! Dunna yer want me?'

'I wish I needn't go! I wish I could stop and have breakfast with you.'

He looked at her searchingly.

'Shall yer?' he said.

'No!' she said, very low. 'I'd better go.'

They went through the dewy morning wood. Everything was morning.

'We are lucky to have each other!' she said, suddenly catching his hand for a moment.

He hesitated in his walk. Then he went on without looking at her.

'Ay!' he said, in a blank voice.

At the gate she said to him hurriedly: 'Another time! We'll have another time like this.'

'Ay! We mun!' he said, closing the gate behind her.

She hurried away across the park, out of his sight.

There was a letter from Hilda, saying she would call for Constance in the beginning of June, and they would both go to France for two or three weeks with their father, old Sir Malcolm. The old painter had travelled a good deal with his daughters when they were quite young, and even now he would sometimes go off alone with them for some jaunt, leaving his second wife, the girls' stepmother, at home. But Constance had not left Wragby since the end of the war — since Clifford came home.

The trip to France was no new proposition. Hilda had been insisting on it for months. And now it was to come off. Constance had consented to go. She thought she might be pregnant. She wanted to be alone a while. Time went by so quickly. Already it was the last days of May.

'If you want me one little bit to stay at home, Clifford,' said Constance, 'I won't go. I don't care about going. Really I don't.'

And it was true. She didn't want to go away from the other man, not out of contact. She couldn't bear to think her contact with him might be broken. And she didn't want to leave Clifford if Clifford would be unhappy. Yet in spite of these things, she knew she would go. It was her destiny.

Clifford thought it was a put-up job of Hilda's, to get Constance away from him and probably entangled with another man.

'Oh, I want you to go!' he said. 'But I want you to come back —you know that.'

'I shall come back,' she said very quietly. 'But I needn't go, you know.'

'Yes!' he said, looking at her searchingly. 'You must go.' He too felt it was destiny. If Hilda had got some other man ready for Constance — some old friend probably from Scotland, since the Scotch hang together, and if Constance had a brief affair with the man, and perhaps a child was the result: well, he, Clifford, had no right to interfere. He was no fool, neither was he a conventional die-hard. He knew in his very soul that unless there was some development — such as a child born — his life and Constance's would not run on together. He was shrewd enough to know that she would not always live as a married nun. She was not that type; And that was why he wanted to keep her. He loved her for her warm, still, physical womanhood. He hated women on a higher plane. It needed Constance's strange warm vagueness to keep his life warm. The women who didn't need sex and physical love just got on his nerves.

Moreover, he was sufficiently educated to know that if he kept Connie a married nun, vague and uncertain, during her youth, there would be some miserable recoil later on, some physical derangement. She was the wrong kind of woman for permanent sisterhood.

So he schemed and schemed that she should go, but that also she should come back. He needed her! He became irritable and a bit insane when she was not there.

'You must go!' he said. 'But shall you come back?'

'Oh, I shall come back!'

She seemed so sure. How curious she was! What was there in her mind? — Or if not in her mind, in her emotional psyche? What was she after?

'You won't let Hilda get you away from me altogether?'

'No! Besides, Hilda would never try.'

'I'm afraid she might. She hates me.'

'Hilda hates you!' exclaimed Constance. And even...

(Pages 195—196 of the original manuscript missing)

'You won't mind, will you?' she said to him. He looked at her quickly, cautiously, again.

'It wouldna be no good me mindin', would it?' he said.

Her heart sank a little. He too was angry. She was beginning to know him — and to understand his changes into dialect. When they were merely two people together, quite pleasant, he spoke more or less good English. When he really loved her, and cooed over her in the strange, throaty cooing voice of a man to his tender young wife, he said 'thee' and 'thou'. And when he was suspicious or angry, he used the dialect defiantly, but said 'you' — or rather 'yer' — and not 'thou'.

'Why not?' she said, looking up at him with the same candour that so baffled Clifford.

He smiled a little, uglily.

'Yo'd take a lot o' nose o' me mindin', shouldn't yer?' he said sarcastically.

'Why!' she faltered. 'I wouldn't go if you really minded.'

He looked at her suspiciously.

'Yi!' he said softly. 'Yi yer would! Dunna tell me.'

She too was nettled. Her colour rose.

'But I wouldn't. If you said you minded very much and you'd rather I didn't go, I wouldn't go.'

His eyes, with tiny pupils, watched her keenly and mockingly.

'An' how shouldn't I mind?' he said softly.

'But!' she faltered. 'It's only a little while! And it's so long since I've been away from Wragby. I've never been away — since I came —' She looked at him pathetically.

He looked at the ground. Both were silent.

'Tell me why you mind!' she insisted.

'Eh, dunna bother! Yo' go!' he said, staring away into the wood.

'But I can't go, if — if you don't like me for going.'

He gave a little laugh.

'Eh nay!' he said in pure irony. 'If I don't like yer! Nay, yer know if I like yer or not. An' yer know yer'll please yerself, no matter whether I like yer or whether I don't. If you want to go yer'll go. All yer've got to do is to say: "Parkin, I'm gain' away for the month of June. 'Appen I s'll see you when I get back."'

He was getting nasty.

'Yes!' she said. 'I hope I shall.'

'What?'

She looked him full in the face.

'I hope I shall see you when I come back,' she said.

He gave the sudden explosive movement she knew in him, flinging back his shoulders and stiffening his neck so that his throat broadened. Then just as suddenly he changed, and became secretive and small.

'An' 'appen yer won't,' he said in a small, hidden voice.

She looked at him in wonder. He too had something on his mind. She saw him remote and obstinate, small-seeming.

'You mean you might not be here when I come back? Why? Where would you go?' she asked in wonder.

He would not answer, but stared away over his shoulder.

'Where would you go?' she insisted.

He still looked over his shoulder.

''Appen ter Canada,' he said in the same colourless voice.

She felt something swiftly sinking inside her.

'Canada!' she repeated. 'Why Canada?'

'I've got a brother there,' he said with common sturdiness, 'as runs a saw-mill and makes fourteen pound a week, an' more — steady!'

The sinking went deeper in her.

'Yes, but you can't run a saw-mill,' she said.

'I can learn pretty soon. There's not much I didn't have to do i' t' war. My brother 'ud soon show me.'

Her mind remained a blank. He must have been thinking about it.

'But why?' she said. 'Why should you want to go to Canada? You're all right here.'

'Ay!' he said. 'I'm a gamekeeper, at thirty-five bob a week. Ay! I'm all right! I'm Sir Clifford's servant, an' I'm Lady Chatterley's —' he looked her in the face — 'What do you call me, in your sort of talk?'

'My lover!' she stammered.

'Lover!' he re-echoed. A queer flash went over his face.

'Fucker!' he said, and his eyes darted a flash at her, as if he shot her.

The word, she knew from Clifford, was obscene, and she flushed deeply and then went pale. But since the word itself had so little association to her, it made very little impression on her. Only she was amazed at the diabolic hate — or fury — she did not know what it was — that flashed out of him all at once, like a cobra striking.

'But,' she stammered, 'even if you are — are you ashamed of it?'

He had been looking at her curiously, watchfully, like a dog that has bitten somebody. His expression slowly changed to one of perplexed doubt.

'Am I ashamed of it?' he questioned vaguely.

'Yes! Even if you are my "fucker" as you call it, are you ashamed of it? There's nothing to be ashamed of in it, is there?'

His eyes slowly widened with a slow wonder, and a sort of boyishness came on his face again. She was looking at him with wide, candid blue eyes. He pushed his hat a little off his brow and broke into an amused laugh.

'No!' he said. 'There's nothing to be ashamed of right enough. If there isn't for you there isn't for me.' He stood laughing at her oddly, still a little doubtful.

'Why shouldn't you take me if we both want it?' she said.

'Why shouldna I fuck thee when we both on us want it?' he repeated in broad dialect, smiling all over his body with amusement as a dog does.

'Yes, why not!' she re-echoed.

He looked full into her eyes, and in his eyes a little flame was dancing with perfect amusement. He pushed his hat off his brow again, then pulled it back.

'It's a winder!' he said.

She only gazed at him.

'It's a winder!' he repeated, the smile still flickering and moving all over his face.

'What amuses you so?' she asked.

'Yo' do!' he said.

'How?'

'Say it again!' he said. 'Say it again! — What does it matter if I —' he tempted her.

'Yes! What does it matter if you fuck me, as you call it? — when you know I want you to! And you want to yourself, don't you?'

He stopped suddenly in his laughter, and his whole bearing changed.

'Ay!' he said seriously. 'You're right! You're right! That's what it is to be a proper lady! There's nawt even to laugh at in it! — And you're right, you're right!'

'Then —' she said slowly, 'why were you so cross with me?'

He took his hat off and looked up at her a little bit like a schoolboy.

'Was I mad with yer?' he asked.

'Yes!'

He hung and his head and ruminated. Then he said:

'Let's go an' sit down. Then 'appen I can tell yer.'

They went and sat in the hut. He fetched her a quick, furtive glance. She looked tired and a bit haggard now. He wanted to hold her in his arms and comfort her, but daren't. He had to explain to her why he had wanted to go to Canada.

'Why!' he said, staring away at the sky, so that he forgot her, and his old feelings came over him. 'Why! I felt somehow — you know I like fuckin' better than anything else — you know that — an' I know it. Yet, yer know, somehow — when yer not there — when I'm by mysen i' th' wood an' i' th' cottage — I sort o' feel — well, what sort of a man am I, here hangin' on at the beck an' call of a paralysed man and carryin' on wi' his wife! What sort of a man am I? If I was brought up afore th' magistrates they'd say I was nothing but a thief and a scoundrel. An' my brother says I'm no better than a servant and a stick-in-the-mud. What am I? Even you, what do you think of me? I know yer like me, I know yer do. It's 'appen not for me to say. But I do, I know you like me. Only likin's likin', and bein' able to respect a man is another thing. Yer can't really respect me — not even as much as you do Sir Clifford. You can't. An' I can see it. I'm not blind. What sort of a mate am I for yer? — except just for fuckin', and there a'most any man 'ud do. I couldn't keep yer an' feed yer, because you've got your own money and can pay me my wage out of your own pocket. I can't make a home for you. I can't go among your sort of people, and don't want to. An' you can't come down to my sort, I wouldn't have it for the world. — What is it? It's no good!'

She laid her hand swiftly on his.

'But why can't we stay as we are? You know I love you — and I think I shall have a child.'

He looked at her as if from a long distance.

'An' Sir Clifford'll own it as his own?'

'Yes. He'll be glad to. Think of him and what he has to look forward to!'

'Ay!' he said. 'He's handicapped!'

'Well then — why can't we go on as we are?'

The long-distance look did not go out of his eyes.

'An' me stop here i' th' wood. I canna!' he said.

'Why can't you?'

'I sort o' canna. I canna abide.'

She knitted her brows in despair.

'But I don't understand,' she said.

He lifted his shoulders and shook his head.

'I can't, I say,' he repeated firmly. 'I can't sort of walk about this wood and take orders from Sir Clifford an' watch every minute of my life for you comin' — I can't! I can't!'

'But you were all right before I did come,' she said.

'Maybe! But I was allers thinkin' about Canada. I was allers thinking I should have to go.'

'But now you've got me, do you still want to go?'
'Yes! More!'

'But why? Do you hate me?'

'Don't yer see —' he said with a peculiar tense smile on his face — 'it makes me feel small.'

'But why should it?' she cried.

'Don't yer see — what sort of a man am I, as couldn't provide for the very woman as comes to him an' couldn't make a home for her an' couldn't be seen with her without lowerin' her — as can't even have his own children owned to for hisn? What should you think of yourself if you was me?'

'I should be so happy to have a nice woman in love with me, I shouldn't think of anything else.'

'Ay, 'appen so! But what if you knowed — you knowed you was only a sort of makeshift! That's all I am!'

'You're not! You're the only man I love, really.'

'Ay, so you say! But you're Lady Chatterley, an' I'm one o' th' servants on th' place.'

'But what does it matter — all that social stuff?'

'It matters.'

'And what do you want? Do you want me to leave Clifford and come and live in the cottage with you?'

'No I don't!' he shook his head with distaste.

'Or do you think I can turn Clifford out, and you can come and live with me in Wragby?'

'What as, your errand boy?'

'Not at all. As Sir Oliver Parkin.'

'Sir Oliver Shit!'

There was an angry silence. After a while she turned to him.

'Then what do you want?' her voice changed. 'Me to go to Canada with you?' she asked, rather small.

He did not answer.

'Is that what you mean?' she insisted fretfully.

'It's not for me to say,' he said at last.

'You mean I ought to want to come with you? — Well, I can't, because I can't leave Clifford. I've sworn I'd never leave him to live alone. And I won't.'

There was a silence.

'Well then—' he said.

'What!' she blurted angrily.

'I can go to Canada alone.'

She looked at him almost in hate.

'How mean! But how mean!' she crooned at last. 'This man that I've loved.'

He stared away, and she lapsed into silence. She rose, and turned to him:

'Very well!' she said. 'You go to Canada. If you want any money I'll give it to you. How much would you like? A hundred pounds?'

'You know I don't want such a thing,' he said sheepishly.

'You seem to think you don't get your dues.'

'It isna that — you know it isn't.'

'How can I leave Clifford? How can I swear not to leave him, and then leave him? What sort of a man is it that wants me to do such a thing? A man who would soon leave me, I'm afraid. — No, go to Canada!'

She turned away. But she knew this one was just the man to take her at her word and go the next day. She registered a grudge against him, then turned to him:

'Are you sorry I ever loved you?' she asked.

He stared at her in confusion of feelings.

'Ay! Maybe yer are!' she said bitterly, mocking the dialect, sneering at him. ''Appen yer sorry for it, like?'

Her imitation was so clumsy, it saved her. He smiled at her.

'Tha canna do't,' he said. 'Dunna thee try.'

'But are you sorry I ever loved you?' she asked sternly. 'Answer the truth — in part you are sorry.'

'Am I?' he said. 'Perhaps I am! In part! — No, I'm not,' he added quickly. And she could simply hear his mind creaking as he pondered. He looked up at her. 'Sometimes I'm mad wi' yer, like, because I feel — small! I can do nothing! — But I wouldn't go back on it. It's my life, if I die tomorrow or live to a hundred.'

'In Canada — with a nice little Canadian wife?'

'Ay! I might do that an a'! But —'

'Ah, goodbye!' she said in utter dreary fatigue.

She could see him trembling as he stood. Suddenly again he pressed back his throat and flung up his hands, his face distorted.

'What am I to do?' he cried.

He was in such evident torture, she was amazed. She went and quickly kissed him.

'What do you want to do anything for?' she said. 'Wait just a month for me: I shall be back. And shall I come to the cottage to you tomorrow night, when Hilda is here? Shall I?'

He shuddered with conflicting desires.

'Yer make a numskull of me,' he said.

'Why?' she cried. 'I don't! I only love you. Wait till I come back from France, and we'll think what to do for the best. Promise you'll wait till I come back from France, and then we can try and get it all straight. Promise me, will you?'

'To wait till you come back from France!' The words sounded so sinister to him. France to him meant the war.

'Yes! Only wait for me and not do anything new till I'm home again — early in July. Will you? Will you promise me?'

He could not answer for some time.

'Ay!' he said unwillingly.

'You've promised — haven't you?'

'Yes.'

She kissed him quickly.

'And shall I come tomorrow night?' she whispered.

'Yes!' he said with a little convulsive shudder.

'Sure you want me?' she insisted.

'Oh God yes!' he shouted.

She laughed a little.

'Will you walk a little way with me?' she said.

He walked in silence at her side. She could feel him growing calmer, falling into the rhythm of desire and of forgetfulness. But she said nothing.

'You won't go away with your sister tomorrow then?' he asked.

'I could persuade her to stay a night — though she said she only wanted to pick me up. She is driving the car herself. Father is going from York to London by train.'

'Would she stop overnight if you asked her?'

Constance knew now his desire was uppermost again.

'Surely! Or she'd do better. She could drop me at your lane end tomorrow evening and come for me again next morning, then we should be really free.'

'You'll tell her everything then?'

'Oh, she knows.'

'And what does she say?'

'She's glad for me.'

'She's fond of yer, like?'

'Very! There are only the two of us.'

He was again left wondering at the strangeness of the gentry. They agreed that he should come up to Wragby after tea, and if he saw a red shawl hanging out of Constance's window it meant danger, and she could not come. If there was a white shawl it meant she would come after ten o'clock, as before. But if there was a green shawl it meant he was to go back to the cottage and down to the lane end at the railway bridge, a good four miles away, because Constance would get down there, at the bridge over the cutting, and walk down the lane to the cottage.

'We're up to some rare tricks, that we are!' he said.

'Do you mind?' she asked. She liked it.

'Me? No, I don't mind, on'y it seems a bit funny, like. — I hope yer'll hang a green shawl out though.'

'Yes! It's the Mohammedan's sacred colour. Well, Mohammed liked love well enough.'

'Did he?'

'He did. Not like Jesus!'

And that evening she talked to Clifford about Mohammed.

'Do you think it was right for Jesus to say to the woman: "Go, and sin no more"? After all, he was only a man!' she said. 'Not a woman himself!'

'Quite!'

'Supposing the woman had said: "Come thou, and sin with me!" Would it have been better, do you think?'

Clifford looked at her — she seemed excited and reckless — and laughed.

'He wouldn't have gone,' he said.

Constance was at first very happy, alone with Hilda. They motored down to London and had a couple of days there by themselves, shopping and going to the theatre.

'It's awfully nice to be manless for a while, don't you think?' said the younger sister to the elder.

'I think it's a mistake, anyhow, to have a man permanently about,' said Hilda. 'Men and women are so different, why should they be chained together? One of them has to give way to the other, and whichever one it is, the result is nasty, in my opinion. Marriage is a mistake.'

Constance pondered this.

'Yes!' she admitted. 'I suppose it is! Men are either dense or exhausting. It's a relief to be away from them altogether for a time.'

'For most of the time,' said Hilda.

But Constance was a little more old-fashioned and shrinking than her sister. Hilda had a certain sombre splendour about her. She really despised men. She despised her father; she had despised her husband, she despised him even now for paying her quite a good income: she despised and disliked Clifford: Heaven knows how she would have despised Parkin. Altogether it was a queer go!

Yet she was very handsome, beautiful and warm-coloured and so womanly-looking, with the same soft brown hair as Constance, and big, slow grey eyes. A sort of Brunhild, waging an invisible war, she lived a great deal alone. She had had her lovers. For her there was no longer any very great difference between one sort of man and another, one man and another. They were like puppets in a show, all different, but all worked in the same way, by pulling wires and letting go. And sex she despised as a sort of fraud: more wire-pulling.

She had a strange power of her own, however, silent and inexplicable. Her husband was in Parliament. She had lived in the political world. And men had talked to her a great deal. In the end they had all seemed to her conceited puppies. And almost invariably she made them feel it. Only in some of the tough, socially highly refined members of the aristocratic families, men who held permanent jobs and were not very much heard of, because they had no need to run after popularity, did she meet her match. They were extremely well bred and subtly insolent to her. Secure of their positions, having nothing much to win and not afraid of losing what they had got, inwardly cynical and empty, they had a strange cunning which made them aware of any subversive potency in any individual, and they had a strange, cold, almost insect-like power of paralysing the same subversive potency when they came across it personally.

These were the only men who had been able to confuse Hilda completely and make her feel small. Therefore they were to her the most typical men. Other men were fools in comparison, because they had not this strange cold cunning, a sort of cold, insect-like sapience, and a cunning of knowing just where to bite and leave the numbing venom. They had made her know she was plebeian. And that had been her defeat.

For a few days, however, she was very exhilarating company, for she was very clever. And it thrilled Constance to look on London as a sort of macabre farce, a sort of monkey show with the men for the complacent monkeys and the women for the spiteful ones. To be a spectator in cruel remoteness.

Sir Malcolm arrived, and was a very complacent old monkey. He came of a decent Scotch family of country squires and was incurably conceited but not very boring. He had been made a knight for painting 'historic' pictures. But he had a Scottish oddness and a fund of curious information, a leaning towards the lurid and the 'wicked' aspect of life, and was still quite handsome, with silky white hair, ruddy face, and a little white moustache. The clue to his life was that he had never really put himself out for anything or anybody, and nothing and nobody had ever really put him out. He had a silent, knowing little smile sometimes, and a suave diffidence always. He was fond of his daughters because he was head of their clan. He preferred not to know anything more about them than that they were fine girls whom you handled with gloves on. But he liked the company of young and handsome women: he had married rather late, in the first instance. And the peculiar bond of clan made things easy between them. They none of them ever became personal with one another. They remained just tribal. And that simplifies matters.

It was this Scottish tribal feeling which was their strength and their weakness. Alone, quite alone, they were each one of them a little at a loss, as if cut off from one another. Together, or even with other members of the family, they felt immensely reinforced. And yet they had very little personal contact: even Constance and Hilda. It was female, tribal, and family, what was between them.

They were in a smallish hotel opposite the Louvre palace, on the left bank of the river. In Paris Constance always felt herself settling back into the historic past. Paris, however modern, was, at least by the river, medievally modern: in this respect it seemed to her like Edinburgh: they were both medievally modern. And she liked it. At first she always liked it very much. One relaxed and sank back in some way upon the past. One was not kept up to the scratch so relentlessly as in England.

She liked to walk in the streets on the left side and to sit in the Luxembourg Gardens. How beautiful the midsummer flowers were in the Luxembourg Gardens, so brilliant and so purely decorative! Not at all wistful and a little amateurish as the very lovely and abundant flowers were in Hyde Park! Not in the very least like the pathos of the gardens at Wragby. Fine, splendid, showy, jaunty! She liked them very much. And the thin-legged boys playing games with a ball and crying out with such pseudo-sportsmanlike alertness — they might have come out of a Fourteenth Century picture, the clothing merely a little different.

For the first time, even, she rather liked the way the men looked at her: looked at her to see what she would be like to sleep with. She didn't mind the flâneurs strolling past Hilda and her herself, looking always up and down, at the body of the woman. She rather liked being just a woman in the body.

And there was often something comely and attractive about the men. They were usually well nourished, but then she preferred them so. And their eyes, if bold, were not hard and fishy. Sometimes there was a soft physical warmth in them. Often they were vulgar. But fairly often there was a certain male humanness that she liked.

Then, after about a week the excitement passed, and though Paris did not cease to be sympathetic, it became depressing. These men, these men, like creatures roving restlessly in Hades, in a sort of afterlife, seeking for something in a woman that they had really ceased to want, they were depressed and depressing. They were really terribly disheartened. Only they kept up the old woman-hunt, which no longer really interested either them or the woman. Only they could think of nothing else. In their souls they could discover no new impulse.

'These Frenchmen take an awful lot of pains chasing women they don't really want,' she said to Hilda.

'Do any men really want women?' said Hilda. 'Don't they all do it because it's been done since time began, and they're bored, and it's a stop-gap for their boredom, for a while.'

Constance pondered for a time.

'And because they don't know what to do with themselves when they're alone,' she said.

'Even less than women do,' said Hilda.

'Seems sad, doesn't it!' said Constance.

'It's a great bluff, the man and woman thing. It's like fox-hunting: a silly sort of amusement for satisfying atavistic instincts.'

Constance looked at her sister in fear. She was a little afraid of Hilda's cruelty.

'I don't think it's that quite!' said Constance. 'There can be always something new in the physical connection between men and women, don't you think? Don't you think a new element enters it, and that's what keeps life fresh?'

'If you speak from experience, it may be so. I myself haven't had the experience.'

Constance pondered this. Was her experience such? Was her experience with Parkin just the experience of woman since time began? And would it die down to nothingness the same — or end in something miserable, perhaps a bit squalid?

Yet as she watched the Frenchmen in Paris — or in Fontainebleau or in Chartres or in Orleans, as they motored south — and saw them handsome fellows, often real typical lovers of women: why didn't they move her personally? Why did she think so many a time: I should love that one to be my lover if I was somebody else? He'd be such a handsome lover for another woman: 'jeune, beau, vigoreux,' as the song says. But never for herself. The tiny special spark was always missing.

And there had to be that tiny special spark. And she realised, as she travelled, that she would easier find it in some rare Englishman than in a Frenchman. It was the spark of the great adventure, the power to change nature from the inside. Often she thought of what Clifford had read and pointed out to her: 'Nature is a lot of fixed laws, and human nature is a composition of old habits and fixed feelings. But inside nature there is a spark which sometimes flies into consciousness and causes the shrivelling of old feelings and the kindling of new ones, and displaces old habits and makes a little creative chaos out of which a new nature of man emerges.'

Constance in her own mind was determined that this spark did not fly out of nowhere into somewhere, but flew forth from the perfect contact of woman with a man. That was her philosophy.

And was there not something fine or pure or vivid in Parkin's nature as a man which would strike the right spark of her, the woman? Or was she fooling herself?

Perhaps all women in love had imagined it so. But perhaps it was always true. Maybe the danger lay in not sticking to the truth of it: in letting old habits and old feelings and old laws put out the spark.

'I've got to make up my mind —' this was her continual thought —'whether to take Parkin absolutely into the inmost part of my life or whether to think of him as just an escapade.'

She knew she didn't think of him as just an escapade. But she could not yet open her soul's last secret recess to his embrace. 'I daren't let him spring his seed right in there,' she thought.

And she did not want to leave Clifford to go to live with the other man. 'If we were just naked man to naked woman I might want to,' she said. 'But we are both clothed around with so many clothings, and so different. It's like asking a tortoise to risk breaking his shell to get a new form for himself.'

She didn't want to leave Clifford, to be stuck down among the working classes. Neither did she want to go to Canada and be a colonial. That, perhaps, even less. She had the greatest aversion to the thought. With intense tenacity she stuck to England. The personal escape into the colonies seemed to her a vulgar move, a step into nullity. The mystery did not lie that way. Parkin need never offer her that. If he wanted it, he must go alone. She would let him go.

She did not want to leave Clifford. He stood, socially, for the best humanity has achieved in the collective sense. The whole habit of life was least humiliating that way.

And she did not want to leave the ruling class to enter the subservient class. That too she knew. If she had to belong to a class let it be to the ruling class. Of course the present ruling class might be overthrown. Privately she felt that it would be. But until there were some signs of a new rule she would stick to the old.

The amorphousness of the colonies was merely vulgar. And she herself was no bohemian, and Parkin was no artist. He belonged more to a class — his own class — than Clifford did to his. Clifford, in his very Platonism, was somewhat beyond class.

Yes, and Parkin was beyond class in passion. She had to admit that. Once the queer, passionate lights began to glow and shift in the man's eyes, there was no ladyship nor anything else except a kindled womanhood.

At this thought Constance always cringed a little. She lost her prestige. And she cringed a little. 'Ma chuckie! Ma chuckie! Ah want thee that much!' She heard the curious, crooning voice of the keeper and felt his hand beneath her hips, pressing her up at him with an elemental power, and she shivered. She shivered with reminiscent passion but also with a sort of shame. Such a loss of prestige! 'Ah want thee that much!' Even that which was almost awful to her, filling her with a sort of awe, was also rather ridiculous. 'Ah want thee that much!' — And even want is pronounced to rhyme with chant or with pant! — She felt a fool in retrospect. After all — she wasn't just 'his chuckie'. After...

(Pages 224 — 225 of the original manuscript missing)

daily newspapers or journal. Yet she would have missed them if they had not come home. And she replied with abrupt little letters, which she squeezed out rather with an effort. From Parkin, of course, she could not hear, because she had never written a word to him, and he had no idea where she was.

She heard of him, however, from Clifford. It was towards the end of June, time old Sir Malcolm was thinking of returning to his wife in Yorkshire. He was due back the first week in July, due to take his middle-aged wife to Scotland. But he was still gay-dogging and deferring.

'We've had a mild local excitement,' wrote Clifford. 'The game-keeper Parkin's wife came back to him unexpectedly and, it seems, unwelcome. He turned her out of the house and locked the door on her, but when he returned from the wood in the evening he found her in bed without even a nightdress on her rather battered nudity. What happened I don't know, but he retired to his mother's house in the village for the night. It appears the woman had broken a window pane and got into the cottage. The collier she lived with had turned her out, got tired of her. So she came back to Parkin. He, apparently, declares he will not go within a mile of her. She, on the other hand, declares he got into bed with her before abandoning her to go to his mother in the village. The heavenly hosts being sole witnesses, this matter remains to be threshed out. I am sorry to treat you to this especial bit of local garbage, but Mrs Bolton, our particular garbage bird, our sacred ibis, our intimate buzzard, suggested that Her Ladyship might like to know. For my own part, the conjugalities and amorosities of Mr and Mrs Parkin are not my concern, I only do not wish that an excellent gamekeeper should be spoiled for me.

'I like your picture of Sir Malcolm in the sea, with his white hair washed over his forehead, looking like a bonny babe in a bath. He is one of the most mortal of mortals. He washes off his immortality every time he washes his face. It is strange that a man so utterly devoid of immortality — I should say void — can be your father. But this is but one more proof that immortality is a gift from the Immortal Sphere, and mortals cannot hand it on—'

At first this letter did not penetrate into Constance. She was so strung up to the world that surrounded her, the social world where every individual is tense, holding his own or her own against the rest and scrambling over the faces of the others to assert some kind of valueless superiority; living, dressing, acting only to acquire some peculiar temporary prestige, some meaningless power of veto, some equally meaningless power of suggesting plans for the general amusement: that the whole world of Wragby and the woods seemed unreal.

Here in the villa by the sea everything was social and artificial. The landscape itself was not quite so theatrically stagey as Monte Carlo or Cannes, but it served the same purpose, as back curtain to the social events. The very sea was like a huge bathtub set out by the servants each morning.

And with a queer tightening of the nerves Constance had entered right into this world. She was on the stage of social events. She held her own in conversation and repartee. She dressed in her own way to please herself. And by exerting the peculiar heavy sort of power that was in her she held her own and gained ground in the shifting company. She enhanced her own prestige in the temporary crowd. People would always name her as having been one of the guests. In a world which fights solely and simply for that unpleasant substitute called prestige, a shoddy sort of superiority that is the margarine which butters the social bread since the war as a substitute for the old superiority of rank and talent, she knew how to hold her own.

At the same time somewhere she was ashamed of it all. It was too shoddy and shameful. Even Clifford's megalomaniac immortality was better.

But somehow, having got into the swim, she couldn't get out. She half-wanted to leave, to take the train home. But again, she didn't want to go home, home to Clifford and his insistent immortality, home to Parkin and his insistent desire. Here, at least, she was free. She was bound to nobody, intimate with nobody, dear to nobody, and nobody was dear to her. So she was free.

She knew it was a tawdry, a squalid freedom, tawdry as the pink geraniums and squalid as the awful and inevitable bridge and poker parties. She could see the squalor of the card parties playing for high stakes, plainly enough. She could feel the squalor of the remorseless and incessant fight for a margarine 'superiority' among the guests. But she was in the swim, and she could hold her own, she did not finally want to break away.

'The thing possesses me like some evil spirit possessing a maniac. We are all maniacs,' she said to herself.

She told Hilda of Clifford's letter about Parkin.

'Well!' said Hilda after due consideration. 'If you're going to have the child you've got what you want. It is perhaps the easiest way out of the intrigue.'

The easiest way out of the intrigue! My God!

Constance began to hate the child which she was not even sure was conceived within her. It was not the child she had wanted. The child was merely another substitute for something she knew she wanted without knowing exactly what it was. What did the child matter, if she lost — what? Something hard and angry rose in her and refused to allow her to know what it was she was losing.

A man who did music came to the villa for a few days. He was not young, nor handsome nor famous: a smallish man with an ascetic grey sort of face and a weak digestion, a restless, nerve-wracked creature who would have been a nonentity save for some little power of music in him. He made no fight for prestige, didn't care what the crowd thought of him and was thoroughly miserable, though fairly used to such bunches of company, and therefore used to being thoroughly miserable. He played the piano well — but unwillingly: and his own compositions in the dainty Elizabethan style of music were charming if not memorable.

The second evening he sat down beside Constance on a sofa in the music room.

'My God!' he gasped. 'What an awful place!'

He seemed to be talking to her as if she were a tree he could commune with.

'Rather awful!' she murmured somewhat against her own will.

'Why is it that these places are always so ghastly?'

'Which places?'

'These big smart houses where you meet everybody, and never anybody that's alive. I shall go mad! I am going mad. I know it.'

'Why don't you stay away then?'

'Yes, why don't I? It's like drink, I suppose. My stomach is too weak for alcohol, and my nerves are too weak for drugs, so I suppose I do this sort of thing.'

'What do you get out of it?'

'What does one get out of it — except a sort of conceit at staying in a house with six footmen and four motor cars? It's just conceit, you know, just conceit.'

'And is it worth it?'

'One must always pay for one's vices: I'm insignificant really, so I think if I have a valet de chambre and sit next to the Duchess of Toadstool at dinner I become significant. I know it all. I know it's driving me mad. Yet I do it.'

'But why? Why do you if you know all the time?'

'Oh, because it's my vice. I'm egoistic: we're all egoistic: everybody in this house is a sheer materialistic egoist. We play each other's game. It flatters us. And we're all going mad.'

'Am I too?' asked Constance, amused.

'You must be or you wouldn't be here. Only perhaps it will take longer in your case than in mine. And they won't shut you up so soon, because you've got a background, and I'm one of the bits that come unravelled off the loose end.'

Constance, though amused, was rather impressed. 'But why don't you do something quite different?' she said. 'If you know it is sending you quite mad why don't you break away?'

'What should I do that is quite different? I was Red Cross-working during the war, and that deranged me more than ever. — Besides, perhaps I want to go mad. Very few people who are going mad want to be cured. They are in love with their own derangement. They are proud of going mad. They would hate you for curing them: just as the maniac hated Jesus.'

Constance laughed at him, he was so funny, half-serious, half-taunting. Yet that in itself was perhaps an incipient state of madness.

'Is everybody going mad then?' she asked laughing.

'Most people, yes!'

He looked at her with serious, rather beautiful blue eyes in which she could see the purity of music.

'But which people aren't?'

'Those people whose souls are warm. Our souls are cold — at least mine is, and all the people's here. We've all got cold souls, and it's worse than having cold feet. We're so awfully nice and apparently unselfish, but we're crawling about in cold herds like crabs and lobsters, really, eating putrefaction in perfect cold egoism. We should all go scarlet if we were boiled.'

The last was really amusing.

'But we shan't be boiled, you see,' she said.

'Who knows!' he retorted. 'They may boil us one day.'

'Who?'

'The people who've still got some life in them, some warm passion.'

'And where are they?'

'Oh, down among the lower classes mostly. And odd ones here and there. We're killing them off as fast as we can. We killed most of our lot during the war. That's why we had a war: to kill off the generous, and leave the cold-blooded and the charitable.'

'But you don't sound very charitable,' said Constance.

'I don't feel it. But my blood has gone cold, below a certain degree. And now I am going mad.'

'What a queer fish you are! Do you like to think you are going off your head?'

'Yes! It's a sort of revenge on my head for being too much on top of me. It's a sort of revenge I have on myself: going mad. — But when the head chills the blood below a certain point people always go mad. The Americans are all mad, or going mad. Now Europe is going coldly insane. If the warm-blooded people, who are mostly slow and rather stupid, because they believe that everybody is warm-blooded like themselves — they can't conceive that lobsters are cold — they only see them boiled, when they look so ruddy — What was I saying?'

'If the warm-blooded people don't do something or other —'

'Oh yes! If the warm-blooded people don't wake up and begin to exterminate us cold-blooded ones, we shall destroy the world. We shall destroy the race of mankind.'

'Would it be a great disaster?'

'From our cold-blooded point of view it would be a great blessing. We hate ourselves, so we hate everything, and only hate makes us so well mannered and so grimly philanthropic. We want to buy ourselves off, buy off the day of our own extermination. And every one of us hopes he will be the last man left alive. So we keep up appearances. But we eat putrescence.'

Constance was a little afraid of this mad musician. Most of all, it sank in her like a stone that he classed her among the cold-blooded ones. She looked round the music room, at the well-nourished young men with rather fat thighs and sleek dress suits, laughing with young smart women in silvery, metallic fabrics and naked knees, and she said:

'There are plenty of love-affairs going on, even here. So the human race does not look like dying out.'

The musician glanced round with extraordinary aversion.

'They are all eating putrescence!' he said.

'But why? Perhaps some of them are warm-blooded,' she said.

'The lobster looks ruddy when he's been boiled.'

'But there's no question of boiling. There are really warm-hearted people everywhere.'

'There may be kind-hearted crabs, but there are no hot-blooded crabs as far as I am aware. Hot blood is the part of those with the milk of kindness. Even tigresses have milk. These women have no milk. They are fish. There are kind-hearted people in this house. But there are no hot-blooded ones. We've killed them all off or driven them out.'

'Why?'

'Because they are dangerous. You never know what they will do.'

'Do we know what these will do?'

'Oh yes! They will destroy all life ultimately. But they will destroy it according to formula. And that is better than if they destroyed the social fabric without a formula. So we think, who love a formula above everything because it is compatible with our own egoism, which invented formulas as well as everything else.'

'Look at the Russians!'

'They had a formula: a cold-blooded Jewish formula. That is why we are able to despise them. A real revolution goes beyond a formula.'

'And will there ever be a revolution?'

'Perhaps! and perhaps not! If we are quick enough to stifle and exterminate all hot-blooded people, there will never be a revolution. Only, as in Russia, subversion under a formula.'

'But can the blood change hot or cold or what you like?'

'You can chill the hot blood — but the animal usually dies. You can never warm the blood of the cold ones. That is the miracle even Jesus couldn't accomplish. He could only call forward the hot-blooded ones, and make them active.'

'But there are always both, cold-blooded and hot-blooded people in the world at once. Why shouldn't they get on well together? They do really.'

'They are always in conflict. Cold blood always wants to subjugate all hot blood. And hot-blooded ones have great fits of exterminating the cold-blooded ones. But the cold-blooded ones are cunning, and they never rest till they have made servants of the hot-blooded ones. Then they go too far. Then comes the retribution: and it all starts again.'

'And the hot-blooded ones are always servants?'

'Ye Gods, no! Alexander was hot-blooded, so was Jesus, so was Socrates, so was Caesar, so were Tamerlane and Attila, and Peter the Great and Frederick the Great and even Voltaire. But since Napoleon we've had the slow but awful triumph of the cold-blooded ones in every country, fascist or democratic or bolshevist, all alike: different displays of cold-bloodedness.'

The little madman took his departure the next day. But what it all meant to Constance, as she realised with growing anger and perplexity, was that she would have to choose between Clifford and Parkin. There seemed no earthly reason why she shouldn't have both men, situated as she was. Only for some unearthly reason, apparently she couldn't.

She did not want to choose between them. She wanted both. She wanted to have her cake and eat it. It infuriated her to have to say: I will take this one, I will forfeit the other. She was extremely angry with Parkin for putting her in a dilemma. She was so extremely angry with him, because she could not forfeit him. She couldn't let him go. As for Clifford, it was not just the man in him that she clung to. It was all he stood for. And she could not forfeit all the things he stood for. She felt inclined to do as Hilda had done and cut clear of everything. She was deeply angry inside herself.

She wrote to Clifford, announcing her return, and also to Mrs Bolton, asking for news of Clifford, and casually, for further news of the gamekeeper scandal. For Clifford had forgotten to mention anything further.

'You will be pleased, I am sure, My Lady, when you see Sir Clifford, for he has made great strides. He seems greatly improved in health and looking forward to having you home again, I am sure. Indeed it seems a dull house without My Lady, and we shall all welcome her bright presence among us once more, I can say it for all at Wragby, from the highest to the lowest, for you are quite loved by everyone.

'About Mr Parkin. I don't know how much Sir Clifford told you. It appears the wife came back one night just after dark, saying the collier had thrown her out that she lived with. I heard she had been carrying on with the new policeman, a great big ugly fellow as speaks so broad you can scarcely make out what he says, broad Scotch I suppose. It appears the collier threw her out, and the policeman wouldn't have anything to say to her, so she went back to Mr Parkin. It was just about bed-time when she got to the cottage. But Mr Parkin wouldn't have her in. He gave her ten shillings and told her to go and locked the door in her face. But she wouldn't go, brazen as she is, she knew where she would be best off. She kept knocking and calling all the time, and the dog barking and growling, so at last Mr Parkin, he slipped out into the wood by the back door and left her to knock. But when he got back in the morning, she'd broken a window and got in, eaten everything she could lay hands on in the pantry, and was there lying in bed without a stitch of a chemise or a nightdress on her, showing the low woman she is. Well Mr Parkin he tried to make her get up and go, but she wouldn't, so he went and fetched his mother. Old Mrs Parkin couldn't do anything with her. She swore Mr Parkin had been in bed with her, and he swore he hadn't. And there she lay in the bed without a stitch on her, nor would she get up. So Mrs Parkin and her son Oliver took all the food and everything they could out of the house, and they put a few things in the hut in the wood and took the rest to Tevershall, and left the woman lying in bed without a stitch on her, and a bare house and both doors locked. So I suppose she got up some time, for she was at the Three Tunns that afternoon, raving and carrying on and calling Mr Parkin all the blaggards and the b's. It seems somebody told her to go to the police-station and get a summons to force her husband to take her back and keep her, so she went and kicked up a shine there, and then she went to Mr Linley, because he's the J.P. now. So Mr Linley sent for Mr Parkin and asked him if he'd take her back. He said he'd see himself dead first, and her as well. Then Mr Linley asked him why he'd never applied for a divorce or a legal separation, and he said he'd never thought of it but he'd give his last penny to get a divorce from her. So she said he couldn't, because he'd been in bed with her that morning, and he vowed he hadn't, and she had a lot of nasty talk about showing the sheets and etc. So

Mr Parkin lives with his mother now and is trying for a divorce. Sir Clifford is helping him all he can. That woman lives in the cottage, and vows and declares she will stop any divorce, and that he is a bad one and an underhand villain, and she will tell the judge a thing or two about him, a lot of low talk. Mr Parkin's mother is very upset about it all, and she says she's afraid Mr Parkin will do himself some injury. I believe Mr Parkin wants to give Sir Clifford notice to leave. He wants to get out of these parts, for that woman says she'll not stop plaguing him till he's underground, for he has been her ruin. More likely the boot is on the other leg. But she hates him, you can see that. The collier and the others are nothing to her now, it's nothing but that d—d Oliver. Old Mrs Parkin says she's quite capable of murdering him one of these nights in the wood, but I say he's not the man "to let himself be murdered by a woman," though she's like a madwoman. She even came up to the Hall, but Sir Clifford gave orders that she was to go, and if she didn't go quietly Benson and Field were to tie her up and carry her to the police-station and give her in charge. Now Sir Clifford is getting an order to have her evicted from the cottage, as Mr Parkin is domiciled with his mother. But there's no mistake, that woman is like a madwoman. She is older than Mr Parkin, and it may be her time of life has something to do with it. But if ever a woman was possessed by a demon it's that one. And all against Mr Parkin. I'm sure, My Lady, it makes me feel bad to hear the things she is going about saying about him, awful things, fearful things. Of course nobody believes her altogether, but something's bound to stick. Sir Clifford says we will have her in gaol, but she doesn't care about gaol nor anything else. She only wants to come up before a judge to vilify Mr Parkin and tell all the vile things he did to her when they were married, immoral things and horrible for a woman to go about saying. But Sir Clifford says she won't be allowed to say anything at random before a judge, they won't let her. Such women should be shut up, for there's more talk in the place now then I've ever known, and such awful things. My Lady, it is shameful. But she is not responsible, she is evil mad —'

This letter went home to Constance. She felt a fetid black smoke of vulgar ignominy pouring out of it, covering her with smuts. She could not yet make out whether her own name had been spoken in connection with Parkin's. It seemed not. Yet she recoiled from the fetid scandal of the whole thing.

Yet somewhere, as in a tiny convex mirror, she had a sharp little image of the man her man. It was an image tiny as a little flake of light yet vivid as a star: his male, naked purity. She hardly thought about him: she was angry altogether. Only this little image persisted like a spark which dances before the eyes even when they are shut. And she knew perfectly well, as a woman does know when she is not befogged and falsified, that a passionate man remains pure so long as his passion remains unmixed and uncontaminated by his ego. She did not mind, really, what things Parkin did or had done. She only minded the sharp intensity of his passion for her.

At the same time she loathed the squalor of other people. Not the wife so much. She understood the demon of a wife. The woman no doubt loved him and knew he despised her. The extent of her reckless defamation showed the extent of her morbid love for him, and also, the extent to which he was cold to her, despising her. In her present state the woman didn't care what happened to her, poor thing. If she had been tortured on the rack she would have persisted just the same. She was like a dog with rabies, and death would be really the only solution. Constance was sorry for her in a way. But she shuddered with horror at the thought of her.

And into this awful stew Constance was by no means anxious to return. It was already the first week in July. Sir Malcolm really wanted to be in Scotland by August because then the fun would begin there — and Biarritz was already empty, it was out of season. The house party in the villa was slowly breaking up. The old artist decided to leave on the fifth.

Constance and Hilda, however, proposed motoring round the Bay of Biscay up to Brittany, and crossing to Southampton from Le Havre. It would be a new road. Their father agreed, stipulating only that he must be home in Yorkshire by the twentieth of the month.

Constance telegraphed the date of her departure to Clifford. The day before she left she had a letter from him, and another from Mrs Bolton. Clifford wrote:

'I was delighted to know you are actually leaving that place. Once you set your face north, I shall feel you are really coming. It will be marvellous to have you back, though I am not going to complain for one instant of your absence. I have been looked after most assiduously by the excellent Mrs Bolton. She is quite a curious person, and difficult to understand. One of God's freaks, I should say. She regales me with a great amount of Tevershall gossip, and makes me feel how near I am to the jungle. Nothing seems to surprise her. She takes the offensive Mrs Parkin Junior as calmly as she takes you or me. No fish is too weird for her aquarium. But of course, she is not quite normal. After a few hours of her gossip I emerge into the comparative paradise of Plotinus or even of Hegel and feel I am breathing again. It is surely absolutely true that our world, which seems to us a surface, is only the bottom of a very deep sea, and all our trees are submarine growths, and we are submarine monsters. Only the soul at times rises through the fathomless fathoms under which we live, far up into the other world, the true air, the veritable light. Then one feels like a kittiwake that shoots into the air with ecstasy after having preyed upon the submerged fishes. It is our mortal destiny, I suppose, to prey upon the horrible subaqueous fauna of the human submarine jungle. But our immortal destiny is to escape, once we have swallowed our catch, up into the bright ether, bursting out from the surface tension of Old Ocean into real light. When I talk to you I feel myself plunging down, seizing the wriggling fish of the human secret, then up, up again, and out of the liquid into the ethereal. It is a great game. But with Mrs Bolton I can only plunge down among the seaweeds and the pallid monsters and stay there. I cannot soar again till she has gone.

'We have had a great lashing of sea horrors in the Parkin scandal. I don't know if you remember, I told you his truant wife had come back at him, to use an Americanism, and he found her stark naked in his bed. Since then he has been more or less in retreat behind his mother. The truant wife fortified herself for a week in the cottage, but I had her evicted. Since then, she has been sleeping somewhere in Dakin's Row and spending her waking hours raising Cain. She has besieged old Mrs Parkin's house and has seized her own daughter. The daughter, being kitten of the cat, bit and fought so hard that she received a smack in the face which sent her into the gutter, whence she was rescued by the indignant grandmother. The truant wife then proceeded to her favorite haunt, the Three Tunns, and blew off steam, as the colliers say. She has aired in minute detail every incident in her married life with Parkin that respects to his discredit. It is a curious recital. The virtuous Mrs Bolton will give me none of these details, she only says it is "too shameful to mention". Doctor Smith, however, who is a humorist in these matters, has kept me informed. It is a curious, almost medieval assortment of sexual extravagance and minor perversities, for which I should not have thought our friend Parkin sufficiently imaginative. But it seems that these minor sexual perversities are of all time and circumstance, like fleas and bald heads. It throws a new light on our gamekeeper. I had thought him merely commonplace. Now I see that he too is a little subaqueous monster, incapable of existing without committing absurd and inadequate minor enormities. He has been to interview me several times in regard to this uproar with his wife, and I have been amused to watch him. He is somewhat like a dog with a tin can tied to his tail. Of course I pretend not to notice the tin can, but it rattles obviously when he moves. When I told him not to trouble about the things his wife says of him, he replied: "Them as listens to such things is worse than them as does 'em!" and at that he shuts up like an oyster. He is, however, applying for a divorce. His wife declares she will prevent him and have him in gaol. At present, however, she is herself locked up. She got drunk and attacked our friend Parkin with a large full bottle of Worthington. He defended with the butt of his gun but not before he had got a bad knock on the head. Our friend, the J.P., Arthur Linley, Esquire, had her arrested by the new police constable who is popularly known as the "Meat Fly"! The truant wife managed so to offend our estimable manager, Linley, that he gave her fourteen days. Now I hear she has sworn by all the gods that she will "do him in": meaning Parkin, not Linley. In fact, it is a great scandal, such as visits a village like Tevershall once in twenty years. Of course, we shall have to stop that woman's mouth, it has gone far enough.

'The unpleasant part of it is, Parkin insists that he must leave my service and wants me to let him go at once. I insist he must find me another gamekeeper, or else stay his three months. He suggests his nephew Joe, but that boy is altogether inadequate. When he said he'd got to go I asked him why, precisely? And I told him he ought not to mind mere talk: though I must say I think the bottle of beer hit him hard. He replied: "I'm goin', Sir Clifford, an' I wish you'd tell My Lady I'm not ashamed o' what I've got atween my legs, not if everybody tries to make me. But I'm not goin' ter live nigh to 'em neither." — I told him: "Live it down, man, live it down!" But I'm afraid he saw I was amused, for he said: "Ay, yo' maun laugh, Sir Clifford, but it's not for a man in your shapes to laugh neither." — Which was impudence, but I suppose I provoked it. I said to him: "You'd laugh, you know, Parkin, if you heard those things about one of the colliers, for instance." And he replied: "Ay, 'appen I should! An' I sh'd expect him to stop me across t'mouth, an' a', if he got a chance an' saw me!" — So I left it at that, and accepted his notice, provided he can get another man to go with the callow Joe. I'm afraid if he stays he'll be slapping more people across the mouth than will be good for them or him. He's held himself in remarkably well, considering. I think he must feel a little more guilty, or at fault, than he allows. —'

Mrs Bolton wrote rather briefly.

'I saw Mr Parkin yesterday looking very poorly. What with all this harassment and that blow on the head with a quart bottle of beer. His mother told me he was sick for more than an hour after it, vomiting and retching, and he does look very poorly. But he never says anything to anybody, can't hardly get a word out of him. I said to him I was awfully sorry to see him looking so badly, and it was a shame. He asked me if I knew when your Ladyship was coming back. I told him what I knew and said I was writing to you. He asked me if I thought anybody had mentioned this affair to you, so I said Sir Clifford had, and I had myself. So he asked me to tell you he was leaving, but he shouldn't be going to Canada yet, he would stop on and get his divorce from that woman first. I'm sure no man would want to be tied to her a day longer than he need. I told him I'd be sure and tell you, and I'd let him know if there was any message. He bears up just the same and looks you in the face to see what you're thinking. But I'm afraid he's poorly. It's bound to be a strain on a man, such things said about him, and everybody talking behind his back —'

Constance replied to Mrs Bolton:

'Tell Parkin I'm very sorry all this has happened. Ask him not to go away without leaving his address, because I want to bring him a little present from France, to thank him for being so kind to me in the spring when I was so run down, and he let me feed the baby pheasants.'

And the next day they set off in the car, northwards, home to it all. There is no escape in this world. The only way to get ahead is to go through with the thing no matter what it may be, and come out the other side.

It was full summer, and hay harvest, and the lonely country of France. Constance felt herself seized with one of the violent revulsions she had sometimes from the civilised world, the world that man has made, and that everyone has to live in. She felt it would be good and clean to be dead, to get away from it all. As for rising above it into any kind of immortality, that thought sickened her worse than ever. She wanted no immortality wherein she would remember, just as she wanted no sleep with tormented dreams. Whatever came after let it be utterly different, as different as profound sleep.

Yet the country they drove through was strange and fascinating, as if the world had forgotten it. How strange and remote France was! And sometimes they stayed in a village inn where the men came at evening and drank wine. She heard the guttural sound of the dialect, and a certain nostalgia came over her for the warm blindness of life like theirs. She saw them sitting with knees apart and loosely clenched fists resting on their live, animal thighs. That was how Parkin sat. And there was something in it so utterly restful and warm to her woman's soul. She wanted that, to sink back into the half-dreamy warmth of the unawakened life. She felt she had been wakened too wide and too long. She wanted to sleep again, the warm sleep of life, with a man who would go powerfully through the passion of life without waking her, yet always there in her life as if they were sailing in one boat.

She saw the peasants, the fishermen, the wood-men, and saw they were gradually being wakened into the nervous misery of the civilised life. They were coming under the influence of the towns. Their life was passing away.

And she was afraid for herself. She dreamed at night that she had been arrested and had to stand up before a judge, to be tried as a criminal. She could not make out quite what her crime was. But it was something shameful.

When she thought about it awake, she knew it was the Parkin scandal. And she realised how frightened she was. She was frightened with an old Mosaic fear, afraid of the horrible power of society and of its commandments which she had broken. She felt she was dynamically an enemy of society, and that she was terrified. She had all her life had a secret fear of people and of the ponderous crushing apparatus of the law. Now, for some reason owing to the Parkin scandal, the fear became acute and almost overmastering.

And still she distinguished it from a sense of guilt or wrong. 'No!' she said to herself. 'I don't feel guilty or wrong. On the contrary, I feel it is right what I have done, and will do. Yet I feel paralysed with fear. I feel as if they had got me under. I feel as if they had got me down.'

She laboured under this sense of having been got down, subtly caught and pulled down by the vast mob which is civilised society. She couldn't rise. Her spirits would not rise. She wished she were going to the moon rather than back to Wragby. Heavily her soul dragged on, feeling impotent, humiliated, enslaved.

Then she thought of Parkin. He would be having the same experience, only worse. She knew his peculiar shrinking — from the mass of people, a shrinking which lay beneath his violent aggressiveness, which last was only the cornered dog showing its teeth. She knew how he would suffer, having his nakedness uncovered by that foul woman, his wife. — 'Minor sexual perversities,' Clifford said, and seemed amused. She didn't quite know what he referred to, but she knew that every woman, and hence every man had private sexual secrets which no one had any right to betray. 'The biggest part of my life,' she said to herself, 'is secret, and the first business I have is to keep the secret, and to respect the secret in other people.'

But now Parkin would be exposed in his private intimacies, and the whole place would be grinning and jeering at him, and many would be indignantly crying shame, abomination. She knew what it meant! And he had to pass back and forth through the long, dismal mining village, if he was living with his mother. And all the people would be trying to throw him down and cover him with obscenity as if with excrement.

'I'm not ashamed of what I've got atween my legs.' He meant his penis. She thought of the naked man, the passion and the mystery of him: the mystery of the penis! And she knew, as every woman knows, that the penis is the column of blood, the living fountain of fullness in life. From the strange rising and surging of the blood all life rises into being. Whatever else it is, it is the river of the only God we can be sure about, the blood. 'There is a fountain filled with blood,' said the hymn. And it is eternally true. And every man is such a fountain. And it is not the dead, spilled blood which will wash away all sin, but the living rush of the ever new blood ever renewed. Dead blood can but stink at last. It is the living blood that is the living side, which washes away the old corruptions. And the symbol of the rush of the living blood is the phallus, and the penis is the fountain of life filled with blood.

And with the mystery of the phallus goes all the beauty of the world, and beauty is more than knowledge. Knowledge is so often an illusion, and even when it seems sure, its power to sustain us goes dead. The knowledge of the movement of the stars and the laws of celestial gravitation is wonderful, but the beauty of the stars in their motions is still more wonderful, and it is the penis which connects us sensually with the planets. But for the penis we should never know the loveliness of Sirius or the categorical difference between a pomegranate and an india-rubber ball.

Man need not sacrifice the intellect to the penis, nor the penis to the intellect. But there is an eternal hostility between the two, and life is for ever torn across by the conflict between them. Yet man has a holy ghost inside him which partakes of the nature of both. And hence man has a new aim in life, to maintain a truce between the two and some sort of fluctuating harmony. Instead of deliberately, as science and Socrates, Christianity and Buddha have all done, deliberately setting out to murder the one in order to exalt the other.

What are we when the phallic wonder in us is dead? We are wretched things, and evil. What are we when the penis is the mere tool and toy of the mind? We are perverted and vicious. It is the penis alone which saves men from utterly destroying the world, and the phallus alone is the symbol of our unison in the blood. The cross, as the symbol of the murdered phallus, is an evil symbol and carries evil wherever it goes.

Poor Parkin, they could hurt him so much more than they could hurt Clifford, for example. One could not really hurt Clifford, in the wincing, sensitive way in which one can hurt a physical man. One could only offend him or hurt his self-esteem or abandon him to his own dreariness. He was dreary really. In spite of all his subtlety, he was tough and insentient. It was so like him to join in the laugh against his gamekeeper. He would join in a common laugh. There was something so vulgar about it.

She felt a great wave of distaste go over her against Clifford. He was so cold, so egoistic in a polished way, and so insentient in a refined way. She loathed his refined insentience, his refined lack of feeling. He could talk about 'minor sexual perversities' so glibly, without for a second remembering his own. He could laugh with that vulgar superiority, as if he himself verily never had had a penis. And verily, she thought, in the magic and the sacred reality of it he never had. He had had an organ, a toy and a tool for his own ego.

She was so sick of people with their egos. It made them all so tough, so leathery-hided, so aware only of the surfaces. It made them so subtly bullying. In a curious way Clifford bullied the whole place at Wragby, even his very tolerance was a cold denial of life. Ugh! She was so weary of it, the cold emptiness of that way of life, the toughness, the insentience, the negative sort of tyranny. A tyranny of negation: the warm blood must not flow, it must be chilled.

'I won't!' she said to herself. 'I won't take Parkin's child and hand it over to Clifford! It shall not be a Chatterley and a baronet and a gentlemen and another cold horror. If I've warmed my hands at the fire of life I won't spit in the fire. And Parkin is my fire of life, and he warmed me all the length of my body and through my soul. I've been denying him lately, and I've felt beastly because of it. I won't deny him. And I'll go home and tell it him. And I'll tell him his penis is more beautiful to me, and better, than all the bodies of all the people in Tevershall and Wragby.'

So she settled the question: not in these set terms but to the same effect. How does one think when one is thinking passionately and with suffering? Not in words at all but in strange surges and crosscurrents of emotion which are only half-rendered by words.

Having worked herself up into a state, Constance decided to go straight home by train via Dieppe.

'What difference will a few days make?' asked Hilda.

'I want to go,' said Constance. 'I feel it is time.'

'Time for what?'

'I don't want to leave Parkin in the lurch,' said Constance, who had told Hilda roughly about the scandal.

'What do you mean by not leaving him in the lurch? What can you do for him exactly?'

'I can be there.'

'But — why should you be? Much better stay out of it, it seems to me.'

Constance looked at her sister with those blue, candid eyes which always looked most innocent when she was battling for her own way against opposition.

'I've thought it out. I can't let him go out of my life. I've thought it out. I must live with him.'

It was Hilda who blushed slowly and deeply.

'I think you are very foolish,' she said. 'Why must you live with anybody?'

'I want to so much — with him,' said Constance.

Hilda turned aside and sat down.

'Aren't you being foolish?' she asked quietly.

'No, Hilda!' said Constance, still reasonable.

'And supposing he doesn't want to live with you? Supposing he's had enough?' said Hilda.

Constance watched with those big blue eyes.

'But you see, Hilda, he hasn't,' she said.

'How do you know?'

There was a pause.

'Well, goodbye, Hilda!' said Constance. 'I'll get a taxi to the station.'

She crossed by the night boat. It was a still night, and warm. She sat on deck and looked at the stars and the night. She felt a great turmoil outside but a great quietness inside. The yearning that had been tearing at her for weeks now, like a distraction, seemed soothed. She was very still, and the journey passed like a dream.

By one o'clock she was at Uthwaite, where the car would meet her. And on the station platform — Oh God! — was Clifford on crutches? He had learned to go on crutches since she had left! His face, ruddy and healthy-looking, and with that inhuman birdlike keenness, was watching the train as he himself leaned against one of the iron pillars that supported the station roof, his crutches under his armpits. Those eyes, those keen light-blue, hard swift eyes, of an English gentleman! She almost felt them strike her as they lighted on her face. And a curious flame of triumph filled them, inhuman. He was triumphing in his new victory over fate. Poor Clifford!

The man-servant hurried forward to help her. Clifford remained with his back against the pillar, watching tensely. She hurried forward to him.

'Why Clifford!' she said in her breathless voice.

'How are you, dear?' he said, as he leaned a hand on her shoulder and bent forward to kiss her.

It was almost with surprise that she realised that he was an actuality. He had become a sort of shadow while she was away.

'But can you really go?' she cried, looking at the crutches.

'In a fashion,' he said.

'But how wonderful! How — ?' she could get no further. She was panting, and her cheeks were bright red.

'Mrs Bolton inspired me. Oh, she's an amazing woman when she likes.'

'And — and have you been out before?'

'Not to Uthwaite. This is the grand celebration of your arrival home!'

He was looking round for Field, his man. Field was a square, powerful, taciturn young man of about twenty-five, with a round and babyish face. He came up saluting.

'Are yer ready then, Sir Clifford?' he said.

'Quite ready.'

The chauffeur took his master from behind and slowly eased him erect till the crutches balanced. There was a queer tension in Clifford's face, fear and excitement.

'Let go!' he said.

And then, with strange swift strokes of his crutches, Clifford was poling himself along the station platform, his dead legs swinging in peculiar inert swoops between the crutches, yet holding firm long enough for their owner to plunge onward in another stroke of the crutches. It was an uncanny, fearsome sight. Field, who looked squat because he was so broad and fat, trotted strangely alongside, watching every second, never for an instant taking his eyes off his master. And Constance, left behind, hurried along in amazement, amazement at Clifford's new daring and at the chauffeur's dogged, almost passionate absorption in the new feat.

She emerged from the station in time to see Clifford taken bodily round the waist and lifted into the open car, heaved up in the most amazing fashion. And there he was, sitting in the car like anybody else, his crutches beside him, the chauffeur holding the door for her and saluting.

'But Field, it is too wonderful!' she said as she entered.

'Wonderful, my lady, eh?' said the man, beaming a broad smile on his fat face, and looking at Sir Clifford with such pleased pride, as if the baronet had been his own precocious offspring. Then he hurried to secure the luggage. And Constance thought to herself how marvellous it was that one could have such attention and such service for two pounds a week. But then it was obvious the man took an abiding pride in the achievement itself.

'Well?' said Clifford, looking round at her benignly. 'You look blooming. Have you had a good time?'

'Oh quite!' she said.

'Only quite?' he asked ironically.

'Well, I thought I was having a perfect time — such sun and bathing! But I wasn't really. I was deceiving myself.'

'In what particular?'

'Oh, I don't know. I wasn't interested at all, not in anything we did: I mean, not altogether interested. — But you, you are the wonderful one! Why didn't you tell me?'

'I was afraid I might raise your expectations too high. Are you at all glad to be back?'

'Very!' she said. And as she looked round at the spoiled mining country, she spoke with truth. It was real to her. It corresponded with something real in her.

'That's good hearing!' he said, watching her keenly. There was something about her that puzzled him and allured him.

'So you really didn't mind coming back?' he persisted.

She glanced at him.

'I wanted to come,' she said.

'It's almost too good to be true,' he said. 'I can tell you it's most amazingly good to have you back.'

She felt, somehow, he wasn't quite sincere.

'You didn't mind my being away much, did you?' she said.

'Of course I minded! Of course I minded enormously. But I made up my mind not to mind overmuch, and I got through a frightful lot of work.'

He began to tell her about a new experiment he was trying in the mines. And she could see that this was where his life lay now: in the mines, in his mastery of them. He was determined that High Park, at least, should be exploited down to the last possibility and made to pay for many years to come in spite of all obstacles. He had become a larger shareholder in the mine, having bought out one of the members of the company. And he was risking almost everything on his new experiment with chemical by-products.

'I've actually been down High Park once,' he said. 'I sat in one of the tubs and was hauled out to the leading stall. It looks to me all right, you know. Since the war the mining proposition in England is a new one, and I think I know how to tackle it in our own case.'

So that was it! He had not learned to go on crutches for her sake but for the mine's sake: because he wanted to get to the coal face and inspect the conditions. It was the new fight for supremacy, for his master's rights and his master's fortune, which fascinated him. The real return for his money and his efforts he might not see for some years to come. But he was looking ahead.

'You feel so confident of the future?' she said, looking at him with wide, quiet eyes.

And she saw a shadow of hostility cross his face. He looked away from her.

'Why not?' he said. 'If we make the future we can be confident of it.'

There seemed something mechanical in this making of the future. He left out the human factor too much. Men could become exhausted as well as seams of coal, and humanity could cease to be a paying concern as easily as mines.

'I suppose that's true, 'she said.

'Why doubt it?' he cried.

'I haven't any strong faith in the future,' she said. 'I mean I don't think things will go on being the same.'

'Precisely! That's why we have to go in and make the change in time, so that we shan't be left.'

But she was meaning something else: something in life: something in the way of human feeling.

'And even supposing I'm not a good life for an insurance agent, there's Wragby, and there's you, and possible future developments in your direction.'

What did he mean by that? Perhaps his hopes. that she would have a child. She could feel in the silence that he was inquisitive about her. Questions he would never put audibly he was putting silently, almost forcing her into some kind of speech, some kind of confession, But she held herself mute.

And by the time they were approaching Wragby he was tired. She watched the life in him go grey, and she realised that he was not so vital as he seemed. His hold on life was tense, but there was a numbness somewhere, a partial deadness. He was very glad to be helped indoors. He was wheeled to his room in his chair. And he was almost oblivious of her again, oblivious of her return, of everything.

'You will rest now,' she said to him soothingly. 'And so will I. I am tired too.'

But he did not answer. He was unaware. This too had happened during her absence: except when he deliberately remembered her, she did not exist for him.

She rested; during the afternoon. At tea Clifford was still tired. The great effort of the day had exhausted him.

'It's marvellous having you back, you know,' he said. But she felt the tiredness in him, the absentness. He only spoke in a sort of premeditated way. So she talked to him quietly, desultorily, about France and about the people at the villa near Biarritz. She could see that in his mind he was searching for some possible lover among the company of bathers and dancers and tennis players. He lingered over the account of the mad musician. She was almost tempted to invent some fascinating personality that would give his mind something to play on. But she refrained.

And at length she asked:

'But you've had a quite exciting scandal here. What is the latest development of Parkin and the truant wife, as you call her?'

'The truant wife was peacefully in gaol for a fortnight. She came out some days ago, with money apparently. I don't know the details. To tell the truth, I'm a little tired of the affair.'

'And has Parkin gone?'

'He is due to go on Saturday, having procured the mild Joe and a returned Canadian called Albert to look after the wood. I hope they're on duty at the moment, the pheasants seem splendid this year.'

'And will all three be in the wood? It seems so many.'

'Probably not. In fact, Parkin himself may be in gaol this time. I haven't inquired.'

'What for, in gaol?'

'Why — oh, I'm tired of it — for having a regular stripped fight with Marsden on Sunday.'

'Who is Marsden?'

'Marsden is the lucky collier who threw out the truant wife, and now, apparently, has taken her back, having no one to cook his dinner for him in the afternoons.'

'And why did they fight?'

'Who?'

'Parkin and Marsden.'

'As two dogs will, over a coy female, I suppose.'

'And what was the result?'

'As a sporting contest, I can't say. I only heard that they spent Sunday night in the lock-up. But Parkin is supposed to have been on duty in the wood last night. I am finished with him on Saturday.'

'And what will become of him?'

'I haven't asked. Find work, I suppose.'

Constance finished her questioning. Clifford was tired, and apparently Parkin had offended him. At any rate, he had dismissed the fellow out of his emotions. Clifford was like that. He could blow out his feelings as one blows out a candle, and re-kindle them at his own convenience. If, indeed, one could call them feelings. In the vital sense, Clifford had no emotions. He had feelings as he had clothes, to cover his naked intention. Having virtually got rid of Parkin, after having been either thwarted in his will or injured in his self-esteem by the fellow, Clifford now blew out the candle which represented the gamekeeper in his own consciousness and emotion, and there was no Parkin. It was quite final. For Clifford there was no more Parkin. The candle was not only blown out, it was stone cold, and thrown in the waste box with other candle ends, the dead ends of feelings for people who had ceased to exist in Clifford's mind.

'But he has worked very faithfully for you,' said Constance.

'Quite! And now he chooses to work for me no more, and informs me he is no man's servant.'

'Why?'

'Who knows why? He is a malcontent in any case. I suppose he feels he is too good to serve a master.'

'He used to wheel your chair very nicely.'

'Did he?'

'Yes, didn't he?'

'He wheeled my chair, it is true. He could hardly do less when asked. As for the niceness with which he did it, I only know I never noticed it.'

'Then perhaps you ought'

'What?'

'When people do kind things for you you ought at least to know.'

'I never ask them to do kind things for me.'

'But Clifford! Look at Field! He is kindness itself.'

'I hope not. He gets ten shillings a week extra for the small amount of personal service he does me.'

'But the way he does it: and he's so pleased —'

'My dear child, then he experiences his own pleasure. I don't choose to mix up my feelings with my servants' feelings.'

'You should at least be aware of them.'

'On the contrary, to be aware of them is the greatest mistake any master can make when dealing with servants.'

'Parkin was hardly a servant.'

'Well! — say gamekeepers then. You change from Field to Parkin like a hare on a course. And by the way, why do you never put up such a good plea for the women servants?'

'I would, if there were occasion.'

'Occasion! Occasion! my dear child! There never was an occasion that wasn't made.'

'I shall go and see old Mrs Parkin.'

'Do, if it will amuse you to hear more unsavoury things.'

'They won't tell me unsavoury things. But I shall go and ask her what Parkin is going to do when he leaves you.'

'Do play the benevolent lady of the manor, if it amuses you.'

'Yes, I shall go now.'

'Have the car.'

'No, I shall walk.'

She did so, on the hot July evening when the miners were standing about in gangs or sitting on the kerb-stone. Very few of them took any notice of her. None touched their hats. Only some tradespeople and the schoolmaster bowed obsequiously — and even then, not the tradespeople from whom she bought nothing. These, like the colliers, ignored her: but not at all in an unfriendly way. She did not mind walking past all the miners. Their pale faces were not unkindly, nor were their uncouth, slightly distorted bodies. A certain peculiar warmth came from them to her, like the scent of pit clothes: a certain strength.

Old Mrs Parkin was tidy but flushed with heat. The little kitchen was hot as an oven. There was a good smell of newly baked loaves.

'Oh, Lady Chatterley! I heard you was away.'

'Yes! I'm back! May I come in?'

'You'll be broiled alive — it's bake day, and with two men as won't eat baker's bread —'

Constance sat down. The old woman waited to hear what she had come for.

'Is Parkin going away?' Constance asked.

'You mean Oliver?'

'Yes.'

'He's thinking of it, I believe.'

'Where is he going?'

'He's never let on.'

'Where is he now? Is he at the wood?' She had espied his nailed boots and leather leggings in a corner under the sofa.

'No! He's lying down. He's going out tonight.'

'Could I speak to him?'

Constance's heart suddenly went white-hot in her breast, and she felt she would faint.

'Well — he's having a bit of a rest before he goes out. Was it anything from Sir Clifford — anything particular?'

'Nothing from Sir Clifford. But I should particularly like to see him for a moment.'

'Well — I don't know as he'd want to see yer, if I maun tell the truth. He's got his mouth all cut and two of his teeth gone where that great bullying collier caught him one. — But Marsden'll go cock-eyed while he lives, so there's some comfort in that.'

The old woman had risen. She turned to Constance.

'Do you want me to call him then?'

'Yes please.'

'Am I to say as it's you? — I won't guarantee as he'll come.'

'Yes, say it's me.'

The old woman marched through to the inner room, and opened the stairfoot door.

'Oliver! Oliver!' she called crossly.

Constance heard a grunt from above.

'There's Lady Chatterley come an' wants ter speak ter yer. Are yer gettin' up?'

Constance heard the remote voice call sharply:

'Who?'

'Lady Chatterley! She's in t'kitchen. Art comin' down? She's waitin'.'

For an answer they heard a thud on the ceiling overhead.

'He's comin',' said the old woman, returning to the kitchen. Constance's heart beat terribly, and she felt faint.

'How hot it is!' she murmured.

'Hot enough without havin' to bake of a day like this!' said the old woman. And she crossly took up an old curved piece of sheet iron that was blacked glossy and smooth like a shield, and hung it on the bars of the fireplace in front of the fire. Constance little knew how familiar the clang of the little metal fire-screen was to Oliver. She heard his stockinged tread thudding down the creaking stairs, and she sat motionless.

As he came through the inner doorway she rose unconsciously to her feet. She only gazed at him in a sort of fear. He dropped his head and peered at her under his brow, so that she should not see his mouth. Then he moved forward into the kitchen and went and sat in the man's armchair near the fire, keeping his face averted from her, not looking at her.

'I only got back today,' she said, labouring with her breathing.

He turned slowly in his chair and looked at her, showing the whole of his face. His mouth and right cheek were bruised and swollen, his fierce moustache had a piece cut out of it. But she only saw the hard, almost hostile questioning of his eyes and the peculiar little patches of deadness on his cheekbones caused by misery.

'You are going to leave us?' she asked, still nervously standing by the door.

He remained seated, looking at her, conscious of his disfigurement. But his voice came harsh and strong.

'Ay about that!' he said harshly.

'Have you got other work?'

'Soon shall have,' he said in the same strong voice.

'Where? Where will you go?'

'Sheffield!' he said — and he seemed, in his harsh distance, on the other side of the moon.

'What will you do?'

'Me? What shall I do?'

'Yes. What work will you do?'

'What work shall I do? I shall drive a lorry, if I'm lucky, wi' a man as was my mate in th' war.'

His voice was so harsh, and his tongue seemed so thick, she would not have known it was he speaking.

She remained standing, and he remained seated, his feet, in their grey stockings, wide apart, and his face turned to the screened fire. He reached forward and with a quick cat's-paw movement jerked the screen by its brass handle and unhooked it from the stove bars. But it burnt him, and he let it drop with a clatter. The old woman, hastily taking a cloth, stooped and picked it up.

'A fool's thing to do with a red-hot screen!' she said. 'If you've burned yourself it's your own look-out.'

But he did not answer. He now stared into the glow of hot coals, red-hot, that half-filled the grate.

'Will you go on Saturday?' asked Constance.

'Or else Sunday,' he said, but his voice was dulled now.

'I brought you a silk handkerchief from France, to thank you for letting me feed the little pheasants when I wasn't well in the spring,' she said to him, panting a little as she spoke. 'Shall I bring it to you to the hut?'

He turned suddenly to the old woman and said in the voice of intimate authority which the ordinary workman uses to his women: 'Mother, step down to Goddard's an' get me an ounce o' cavendish.'

He fumbled in his trousers pocket for the money. She took it crossly, grumbling about running his errands for him. But she went out just as she was, in her apron, into the street.

He waited till she was well gone. Then he said in a small voice, sarcastically: 'Yo've 'eered all about our dustup, 'ave you?'

'I've heard about it. I'm very sorry.'

'Ay! Summat ter think abaht.'

His eyes were hard and unyielding, but there were little white patches on his cheeks, on the cheekbones, which troubled her more than his cut and swollen mouth and the missing teeth that showed their gap when he spoke, his tongue clumsy.

'I —' she said stammering — 'I mind about it awfully. I don't want you to go away.'

He hung his head, and she saw the veins stick out in his loose, hanging hands. Then he gave his head a tiny shake as he looked up.

'I canna stop now,' he said.

It was the finality of destiny, and she accepted it.

'But shan't I come to the hut to you before you go?' she said. 'Shall I come tonight?'

The hardness of his eyes darkened to misery as he watched her.

'Yo' dunna want ter do that,' he said dully, as if to a child. 'You niver know who's follerin' and doggin' me now. Nay, yer dunna want ter do that.'

He spoke with a kind of dreary indulgence, as if to a child that didn't understand, and he himself were stupefied.

'But I don't want you to go away from me. I'd leave Clifford and come and live with you if you'd have me,' she said to him.

He looked at her, then looked round anxiously. Then he rose and came and stood in the open doorway, looking across the little brick yard into the street. In the full light his face was a sorry specimen.

He turned and said in a low voice:

'You wouldn't do such a thing though, would yer?'

'I would come to you if you wanted me to,' she said.

His eyes slowly softened but still were dulled with misery. And he shook his head.

'Yer don't want to do anything like that, you know. You aren't mentioned. You keep yoursen out of it,' he said in a gentle voice, still as if to a child.

'But I missed you so when I was away. I don't want to miss you all my life,' she moaned.

His eyes looked at her, wondering if she really meant it. Then seeing suddenly the soft, lovely appeal of her face, his heart all at once ran into flame that tortured the stiff mask of his face and of his soul. She saw the light leap in his eyes and drop down.

'Yo' canna want the likes o' me,' he said, unbelieving.

'Don't you care about me?' she asked in the queer moan.

He looked at her, afraid. He was afraid of caring for her.

'Me! What's the good o' me carin'?' he said.

'Care for me! Care for me!' she moaned.

'Ah ber though!' he began with his old jerk. 'Dost want it?' The old, impulsive passion was spreading through him again.

She could only nod, nod, nod her head.

He heaved a deep sigh, fascinated. He knew! And he didn't want to know.

'Ay my God!' he jerked. 'If a man knowd what he should do! — Yo' mun leave me alone, yer know.'

'Can't I come to you?' she said, still in the queer moan.

'When?' he asked, looking down into her eyes. She saw the sudden slight tremor go over him.

'Tonight! to the hut!'

He gazed into her eyes, and a funny light, like a smile, had come into his own eyes. Then he went to the yard entrance and looked down the street. He came back.

'There's my mother!' he said in a low voice, warning but reckless. 'Ay, come if yer like. But dunna come afore midnight. An' if there's any other bugger i' t' wood afore then I s'll put a bullet in 'im. Come if tha' wilt. I s'll be theer.'

She looked up at him.

'I shall try to come,' she murmured.

The old woman appeared in the little brick yard.

'Ta'e thy 'bacca then, an' theer's a ha'pny change.'

He took both without a word.

'Well, if I can do anything for you I will: and I'm sure Sir Clifford would,' said Constance, moving through the door.

'Ay! Thank yer!'

'Good evening!'

She was gone, leaving him to explain to his mother what he liked.

'What's 'er want?' asked the mother.

'Ter know if I've got a job.'

''Appen so! An' what besides?'

'Nowt, as I know on.'

The old woman stared at him.

'Well!' she said. 'Tha'rt a picture, tha art.'

He took no notice.

As a matter of fact, the hot, defiant blood was rousing in him, and he felt, if Constance liked to risk herself, let her.

She spent a quiet evening with Clifford, but they were not in harmony. She found in him a certain arrogance, and he resented in her a certain heavy, cloying emotionalism. He told her that Linley, the pit manager, was retiring, and they had found a younger man, a man with energy and will.

'He'll put some discipline into the work. It's drive we need, and discipline. These ca'canny tricks have got to stop.'

Constance herself had no belief in the ca'canny method. At the same time she saw in Clifford the arousing of a new naked will which would compel work from men. He was clever, almost weirdly so. If the men had ca'canny tricks, he had ca'uncanny ones. And who would win?

She looked at her husband's light-blue eyes in a sort of admiration but also with dislike. He was a kind of robot after all, and she was not with him in his assertion of will.

'But do you think those methods will work?' she asked.

'What methods precisely?'

'Bullying.'

'There is no bullying to be done. Discipline! If you call discipline bullying. The mines have got to pay, or even the miners starve. And if the mines are going to pay the men must work for it like everybody else. They must. And we will see that they shall.'

'But you're not really thinking about them, whether they starve or not.'

'Am I not? And if that is not the first consideration with me, let it be so with them. They must submit to my control or ultimately they must starve.'

'Perhaps they'd rather.'

'Starve? Then it shows what fools they are, and that they must not be allowed to have their own way.'

She was silent for some time.

'I don't believe in that sort of control,' she said sulkily at last.

'Then what kind do you believe in?' he asked witheringly.

'There's got to be some sort of rapprochement. You've got to have feeling for one another.'

'Who exactly?'

'You and the miners. You must draw nearer to one another and touch one another like human beings. What it needs is a warmth of heart between you.'

'But my dear child, we aren't women. We're men. We are masters and men. And warmth of heart, as you call it, like the warmth of sweat, has to go into hard work. You can't hew coal with emotion: especially from a poor seam.'

'I think you can,' she said.

'Oh well!' he threw out his hands. 'It isn't your funeral, you see!'

They became silent, and the evening seemed long and oppressive, because they were opposed in flow.

'What did you do in the evenings when I was away?' she asked.

'I worked a good deal. And the new engineer Spencer came up sometimes. He's a very intelligent fellow and has an instinct for mining.'

'And did Mrs Bolton manage all right?'

'She managed splendidly. She knows very well what I want.'

Constance paused. Then she said: 'And what does she want. If she knows so well what you want, why don't you know what she wants?'

He stopped dead and stared at her.

'Because, Connie,' he said, 'that is by no means my affair.'

She said she was tired, and went up to bed.

If there must be a battle of wills she would fight too, even with her heavy passivity. And she was not on Clifford's side in his arrogance.

She came downstairs and sat in the moonlight in her own small sitting-room that had window-doors opening to the garden. There was a smell of honeysuckle, almost overpowering. At eleven o'clock she just walked out of the garden and into the park. It was bright moonlight.

There was no one at the wood-gate: neither was he at the hut. She had her key. Inside the hut was the bed he used now, of dry bracken and a couple of blankets. She sat down a moment. Then restless, seeing the bright moon outside, she slipped off her dress and went out stark naked into the cool shadows, breathing deep, because she wanted to be fresh. She felt stale and unfresh.

The dog came running towards her, and she heard his footstep. Naked save for her thin shoes, she walked across the moonlight to him.

'I am a little early?' she said.

He did not answer, being afraid of her.

'Turn your face to the moonlight,' she said to him. 'Let me see you.'

He did as she said, and she delicately touched the discoloured, swollen mouth. He stiffened a little. She pushed back his lip and saw the torn place where two of his teeth were knocked out. He was really disfigured. She felt depressed, yet she kissed the swollen place on his mouth.

'My love!' she murmured. 'I'm so angry! Are you?'

'I'm angry enough,' he said.

'Take your things off too,' she said, 'and be naked with me. We're so angry. Take your things off and be naked and angry with me.'

'An' what if somebody comes?'

'We'll shoot them.'

He went into the hut and took off his coat. He had hurried and was hot, But he got his coat off carefully, having a shoulder that was painful.

'Does it hurt you?' she asked.

'Ay, it hurts if I twist it.'

As a matter of fact, he smelled of liniment. She realised the smell now.

'I'd better not ta'e 'em a' off,' he said, hesitating, meaning his clothes.

'Yes, do! Do! I want you to.'

He came naked into the moonlight with her and she saw the discoloured bruises on his arms and breasts and sides.

'Do they hurt?' she asked.

'Eh!' he said impatiently. 'A bit.'

'You smell of Elliman's embrocation.'

'Ay, I expect I do.'

'Do you think I am beautiful?' she asked, standing back from him naked and white in the moonlight. To him the shadows where her eyes were made her ghostly.

'I should think so,' he said, noncommittal, without any feeling at all.

She laughed.

'You don't!' she said. 'Not a bit. And I don't even think you are. We are Adam and Eve naked in the garden and with no desire left in us. But I don't care. I like us as we are.'

She went and picked campion flowers and stuck some in the hairs of his breast, some in the hairs below the navel. And she made a trail of honeysuckle stay round her own breasts.

'Look at me!' she said. 'Do I look nice?'

'You look a figure!' he said, smiling.

'Suppose we walked through Tevershall village like this! — Wait, your flowers are falling!' She fastened long flowers round his thighs and round his neck. 'Suppose we walk through Tevershall village like this! What would they all say, do you think?'

'Eh!' he ejaculated. 'Nawt afresh.'

'Wouldn't they? I wish we could! And I wish I could hit every one of them across the face with this guelder-rose switch for having no nakedness as they should have, for which I hate them.'

She swished the air with the bough and lightly beat him on the body and the legs.

'Does it hurt you?' she said.

'No!' he replied, laughing.

'I'm dusting it off you. I'm dusting you clean.' And she continued lightly to switch him with the leaves of the guelder rose.

'Thy sort o' dustin'!' he said, laughing as the leaves tickled him.

'I hate them all,' she said.

'Tha hates 'em?'

'Yes! I hate them all, that they can't be naked like the moon. Look at the moon!' She put her hands under her breasts and tilted them at the moon. 'Kiss me, moon! Kiss me!'

He saw her white and sturdy, with full thighs, tilting her body to the moon.

'Tha're a rum 'un!' he said.

'You tell the moon,' she said. 'You speak to her!'

He suddenly spread his arms to the sky.

'Ay, come!' he said. 'Come down!'

But she suddenly ran into his arms, and he felt her cold freshness against him and the sprays of honeysuckle between. And the bloom of cold, jasmine-like beauty filled him like another sort of consciousness, her beauty occupied his whole body.

'Open to me! Open to me wide!' he said softly.

She kissed him, and clung to him.

'I'm going to have a child,' she murmured. She felt the pause in him, and the drop.

'Wait for me,' she murmured. 'Love me and hold me and wait for me. I'm going to have your child.'

She felt the long, slow rhythm of his breathing, and crept closer to him.

'Hold me!' she murmured. 'Hold me!'

He held her close, covering her with his arms and looking over her hair at the white moon.

'Folks like you,' he said, 'is more like the moon than this world.'

'But my world is the real world. Tevershall isn't real. They aren't real, all of them. Only the moon is real, and you and me. Say I'm real to you!'

She clung to him in supplication.

He stroked his arm down her tense, chill back, and the silky, cool sense of beauty, the beauty of her, took away his worldly consciousness for a while.

'Tha'rt real an' nowt else is!' he said.

She shivered with pleasure.

'Yes! The moon! And the flowers! And you!' she insisted. 'The wood is real. The sky is real. Only people aren't real.'

'Maybe!' he said. 'Maybe they aren't!'

This was the admission she wanted of him. She shivered again.

'Thar't cold!' he said.

He took her into the hut, and they lay down on his bed, wrapped in a blanket. And immediately she fell fast asleep. He lay with her in his arms, thinking and feeling as he felt when a boy, when he lay and saw the moon through the window, and he felt the dim great trust in his soul. It filled his soul now with the same vast stillness. And he lay with his back to Tevershall, indifferent to the whole of life as it lay outside. Somehow in the circle of his arms was the whole sky, the whole of another sort of life, the great living stillness. All he wanted now was to breathe the living stillness. He cared nothing about Tevershall and the days behind.

He did not sleep. And when the dawn came he woke her. She was warm as in a nest, with him: he had pulled the blankets and his coat over her, and she had slept in complete unconsciousness. Now she must wake, and the dawn was chill.

'Tha maun go,' he said. 'Joe an' Albert'll be comin'.'

'I don't want to leave you,' she said.

'No! Tha maun though!'

'I want to come and live with you,' she said.

''Appen we can contrive!' he said quietly.

She looked at him closely. In his face was that still, soft unfoldedness, like a very fresh, sensitive flower. It was this look, unconscious and unseizable, that filled her with mad love for him. It was so vulnerable, like a flower unsheathed from its defences, in pure living petals and breath of perfume.

And in all the sensitive unfoldedness a quiet repose of power, the power to live and to set life flowing. In the long run he was the master because life was with him. And Clifford, though he had a diabolic will and cleverness, had lost the softness and mystery of life.

But for the time being, the external power was in Clifford's hands, and Parkin was powerless.

So she left him, while he looked after her with the pupils of his eyes widened and softened; and she turned again, to see the mystery and the power in them. She smiled to him, and he nodded but without smiling. He was waiting again for his destiny.

She had arranged to see him again on the next day, which was Friday, his last day in the wood. On Saturday he would come for his wage and depart for Sheffield, leaving the unknown Albert in the cottage. Albert was a Scotchman who had married a Tevershall girl in New Zealand. They had come home for the war. They had five children, all of them to be poked in the cottage. This was as much as Constance knew.

The afternoon was hot and quiet when she walked to the wood to meet Parkin for the last time. How quickly her woodland idyll had come to an end! How soon he and she had ceased to have a home among the trees!

He met her in the big riding. His dog came running to her.

'What shall you do with Flossie?' she asked.

'I s'll leave her with Albert — she'll mind him.'

They turned off down the path towards the hut. When they came to the clearing she said, crossing to the oak tree: 'Let us look at our two nails.'

He came with her. The two nail-heads, rather rusty, were there just the same. She put her fingers on them.

'Side by side !' she said, looking at him.

'Ay!' he replied, turning his face away.

She glanced at him. He seemed to be withheld from her. She went and sat on the log at the hut. He took off his coat, repairing some traps.

'Where are you going to live in Sheffield?' she asked him.

'I'm lodging with Bill Tewson for a bit — him as I was with in the war — drivin' a lorry with the artillery.'

'What does he do now?'

'He drives a lorry for Jephson's Steel Works.'

'And will you do the same?'

'He says he'll get me on somewhere. Then when there's a driver's place comes empty I s'll get it. But I s'll have to be a laborer for a bit.'

'Hard work!' she said, looking up at him.

'Ay — what else, if you're going to earn your living?'

'Why don't you let me find us a little farm that you could work — and I could come to live with you?'

He was silent for a time, pottering with the traps. Then he stood up and looked at her.

'Are yer sure as you're havin' a child?' he asked.

'Yes! I think so,' she murmured.

'An' you don't want to have anything to do with me, like — you know what I mean — while that's comin'?'

'I think it's better, don't you?'

He did not answer for some time. Then he said: 'It's the way o' th' animals, so I should think it's right.'

'Yes!' she said softly, glad to get her own immunity.

'You know as I've put up for a divorce?' he said.

'Yes! When will your case be heard?'

'Not afore September. An' then there's another six months. Brings it about to next April afore I'm clear, all bein' well.'

She looked at him — and realised partly what he meant.

'Yes! I want no more of what I've had.'

She found him a stranger again. There was something hard and decided about him.

'So we mustn't live together before you've got your divorce?' she said, murmuring, looking up at him. His red-brown eyes with the small pupils looked keenly into hers. Today he was hard, and decided on his own way. Even the cut and swollen mouth only made him look more tiresomely resolute.

'Not afore then, whatever happens,' he said. 'I've got to be clear of 'er, if I live. — But you! You don't want to come and live with me, you know!'

'Why don't I?' she said softly.

His face had a peculiar expression of distaste, like a dog that wrinkles its nose in distaste.

'Why don't you? You know, though. You've had me — you know what I am like. It's comin' of a year afore you'll want me again — for that. An' you don't want to live with me. What's the sense of it! You only imagine it.'

'But why don't I want to live with you?'

'Why? Because you'll never make a gentleman of me, any more than you would o' Flossie there.'

'You'll be as much of a gentleman as I want you to be.'

He turned to her quickly with that sudden dangerous move that always made her wince.

'Ay!' he said. 'An' 'appen I shan't — and shouldn't! 'Appen I shouldn't neither: for I've no intentions o' bein'.'

The peculiar expression of vicious distaste wrinkled his face. She eyed him up and down and saw an enemy in him, to her hopes.

'But I don't want you to be a gentleman. I want you to be just a common man,' she said.

'Ay, a common man! An' what about you? Are you goin' to be a common woman?'

'I can try,' she said, looking up at him in innocence.

He threw back his head and shoulders in the violent gesture of impatience.

'What do you say so for!' he cried. 'It's nawt but foolery! You're a lady, you're more a lady than a woman — how can you help it? You're not a common woman, nor ever could be. No more could I be a gentleman. — But what's your idea, about living with me? What's your idea?'

'Well! I thought we might rent a farm — a nice little farm — or something else if you'd rather—'

'Wi' whose money?'

'Mine! I've got three hundred a year of my own.'

As a matter of fact, she had five hundred. But she thought it better to understate it.

'Six pounds a week, like?' he said.

'Yes! A bit more. We could live on that. And if we had a farm or something, you would be earning more.'

'Ay, two folks ought to be able to live on six pounds a week. An' what should you think of me if I was living on your money?'

'I should think a great deal less of you if you let my little bit of money come between us.'

He watched her keenly for a long time. Then he shook his head.

'You're foolin' yourself, you know,' he said. 'You think you can make a nice little place for me an' put me in it, an' keep it all nice accordin' to your own ideas: and say come! when you want me to come, and keep off! when you don't want me: and puss! puss! when you're pleased and summat else when you're not pleased. — But it'd niver work. I've got to be th' man i' my own house. An' you'd have to be my lady no matter wheer you was — except 'appen in Canada, when you'd have to wash it off a bit. But I don't care about Canada neither.'

He came to a stop, angry and clumsy.

She looked up at him, and angry flushes burnt in her cheeks.

'And what about your child?' she said. 'You don't want to make a home for that?'

'Eh!' — he threw back his head. 'That's yours! If it's a child it's yours. — And Sir Clifford's, if he wants it.'

The flushes burnt deeper in her cheeks.

'You mean now you can't get any pleasure out of me, you want to be rid of me — you don't want to think about me any more — you want to clear out to Sheffield or wherever you go, and be free? Perhaps you're not even going to Sheffield! Perhaps you're going to get away to Canada and wash your hands of everything.'

He looked at her curiously for a long time.

'Well!' he said at last. 'I don't see the good of foolery. I'm going to Sheffield to work in a steel works, and count myself lucky if I get fifty shillings a week. That's what I'm goin' to do. You, you're a woman wi' money an' used to money. You're a lady an' used to a lady's life —'

'I don't want a lady's life. I should like to learn to cook and bake and wash. If we had a cottage —'

'Ay!' he said sadly. 'At your own convenience, maybe. But if it was a force-put all your life long, you'd not like it. No, you'd wish yourself back in Wragby Hall. Don't talk! You don't know what it means and you never will: to be a working man's wife and bring up a family on three pounds a week at the best. I wouldn't want you to know what it means.'

'What does it mean that I don't know?' she asked proudly.

'It means drudging and dragging and whittling and worrying and bein' worn out wi' doin' things — an' bein' under.'

'Why should you be so afraid for me if I'm not afraid for myself?' she demanded.

'Because I know better what it means. You've never lived in a collier's kitchen, you know —'

'Good God! — Then I've lived somewhere else. You talk as if a collier's kitchen was some mysterious place like the Spanish Inquisition. Did you find it so awful?'

'Not me. But you would.'

'How do you know?'

'Because I do.'

'Ha!' she cried. 'Men are all alike. They're all gentlemen when it comes to preventing a woman from living.'

'It's like this,' he said harshly. 'You're up, and I'm down. You think if you came down a little bit you could drag me up a long way. If I held my mouth shut you might pass me off. Hell!' He looked her suddenly in the eyes. 'I don't want to be no higher than I am. I don't want it. Not for a woman's sake, nor for anything else. I don't want to climb up the ladder on your money. I want to stop where I am. I don't want you. I don't want nothing of yours.'

She went pale. This was an obstinacy and an imperviousness as bad as anything she met in Clifford.

'But — but why did you make love to me then?' she stammered.

'You wanted it,' he said crudely.

'And didn't you?' she cried.

He turned and looked at her.

'Ay!' he said slowly softly. 'Ay! I've loved it. I know it. — But I shanna ha'e yer tryin' ter ma'e a gentleman on me. There's too much difference atween us. I dunna want ter come up, mysen. — An' I don't want yo' to come down. I don't want it.'

'What do you want then?' she cried.

'Let be!' he said. 'Let be! Let me go to Sheffield an' get a job — an' let's see.'

'But if I have to go on living here the child will be Clifford's!' she cried.

'Well! It'll have a good home — aren't you pleased?'

'Don't you care? Don't you care about your child?' she asked in angry amazement.

'Me? No!'

'But you're unnatural!'

'It'll be thy childt. Tha'lt ha'e it.'

'But it will be legally Clifford's. And if I want to come to you later he can take it from me.'

'Let him ha'e it if he wants it. 'Appen when he knows who th' dad is 'e'll be glad to be shut on't.'

'Do you hate Clifford?'

'Me? What have I got to hate him for?'

Flossie gave a soft little bark, and went running down the path.

'It'll be Albert,' said Parkin softly. And he went on with his trap-mending.

Out of the path emerged a tall, clean-shaven man with a close-pressed mouth and a hard, keen blue eye that had seen all round the world without having been very much interested. He came forward awkwardly yet with the colonial challenge. Parkin stood and waited for him. Albert lifted his hat a little, awkwardly yet with the bacwoodsman's canny self-sufficiency.

'My lady, this is the new gamekeeper, Albert Adam.'

'How do you do!' said Constance. 'Have you moved into the cottage?'

'On Monday, mam!'

The man stood attentive, holding himself suspiciously out of communication.

'Last Monday?' said Constance.

'Yes mam!'

'Do you think your wife will like it?'

'Yes mam! Sure!'

'She was a Wragby girl, my lady. Her father was gardener in Sir Geoffrey's time,' said Parkin.

'And you,' said Constance to the new man, 'have been in New Zealand, haven't you?'

'In New Zealand and in California, mam.'

'And does England seem very small? I suppose this wood seems like nothing to you?' she said.

'A man does seem to be running up again a fence pretty often,' said the new gamekeeper. 'But if the country's small the people's plenty.'

'Yes indeed!'

There was an awkward pause.

'I shall be comin' down th' new warren in a while,' said Parkin.

'You will! Right you are!'

And lifting his hat, the new man departed again without a word.

'Where have you put your furniture, from the cottage?' she asked Parkin.

'My mother's got some — the rest is sold.'

'You've broken up your home?'

'I have that!'

He looked at her curiously.

'Do you like our new gamekeeper?' he asked.

'Yes! He seems plain and honest.'

'Oh, I think he's a good man all right — if you can stand his lingo.'

'Will you write me down your address in Sheffield?' she asked.

'Now?'

'Yes.'

He went to his coat and found an old bit of paper and a pencil. He wrote out the address: Mr W. H. Tewson, 47 Blagby Street. He gave it to Constance.

'Do you think I could come to see you?' she said. 'I could come quite simply, as Lady Chatterley coming to see one of the men who had worked on the estate. Perhaps for half an hour some afternoon.'

'Then it'd have to be Saturday. I'll ask Bill, if you like.'

'And write me a letter,' she said.

He hesitated. Then he replied:

'I'd better not be writing.'

'Send me a letter to Hilda in Scotland, and she'll forward it to me. Will you do that?'

'Ay!' he said reluctantly.

She wrote him down the address.

'And now goodbye!' she said, tears springing to her eyes.

He turned pale. Then he leaned forward and kissed her gently.

'Ay! We s'll see one another afore long,' he said softly.

'I wish you weren't going! I wish you were still in the cottage, and we had the wood for our own! I need you so, whatever you may say about being a lady and all those things. — Don't you need me a little bit?' she asked him.

He pulled on his coat.

'If things was different!' he said. 'If things was different, you an' me, we mightn't have been so fur fra one another.'

'But why need we be so far from one another, now?'

'Because things are as they are. High an' low, an' low an' high — it's further than California or New Zealand, as you met see by Albert Adam. Ay! It's about as far as life an' death.'

'But that's silly. You and I aren't so far from one another.'

'No! Not this minute. In an hour's time where shall we be?'

'I shall be in Wragby.'

'An' me goin' home to my mother's in Teversall. I believe if I wanted, I could be as good a gentleman as any of 'em — if I wanted.'

'Why of course — better!'

'On'y I dunna want, an' there it is.'

He looked at her unhappily, but with some decree of destiny written on his face.

'I only know I love you,' she said. 'I can't see that the other things matter.'

'They matter!' he said nodding. 'Oh, they matter! An' I wouldn't have not even you try to make a gentleman of me — I wouldn't.'

'But I wouldn't try.'

'You couldn't help it.'

She shook her head woefully. It seemed all so obstinately beside the point: like Clifford but at the other extreme.

'Well, goodbye! You will write to me?'

'Yes, I'll write.'

'And let me come and see you?'

'I'll ask Bill.'

'And if not there, then somewhere else in Sheffield: some park, or some tea place. Promise!'

'All right,' he said evasively.

'You don't really want me,' she mourned.

'Oh, I know I love thee an' a'. But when there's a big distance atween two folks what's love? — But I s'll see thee then, i' Sheffield.'

And a little light broke into his eyes as he said it, and he smiled faintly but intimately to her. She waved her hand and went. He made her feel irritated and depressed. Facts of circumstance meant so much to him in his stupid man's mind. To her facts of emotion were everything. But she believed that whether he knew it or not, he loved her and would find he could not live without her. In spite of all the things he said, something would draw him to her.

Two weeks went by. August Bank Holiday, which meant for Constance the outbreak of the war, also passed. Then she had a letter from Parkin. 'Dear Lady Chatterley, My friends Mr and Mrs Tewson say they will be very pleased for you to come to tea here on Saturday if you care to. Respectfully. O.P.'

This was a chilly communication indeed: especially the 'Respectfully. O.P.' Constance was offended and tempted to reply, 'Dear Mr Parkin, I am afraid I don't care to. Contemptuously. C.C.' But then it might merely be clumsiness and not knowing how to proceed. So she sent the reply to Mrs Tewson. 'Dear Mrs Tewson, Many thanks for your invitation to tea next Saturday. I shall come, if I may, about half-past four. Yours sincerely —'

But still, even as she posted the letter, she felt angry. What did the man mean by it! Was this his manner of showing that he was not a gentleman?

However, on Saturday afternoon she drove into Sheffield. It was not much more than an hour's run. She saw the pall of smoke ahead, and it looked ominous. She dreaded something, something in the very atmosphere of this unattractive town. She felt an ugly hostility.

Nevertheless, she did her shopping and called on the doctor with whom she had made an appointment. He was a clever and well-known man, and treated her with great respect. He told her she was going to have a child, but that she was perfectly well in every way.

Without thinking, she took a taxi to Blagby Street. The driver leaned out of the car and said, 'Where?' with such emphasis that she stammered. He seemed to think for a moment. Then he called to another driver: 'Hey, Luke! Wheer's Blagby Street?'

'Up Stanswell Road — after King Alfred — just after th' Crown and Anchor.'

The driver gave a long nod and started the machine.

Blagby Street was one of those steep streets paved with setts and lined with solid lines of dwellings whose roofs go uphill in jagged steps. It was as hard as a stone shaft and there was an endless succession of square windows and doors with two doorsteps on the pavement. The driver pulled into low gear, and the car ground dismally up. There were few people in the street's ghastly rigidity, a few children holding large slices of bread and jam, a man here and there, the queer, ghoulish men of the ironworks, disappearing into one of the little entries between the houses. All the doors and all the windows were shut, though it was a fine afternoon. But they were parlour doors and parlour windows, which Constance did not know.

The car pulled up on the tilt of the hill. Yes, the number on the hermetically sealed door was 47. The window-curtains of Nottingham lace were rigid. In trepidation, Constance paid the driver, realising as she did so that never in her life had she been up one of these streets and never in her life had she entered one of these so-called houses that seemed to her more like the kennels of some gruesome animals. Yet, of course, it was a decent street.

She knocked, standing on the upper stone step. Everybody had turned to stare. The taxi man, swearing, went on up the diabolical hill, crawling with noisy abhorrence. And at last, after a cruel age she heard someone unbolting the door.

It was Parkin, in his shirt-sleeves. He looked tired and pale and somewhat irritable.

'You've come to th' front door,' he said.

'Yes,' she replied, not knowing what he meant.

'Shan't you come in?'

She stepped into the small parlour that was furnished with a 'suite' in green cotton-velvet brocade, a black piano, various 'stands' with photographs, a gramophone, and huge 'enlargements' of photographs. The inner door was open. She heard scuffling in the inner room and saw children peeping.

'Shall yer sit down here or go in the' living-room?' said Parkin.

'I'll sit here a moment.'

She sat on the green cotton-velvet sofa and looked at him. How tired he looked, almost haggard! The heavy work had gone hard with him after his easy gamekeeping life. And he looked a workman now: he used to look different. He had sat down awkwardly on the piano stool, laying his hands on the imitation rosewood table. She was shocked when she saw his hands scarred and swollen, almost shapeless. They had been so quick and light.

'Your hands!' she said, shocked.

'Ay, that's where it catches you,' he said dully, opening his hands and looking at the swollen, inflamed callouses.

But he would not look at her.

'Have you found it very unpleasant?' she said.

'It takes a bit o' gettin' used to,' he admitted slowly.

'But why should you get used to it?' she asked.

He looked up into her face now.

'It's what every man has to,' he said.

She pondered. Every man! To him it was every man. To her, of course, it was just — oh well, no man she ever thought about.

'But you don't have to,' she said.

However, he picked slowly at a half-healed wound on his thumb, and answered not at all.

'Don't do that!' she said softly, and he glanced up at her swiftly, startled like a boy caught in misdemeanour.

'I'm a working man like all the rest of us,' he said into her face with challenge.

'Yes — but — do you want to be? — That kind of work?'

'Oh, I s'll be all right when I get a driver's job.'

'When will that be?'

Again he was slow in answering.

'You never know. 'Appen come New Year.'

How slow he was! How unforthcoming and irritating.

'I went to the doctor here,' she said.

He glanced up again swiftly, he had fallen to picking the wound on his thumb again, helplessly, revealing the state of his nerves.

'You did!' he said. And she guessed that he had been to the doctor too.

'Yes! He says the child will be born probably in February. He thinks it's three months almost.'

He ducked his head and left his thumb alone.

'Have you told Sir Clifford?' he said, very low.

'Not yet.'

'I have to go up for my divorce next week,' he said.

'Do you?' And she asked him a few particulars.

She saw how much this matter of a divorce meant to him.

'Why do you care so much?' she said. 'She probably would never bother you again.'

He stirred rather stiffly and wearily.

'I'll be rid of her anyway,' he said.

It was as if something had stiffened in his soul and would not relax. It was some sense of injustice perhaps: certainly some form of anger which included her as well. She could not soften him.

'Yes, it will be better,' she said softly.

A voice said insinuatingly in the passage:

'I've mashed th' tea.'

'Comin'!' he said, rising to his feet. Then to Constance: 'Shall yer come in an' have yer tea then?'

She could tell he hated the thought of this meal: he would feel a bit ashamed.

'Yes!' she said. 'It's very kind of them to have me.'

He went in front of her through the stairfoot passage, where the coats and hats hung, and where the pantry door opened darkly under the stairs. The living-room door had been shut so that they should be private. He opened it, and she became aware of another small room that seemed full of people, and a table that seemed oversized, spread with a white cloth and many glittering things.

'Oh how do you do? You're Mrs Tewson,' said Constance to a brown-eyed woman in a rather elaborate buff silk dress.

'That's right! On'y we usually say Towson in these parts, though we write it Tewson. Well where shall you sit? You must make yourself at home, you know.'

The woman, rather lean-faced and worn but with nice dark eyes, was pushing forward a chair.

'Hold on a minute, missis, there's me!' said a man in the background. He was medium-sized, pale-faced, but with alive grey eyes perhaps a little impudent. 'How do you do, Lady Chatterley!' he said, holding out his hand. 'I'm Mr Towson — or Tewson — whatever you like to call it: otherwise Bill! Pleased to see you! Make yourself comfortable if you can. I know it's a poky business.'

Constance shook hands with him, laughing because she did not know what else to do. He had queer, bright fair hair that went up from his temples.

'And the children. You must introduce me to the children,' said Constance.

For in the corner in the background was a boy of about eleven and two little girls rather younger.

'Ay!' said the mother. 'There's bound to be th' children. I tried to shunt 'em off, but would they — ! Not when they knowed there was cump'ny! — Come here, Harry, and show you know how to behave yourself. Say how do you do to the lady. Come Dorothy! Come Marjory love!'

Constance shook hands with the confused but honest boy and patted the cheeks of the two girls. The children were pale and nervous-seeming, except the little one: Marjory love!

'But she's a bonny little girl!' said Constance.

'The only one as doesn't shame 'er cupboard,' said her mother.

'Oliver, hadn't you an' me better put us coats on?' said Bill suggestively.

'It's what I've been tellin' 'em,' said the wife. 'But they that obstinate, you can't move 'em. And I'm sure they make one another worse. Now we've got Oliver here — Mr Parkin you know — I'm nowhere. No use what I say.' Bill had gone into the passage and got the two coats. There was a great shuffle, in the small place, of everybody getting to a seat. Constance was seated next to Oliver. Marjory love sat in a high chair beside her father, the other two children on the sofa.

'Not much elbow-room, is there?' said Mrs Tewson. 'I keep on at Bill to get us a bigger house, but it's like movin' a mountain. Let's see — do you take sugar an' milk?'

The tea cups were handed round.

'I can see my husband lookin' at these small cups — he's used to a big one. And so is Oliver — Mr Parkin — they both like plenty an' swilkerin'. But you've got to drink it up slow today, my lad!' she added to her husband.

'Yo'n made it that sweet, looks like I shan't be able to drink it o' nohow,' said Bill.

'Well drink a drop up, an' I'll fill it up. — What shall yer have now?'

Constance felt breathless. On the table was tinned salmon and boiled ham, tinned peaches and tinned strawberries, though it was fruit season: brown bread and butter, and white, and currant loaf —besides various home-made cakes and pastries.

'Have a few strawberries! Oliver — serve a few strawberries, if your hand'll let yer.'

Oliver very awkwardly served a few strawberries.

'Well 'ow do you think 'e's lookin'?' said Mrs Tewson. Constance looked rather blank.

'Mr Parkin I mean. How do you think he's lookin'?'

'Oh! Rather tired, I think,' said Constance.

'Rather tired! Ay! I should think so! It's cruel, you know, when you not used to it. Handlin' that iron all day long, an' those raw edges an' all, oh, it's cruel work at the best of times, an' when you're not used to it it punishes you something terrible. I really thought we was goin' to have him bad, what with a sprained shoulder and his hands in a mess you never saw. But he's got over the worst of it now, he'll soon be hardened to it. An' Bill'll see as he gets a driver's job as soon as one comes vacant. Bill 'as his say almost like one of the bosses, as you may say, in that. — Bill, can't you see to th' child. Marjory love, not on mother's clean tablecloth — no!'

Marjory love was emptying tea and tinned salmon with a teaspoon on to the fine white cloth.

The fine white cloth, the sparkling glass bowls, the bright knives and spoons, the pretty china — it was quite wonderfully refined! Constance marvelled all the time at the queer energy that kept it all going. Only the dessert spoon, with the tinned strawberries, did taste a little of metal.

The elder children were very good. Bill looked after the Marjory love casually, taking her little hand in his huge one and wiping it on her feeder. Then he proceeded steadily with his meal — for it was a meal to him and to all of them. They would not eat much supper.

'You're makin' no tea at all!' said Mrs Tewson. 'Isn't it to your fancy? Oh, you must eat or we s'll think it's not good enough for you.'

This was a dilemma. Constance started on currant loaf.

'How are you gettin' on at Tevershall, like?' said Bill to her. 'I've been over there, you know! Yes! I've stopped wi' Oliver over Saturday night in the cottage at Wragby — 'aven't I, Oliver.'

'Ay!'

'Really! But I didn't see you,' said Constance.

'No! I kep' mysen out of sight. But I seed you an' Sir Clifford in th' park. It's a lovely park, an' a'! But that was afore you took much notice, like, of Oliver.'

'Yes!' she said. And she wondered how much the man knew — how much Oliver had told him.

'Your ladyship never took no notice of me till we raised those pheasants this spring — and then we got sort of friends, if it's not sayin' too much,' said Oliver quietly.

'And if a man's kind to a person, be she lady or be she who she may, she'll feel kind back again. An' that's friends if you like to call it such,' said Mrs Tewson flatly.

'Oh, I consider Parkin and I are friends,' said Constance.

'You do! Ay!' The brown eyes of the other woman looked at her shrewdly, caustically. Constance flushed. She did not realise that Mrs Tewson was offended with her for calling him 'Parkin'. In Mrs Tewson's ears that was almost an insult. It was displaying her ladyship.

'Well!' said Mrs Tewson, after a pause. ''Appen there's friendship possible between them what's higher up in the scale an' them what's lower down. But it's bound to be one-sided. And it's silly to brood over such things.'

This was a shaft at Oliver. He was uncomfortable.

'Do you mind now,' said Bill to Constance, shifting uneasily in his chair, 'do you mind now if I ask you a plain question?'

'Not at all!' said Constance, flushing.

'Do you think there is much difference between people in one walk of life and in another, like? You know I don't want to say nothing I shouldn't, don't you? Ay! Well — do you think there is much difference between your sort of people and people like us? You see what we are — it's obvious. Everybody knows what we are. We're just decent working-class people. What would be the good of pretending anything else. But people like you! We never meet you. We don't know you. We don't know what you're like! And is there very much difference, do you think? Do you think there is?'

He had laid his workman's hand earnestly on the edge of the table, and was leaning forward, gazing at her with those wide, wide-open, perplexed eyes, under his rather thick, perplexed eyebrows. He was intensely in earnest in his wide-mouthed, anxious way.

'Not really!' she said, nervously turning one of her rings. And at the same time she was shrinking in a kind of fear from that pale, forward-thrusting, wide-eyed, intense face that gazed so full into hers.

'No!' he said, slapping the edge of the table. 'Not really! Really, really, we're alike. What I mean to say, our feelings are about the same. — I know we're not refined nor none of that. We're not gentry. But take the most of the feelings — they're the same? Aren't they? Most of your feelings are the same as most of ours, aren't they? I don't mean you personally, because your father was a painter, and artists are more free anyhow. That's how I can understand you might like to come here — something new for you, like, to see us in our own homes. But Sir Clifford! Sir Clifford! He's not free like you are. He's more one of the stuck-up ones, if you know what I mean. I mean — well, you know what I mean — he's more of a gentleman on the snobbish side. I can understand you better, being the daughter of a great artist —' Oh, if Sir Malcolm could have heard! — 'But take even Sir Clifford! His feelings and my feelings, are they so very different?'

Constance had thought many things during this tirade. So! They took her visit for a sort of bohemian curiosity. And they didn't mind, they put up with it. And they had not the faintest suspicion that she was Oliver's lover. The sly little devil, he had not let them suspect in the slightest. Even the woman didn't suspect. They thought it was bohemian curiosity and boredom. She longed to say to their noses:

'I'm pregnant by this Oliver Parkin here: been pregnant for three months.'

At the same time the queer white flame of earnestness on Bill's face opposite her was pathetic, pathetic. Were his feelings the same as Clifford's? Good God, no!

'Yes!' she said in her soft, composed voice.

'Eh?' he started. 'Yes?'

'Yes!' she repeated.

He stared at her with those bright, grey, intense eyes for some moments as his tension slackened.

'You mean to say there is a difference between my feelings and those of a man like Sir Clifford? You mean to say there is?'

'Yes!'

'There is? And a big difference? Big enough to matter?'

'Yes.'

He sat slowly back in his chair, his face very pale and as if bewildered. Then he quickly rubbed his forehead and ruffled his hair so that it stood on end. Then he gave a queer, quick, deep little laugh as he looked round, half-rueful, half-roguish, at Parkin.

'It's what tha towd me, lad!' he said.

Parkin did not answer. He suddenly seemed to Constance such a furtive bird.

'What did you tell him?' she asked softly.

'Me!' He looked her in the eye. 'I towd him folks like us an' folks like you an' Sir Clifford wasn't in the same world an' never would be.'

'But have you found me in a very different world from the world you are in?' she said.

'Ay!' he answered, pushing a piece of cake into his mouth, and speaking as he chewed. 'Different as owt could be.'

He spoke in a curious bitterness and heaviness.

'But need it be?' she said.

He chewed like an ox. Then he said: 'Ay, bound to be! Bound to be from the beginning.'

'Have another cup o' tea, do!' said Mrs Tewson. 'I'm sure these two men here, they'd talk the leg off an iron pot. They don't give a body a chance, Bill was bad enough afore, but since Mr Parkin's come I can't put a spoke i' t'wheel o' nohow, try as I may. A lot o' clat-fartin' ideas an' a' —'

Bill looked at her as if she was a noise somewhere away outside. He looked too as if he had had a blow. He leaned forward in his intense way to Constance.

'Now do leave it alone, Bill, an' offer folks a bit o' something to eat instead of all that talk,' put in his wife.

He caught himself up for a second, looked vaguely round the table, then into Constance's face, and asked simply:

'Shall yer have anything else to eat?'

'No, thank you.'

'You've finished? You're sure now? Don't let me put you off!'

'Nothing more, thank you.'

'Ay! Well now! Let's get to the bottom of this. You say there's a difference, a big difference, between the feelings of a man like Sir Clifford and a man like me. And Oliver says that even you and him are in different worlds when it really comes to: though you come from artistic people who sort of know all the worlds: and Oliver — Oliver's not so simple as he looks. Are yer, lad?' he added banteringly, turning to Oliver.

'I'm a fool of my own sort,' said Oliver.

Bill gave a funny roar of laughter, then subsided again immediately into earnestness.

'We're all that — fools of our own sort,' he said. 'But what I want to know — what puzzles me — is how folks can be in the same country —speak the same language — read the same papers an' all that — an' yet be really, really different in their feelings. That beats me. Take Sir Clifford now. He's got a wife. And I've got a wife. He cares for his wife surely! And I care for mine — don't I, dear, in my own fool's sort of way?' He laughed a guffaw. 'Well then! Well then, where's the difference, where's the difference?'

'You care for the sound of your own voice a lot more than you care for your wife,' said Mrs Tewson.

'Ay! Hold on a minute!' he said, glancing at her as if she were going to make him drop something. Then he turned to Constance. 'Where's the difference?' he insisted. 'Is there any difference?'

Constance was laughing at him and at his driving her into philosophic or analytic corners.

'There is a difference,' she said. 'But it's very difficult to put it into words.'

'Then does it matter? Does it amount to anything?' he asked quickly.

'Your wife's part of your own flesh and blood. Sir Clifford's wife is part of his fortune,' said Parkin harshly.

Constance looked at him in quick surprise.

'Misfortune perhaps!' she said softly, laughing.

'Fortune or misfortune, t'one or t'other,' he said.

Bill looked quizzically at his own wife.

'I might say my wife was part of my fortune,' he said.

'You might, for she's a good investment to you,' said Mrs Tewson drily.

'Hark at that!' he said with his guffaw of laughter.

And it was strange to see him instantly subside into perplexed seriousness, heavily serious, rubbing his brow in a sort of pain. He cared! Something deep in him was troubled. How queer he was!

'But does it matter if people are different?' she said.

'It's like this,' Bill said to her with utmost gentleness. 'There's many of us are socialists in our shop, and many of them are Communists, out-and-out bolshies. And they argue that our feelings, of us working men, and the feelings of the masters and bosses are two different things. They say that we feel for one another, to a certain extent at least. But the masters, they don't feel for anybody, only for their own pocket. Now is it true? Don't men like Sir Clifford have feelings for their fellow men, same as most of us?'

'Oh!' said Constance. 'Clifford is very kind.'

'He is! Kind for his colliers as well? You say so?'

'Yes!' said Constance slowly. 'I'm sure he'd like the miners to be as well off as possible. And I'm sure he'd help any one of them that was in trouble, if he could. He's very just.'

'There! There! You hear that!' said Bill, turning with accusing voice to Parkin. 'If a man's just and wants to be fair, you can't say much against him.'

There was a pause during which Mrs Tewson lifted Marjory from her chair and sponged her face, and the other two children wriggled out under the table and escaped. They had been prisoners long enough, having eaten all they could.

'Now mind Marjory, Dorothy, and don't go down on Stanswell Road, with all them motors. You hear what I say!'

'All right.'

'I'm frightened to death of those motors and buses and lorries. They nothing but a death-trap for children,' the mother said to Constance.

'They are frightening even for grown-ups,' said Constance. And she felt that she too should be leaving.

'Ay!' said Bill, who had been rubbing the hair on his forehead. 'If a man's just — if the owners want to be just and fair — well, I can't do no better myself, can I?'

'If you owned all the coal royalties the Duke of Oakwood owns, it wouldn't be fair for you to give any of 'em up, would it?' said Parkin, in his strange, vibrant harsh voice that somehow had a catlike voluptuousness in its harsh timbre.

'Ay! Well that's a different matter. Perhaps even the Duke would be willing to even things up a bit if the proper way was found to do it.' He turned to Constance, and asked naively, yet cunningly: 'Don't you think so?'

Constance, who knew the Duke, laughed.

'I don't think he believes there could ever be a proper way found to do it,' she said.

'You don't think he'd let go some of his rights, like, to even things up a bit?' asked the earnest Bill.

'He thinks things are evened up enough by what is taken from him in taxes,' said Constance.

'Ay, but that's another thing, that is,' said Bill.

She wondered over his seriousness. And she didn't see any great difference between taking the Duke's money from him in taxes, or taking away his royalties on coal.

'If he sort of felt,' Bill continued, 'something like this, shall we say. — Well! We're all men, all of us together. But I happen to be very wealthy, and many have just what wage they earn. Well! That's not my doing nor anybody else's. The world was made that way before we were born into it. We're not, so to speak, responsible, any of us. But perhaps the time has come to even up a bit, like—'

Here Parkin gave a loud hiss like a torn cat, and Constance laughed.

'Pff!' Went Parkin. 'Hold thy face! Hold thy face! Even up a bit! — Why, they'd rather be hung an' drawn an' quartered, rather than even up a bit; yi, an' rather than own as it would even be evenin' up. They don't think as we're all men together. That's blarney! That's blitherin' sawdust, that is! They don't think as we're the same as they are. They don't think as we're the same flesh an' blood. — An' they're right. They're nobbut sort of fishes, an' what they've laid hold on they'll keep, if you tear 'em to bits to get it from 'em.'

A strange, quiet, but deadly stream of hatred came out of the ex-gamekeeper. He hated Clifford and the gentry who had shot his pheasants at Wragby. He had felt insulted by them, and he hated them. Constance listened in irritation and depression. This kind of hatred got on her nerves.

'Oh but come now! They're men like we are,' said Bill. But even he lacked conviction as he said it.

'Nay they arena'! They're like fishes — there's big red ones like salmon, and long-nosed dirty ones like mackerel, and there's them you can a'most see through like whiting: ay, an' plenty of 'em's red herrings an' all! But they aren't — they arena' —, he shook his head rapidly — 'our sort o' men. I'm not one o' them, an' they're not one of us.'

Bill wiped his brow wearily.

'It seems like it sometimes,' he said.

'But surely,' said Constance, 'there are some quite human people even among the upper classes. The working people can't claim all the privilege of human feeling. Think of your own wife. Think of Tevershall and the people there — they're working-class people — and think how human they were to you!'

'Yes!' he said obstinately. 'I know it. I know it.'

'You surely can't blame the upper classes for your wife and the Tevershall bullies!'

'No!' he said. And he absently picked at the wound of his thumb.

'Do leave your thumb alone!' she said.

213

He looked up at her.

'Ay!' he said, in that harsh, peculiar voice with the metallic tomcat ring in it. 'The working class is devils, and the upper class is another sort of devils. But in the working class you can come to the end of their devilment. An' wi' th' upper class, you canna. They've always got a door shut in your face, an' they're always behind the door, laughing at you.'

'What door?' she said.

'Nay!' he retorted quickly. 'That's what I'm axin' you.'

'You mean even I have a door?' she said.

'An' hanna yer?' he asked drily.

'I wasn't aware that I'd shut it in — anybody's face.'

'Why you canna open it. You sit inside it like a cat in a garret, an' it's niver been opened — since you was a baby.'

From the scullery came the clinking of Mrs Tewson washing up the tea things. Bill sat staring at Parkin in dazed wonder, only half-comprehending.

'I don't think that's true,' she said.

'Yi!' he replied. 'You folks is all doors, an' you keep 'em all shut even with yourselves. And sometimes you open one, and sometimes you open two. But you niver open 'em all, not to God nor man nor the devil. You've always got yourselves shut up somewhere where nothing can get at you: Though a body might think you was open as the day —'

She paused. It was a new idea to her.

'But one must have some place private to oneself,' she said.

'Ay, you must,' he said dully, smoothing the white tablecloth with his dull, swollen hands.

She rose, offended. Really! The man always had some grudge against her.

'I suppose I shall find my way to York Road?' she said.

'Oh, Oliver'll go with you. — Well, it's been rare havin' a talk with one like you. You're a bit of a socialist, like the Countess of Warwick used to be, so you'll take no notice if we say too much. — Shall you come again, do you think?'

'I should like to.'

'These two men's great talkers! An' I can see as you like a bit of discussion as well. I'm not that way, myself, I keep off high subjects. But I hope as you wasn't offended at anything, you know,' broke in Mrs Tewson, who had wiped her hands and hastily taken off her apron, and stood once more in her smart buff silk dress, that hung somewhat sacklike, alas, from her rather stooping shoulders. Unlike both the men, she had no bearing, poor thing. Both Bill and Parkin carried their heads lightly.

She walked down the cruel stone street in silence, Parkin at her side. He wore a navy blue suit and a black hat, and didn't look quite like a workman. There was, for her at least, a certain stillness and distance in his face that was poignant as beauty to her.

'They are nice people!' she said. 'I'm glad they were so simple with me.'

'What else should they be?' he said.

But she was thinking of Lady Warwick! Lady Warwick! Did they see her like that?

They sat in the tram in silence, he with his swollen hands between his knees. He paid the tram fare for her, pushing his hand in his trousers pocket as the working men do. The tram was crowded, and she felt very strange. These people were as strange to her as if they had been Zulus or Esquimo — nay, more alien because their form of sophistication was more weird.

He left her at the corner of the York Road.

'Shall I come again, really?' she said.

'If you like.'

'Won't you come to Wragby one weekend? We could sit at the hut for an hour.

'I shan't come to Wragby — nor to Tevershall — while I'm getting my divorce.'

'Very well! Then I'll come to Sheffield. And we might take a taxi and go for a drive over the moor — or to Buxton —'

He did not answer.

'Wouldn't you like to?'

'Yes! One day.'

'Goodbye!' she said, holding out her hand.

He shook hands with her for the first time.

'Yo' mun take care o' yourself,' he said, 'an' don't you bother about things, you know. When I've got my divorce — '

She waited, but he did not go on. She was disappointed.

'Be sure and let me know how that goes,' she said.

'Yes! I'll let you know.'

She shook again his swollen hand and turned away to the garage. Her heart was sad for him and for herself. But also, she was rather pleased with herself. And she drew a sigh of relief when she was in the modest luxury of her own car, driving away from it all. She was glad she had been. But she was glad to go back to Wragby now. She had carefully fulfilled all her commissions in town, and she sincerely hoped she had bought just the thing Clifford had asked her for, for his radio apparatus. For he was very keen on the radio now, always trying for Berlin or Frankfurt or Madrid, He took peculiar delight in a German lecture or a Parisian opera heard in his own room at Wragby.

There was quite a party for the shooting. Clifford had asked Sir Malcolm, but that gentleman remained in Scotland. However, between relatives and friends from the

Cambridge and Eton days, there was a house-party. Constance enjoyed it too, all the fussing and all the talk. To be sure, the bang-banging down in the wood irritated her, and she conceived a dislike for pheasant at table: remembering the pheasants she had raised with Parkin. She felt one of her nauseas at the imbecile futility of men who could go shooting away at the beautiful half-tame pheasants and call it sport.

'There can be no sport,' she said, 'unless the thing you shoot at may shoot back, If a pheasant had a deadly little rifle under its wing —'

'You want another war—' said Sir Clifford rudely.

He and she did not get on very well nowadays. She was increasingly aware of Clifford's silent will trying to tyrannise over her. He wanted to dominate her stream of life as he had done in the past. But now that her stream of life no longer flowed obediently in the channel he drew for it, having found some sort of natural channel of its own, there was naturally conflict, though it was chiefly silent.

Clifford had taken to going out again. She could not bear motoring with him. The movement of the car acted on his nerves in an unhealthy way, he became curiously tense and irritable, and sometimes whistled to himself unconsciously for an hour at a time, like a madness, gazing fixedly out of the automobile. Then in town, he would get out and swing along the pavement on his crutches with those great, flying, stiltlike strides, the chauffeur running after him, Constance following in dismay. The excitement of it and the risk, and the staring of the half-horrified, half-compassionate people, was very bad for Clifford, It made him afterwards lie exhausted and shattered with nervous irritability. Yet he would do it.

'I shall be in the grave long enough,' he replied, when Constance urged him to stay peacefully at home.

And he always wanted her to drive with him. It became a torture to her at last to sit there in the car with him and his crutches and his poor, withered legs while the running of the machine ran his nerves into a kind of frenzy, and his face became like the face of some clock, registering only degrees of nervous tension, amounting after a time to a species of madness. She had finally to declare that she loathed motoring: which was true. So that if she wanted specially to go somewhere on her own errand, she went without telling him, leaving a message for him. And when she came back he looked at her in his tense way, and said:

'I might have gone with you.'

'Might you, Clifford! But I had so many silly little errands to do that take so long. You'd have been so tired.'

He was becoming much more irritable and abstracted as the weeks went by. The only thing that really roused him to life was the business. When it was a question of the mines he came to life. He spent many mornings at the pit, and many evenings the general manager or the engineer or the underground manager would sit closeted with him. He was like a madman again in his intense concentration on the mining industry. And when a strike threatened, or the market for English coal depreciated, he seemed to have slight accesses of apprehensive insanity, as if the end of the world were really coming.

His one great relaxation now was the thing he had at first so despised, the radio. He had a very expensive set and was very successful in getting all kinds of stations. But he had also a loud-speaker, and this was the bane of Constance's life. He was always looking blindly and abstractedly at his watch to see what time it was, which station would be calling. It became a passion with him to get the distant or difficult calls. Constance heard weird noises in the small hours and sat up in bed in terror. Then she remembered, he was trying to get New York, which would be calling at half-past two in the morning.

He seemed no more like a human being to her. He was really interested in nothing but these two things: business, and the radio. He had a passion, an obsession about the mines, and his strange, pale-blue eyes would be rapt as if in mystery as he thought out plans. And when all seemed to be going well he seemed to feel a strange, arctic sort of happiness. Constance herself was quite pleased for the money to be coming in. But with him it was something different, a sort of queer, thrilling delight like the humming of some sort of insect. It was the sound of bees thrilled with depositing their honey: and Clifford's honey was money.

Yet he was not mean. As soon as money began to come in, he was burning to spend it.

'Have your own car, dear! Have a car of your own and a man of your own,' he said generously when she had to wait a day for the motor car, once.

'Oh no, Clifford! I should hate it.'

'But why? The money is coming in!'

It seemed to be sufficient answer for everything. In quite a short time he had changed like this. She held her breath with amazement. His Plato, his painting, left him as an attack of measles might leave him. His passion now was to build up a fortune and make himself really a personage in the county.

But it was not natural. It was uncanny. He was no longer really human. She looked on him now as some weird bird or some creature whose soul has suddenly left it, while it lives on a sharp, often dislocated will of its own.

So, when pheasant shooting came in he must have a house party. He must have a great bustle round him. It served almost as well as the wireless. There were voices going, going, no matter what they said. And that was enough.

It was as if his soul had suddenly flown away from him and sat, perhaps, in the boughs of some tree somewhere within call. And if there was a noise going on outside him that he could listen to — listen in, as they say — he felt as if his soul was perched inside him again: or at least, as if there was no disjunction.

He was aware of Constance too, by an uncanny second awareness. By the strange owl-like look of his eyes when she came back from Sheffield, she knew that he realised quite well that she had been taking the great journey away from him. Yet there was so complete a rift between what he knew psychically, perhaps by telepathy, and his rational mind that he never for a moment doubted her when she said she had just been shopping. She saw that he accepted her word implicitly, like a child or an imbecile. Yet by his strange, forlorn, owl-like eyes she knew that some part of him was aware.

'Where's her ladyship?'

Those were the first words she always heard when he came in after having been out. And if she herself were out she could simply feel him groping after her through the ether. It was uncanny. Even Hilda had said to her:

'One always feels someone else's presence about you. Is it Clifford haunting you?'

'I hope not,' said Constance, going pale.

And she knew that she had sought refuge in the sanity of her passion for Parkin from the terror she had of the slight insanity of Clifford's fixation upon herself. She did not want to become fixed in her consciousness of him. Even now she could, if she would, come into a kind of communication or at least connection with him at any hour of the day or night merely by thinking of him. Then it seemed that his ghost or spirit became present to her: not to her body but to her own ghost or spirit. They held a ghostly interview.

And she hated it. It frightened her, and she loathed it. She loathed the baleful cold forces of the spirit and of the spirit world. It seemed like the very flame of corruption and disintegration. She prayed to escape from it.

Parkin had been her escape. She knew if she told him of her dread of Clifford and of the haunting obsession of Wragby, Parkin would really pity her and take her away. But she would not do that. She would not reveal her own weakness as far as that.

She did not tell Clifford that she was pregnant. And again, by the strange vacancy of his blue eye sometimes, she felt he knew. She felt that he knew. She felt that he knew, absurd as it may sound, in his shoulders, in his high, square shoulders of a cripple. But in his everyday mind he would never know and never ask, perhaps never even suspect: not until she told him in so many bald words.

She was frightened: inwardly and coldly frightened. And after her visit to Sheffield she admitted it to herself. She was afraid of the uncanny, of the morbid or disintegrative influence in her life. She was afraid of tense, unremitting human wills that turn into ghouls, fixed and destructive influences within the living ether. She recognised her eagerness for the vulgar healthiness and the warm passion of a common man like Parkin. But she dared not tell him so. She dared never let him see the sickness that was in her soul. She must always play the lady, the donor, she who gives the gift. She dared never let him see her as she was, somewhere in her old, tortured soul, as the leper who could be healed only by the bath of living blood.

Clifford had got a shooting party in the house, and was even talking about joie de vivre. 'Amazing fact, you know, but you never experience real joie de vivre until half your corpus is knocked out, really half of you is in the grave. Then you know what it is to have a perfect delirium of joie de vivre, the actual joy of actually being alive. Oh, it's great!'

She heard Clifford saying this to Duncan Forbes. Duncan was a painter, one of the moderns, and she had known him before she knew Clifford. He came from the same village in Scotland as her mother. He was a little older than herself, grave and quiet, though with a sturdy Scotch physique. He and she had always been friends since long before he went to Paris and became queer and modern.

Clifford liked him because he seemed so simple and sympathetic. 'There's a great deal of the child about Duncan,' he said easily. Perhaps there was. But it was of that sort of child which is father to the man. Duncan had a sort of second sight where people were concerned, and he saw through Clifford absolutely. Like some quiet hooded crow from the north, he sat and let the Englishman talk while he himself scented carrion and waited. He saw the macabre side of the affair perfectly.

And it was to Duncan that Constance confessed her condition. 'Don't tell anybody,' she said. 'I'm going to have a child.'

'Of Clifford's?' The question came like a gunshot.

'No! Another man's.'

'Oh!' But it was an 'oh!' of infinite relief.

'I haven't told him yet,' she said.

But Duncan wasn't listening. He was in a brown study.

'My God!' he said at length. 'I had a most horrible shock when you said that. I thought it might be Clifford's, and if that were so—'

'No, no!' she said. 'Far from it.'

He gave a little Scotch laugh.

'Very far?' he said. 'Do you want to tell one how far?'

'How?' she asked.

'Who the "other man" is?'

'No!' she said. 'I'd rather not.'

'Quite! A secret! — But a nice man?'

'Yes!'

'Why don't you go away and live with him?'

'I can't very well. And he doesn't want me terribly.'

'Why not? Does he care for you?'

'Yes! I believe he does.'

'You don't care for him?'

'Yes! I do!'

'Well then!' — For this young man, there was no more to be said.

'There are complications — on both sides,' she said.

'None on yours,' he said hastily.

'Clifford!'

'My God! Leave him!'

She went into a brown study, now.

'What I'm not quite sure,' she said, 'is whether I can let him be the child's father legally.'

'Would he accept it, do you think?'

'He has half-hinted he would — when I said I wished I could have children.'

'Hm, hm! Hm, hm!' The young man mused. 'Quite! Son and heir! Pass it off as his own! Local rejoicings! The young baronet presumptive! Quite.'

'It's not altogether unnatural — poor Clifford!'

'Not at all unnatural as far as that goes. There is to consider, though, as you say, whether you could hand a child over to Clifford: especially if it was a nice man's child. What does the nice man say by the way? Does he know?'

'Yes, he knows. He says: it'll have a good home, won't it?' Duncan gave a quick little laugh.

'That's a point of view. He's poor then?'

'Oh yes! One of the working people.'

'I see-ee!'

'But very nice — he doesn't know life in the least as we know it — not the — the really frightening side of it. He thinks Wragby would be a wonderful home!'

Duncan laughed again.

'Poor man! He doesn't know Sir Clifford Chatterley!'

'He does — as far as it goes — and can't stand him!'

'Hm! That's good anyhow. And what are you going to do then?'

'I don't know.'

'Why don't you set the nice man up in some sort of business and go and live with him?'

'He won't let me.'

'So you've mentioned it to him?'

'Oh yes!'

'And what's the objection?'

'Oh — tiresome! He's just getting a divorce from a very horrid wife — and he wants to be clear there —'

'Ah — I see! The gamekeeper story I've heard from Clifford! Hm! Hm! — Never mind if you've given yourself away. I don't know him and don't care. Go on! He wants to get a divorce from a very horrid wife —! When is he starting to get the divorce?'

'The case was heard yesterday. I saw it in today's paper — a decree nisi.'

'Six more months! And when is the child coming?'

'February — I suppose!'

'I see! A little too soon. — Do you think the gamekeeper — the nice man, let us call him — would marry you if Clifford divorced you?'

'Yes! I think I could make him.'

'What means would you take to make him?'

'I should show him how frightened I was.'

'Of what?'

'Clifford! Myself! Ghouls!'

'Mmm! Yes! Would it have any effect?'

'If he thought I was really frightened, really frightened of the unholiness of — of — I don't know what — of my future — he'd take me.'

'Would he?'

'Yes.'

'You're so sure! Is he so naive?'

'Oh yes! He's not a fool.'

'Can one be naive without being a fool?'

'Yes! Even I can! I feel I'm far more a fool, not being naive — than — than — But of course, he's fooled in a way. He thinks Wragby is terribly important and grand.'

'Quite! That's what I meant'

'But it's only a thin layer of him, the cold crust, that thinks like that. Underneath there's a sort of fire that doesn't care, doesn't know that Wragby exists.'

'One always hopes it is so,' Duncan said slowly, 'with the working people. But one has grave doubts. They seem to have Wragby fetishes very deep in their mental insides. It's only people like us who chalk ribald words on the fetishes and keep them merely for what they're worth — indoor space and a hot bath, and fresh vegetables.'

There was a pause.

'Where is he, by the way — the nice man?'

There came the banging of guns from the woods.

'Hark! They are killing his pheasants!' she said.

'Has Clifford gone in his chair?'

'Yes! He's gone too — with his gun!'

'My God! After the war and all! — and he lets off gunpowder at his own elegant and tame birds! My God! Sits there in a motor-chair and bangs away and bags a few birds, I'll bet!'

'Five yesterday!'

Duncan opened his mouth, and doubled up in mirthless joy. 'I wonder if he cripples any of them in the legs! By Jove, I'll ask him.'

'No, don't!' she pleaded. 'It's all mad, so let the madness go shooting pheasants rather than making scenes at home!'

'Quite! Quite!'

There was another pause.

'Have you any idea what you'll do? Do you think you might stay here and present Clifford with a son and heir? Come to think of it, that's a good joke!'

Constance, however, was gloomy.

'I don't think I can,' she said.

'You don't! If you can't take the child as a joke you'd better not.'

The crimson flooded up her neck and face.

'I can't take the child as a joke,' she said.

'Nor the nice man either?'

'Take him as a joke? Sometimes! But even he's got under my skin, so the joke is against myself.'

'I see!'

'Supposing I — I couldn't go to the other man —' she stammered —'and I had to go somewhere — would you help me a bit?'

'I? You mean come forward as the missing father? That's a good joke too!' But he spoke ironically.

'Would you hate it?' she said.

'I've no idea at all! I've no idea how I should react. I should have to think for ages before I knew what I should feel in such a complicated issue. — You know you and I were once engaged — what a lovely word!'

'Yes, I know.'

'It would be very fitting if we married after all — with a nice man's child thrown in for luck.'

'Yes! Quite!'

'Well! Suggest it to the nice man and see what he says.'

'One does feel free with you, Duncan, to be ironical about everything. It's a relief!'

'But a constant diet of it would be like living on iced cocktails. Yes, I know! And do you know, you make even me more ironical than I usually am. What does somebody say that irony is — the cleverness of a shallow heart? Something equally sapient! You and I must have very shallow hearts so that when we are together the shallowness goes off in sparks. Don't you think so?'

'I don't know what I think. I'm most frightfully tangled up. The world seems like all cheap descendants of the House of Atreus.'

'Well, you have one resource, you know.'

'What?'

'You can make yourself pitiful to the nice man! Save her, Mr Hercules, for she cannot save herself! It would take a man of the people to rise to it. But if it works it's fine.'

'I think I wanted you to jeer at me,' she said. 'It drives me back to my real sanity.'

'Quite! Don't look so blue about your real sanity, though. If ever you do need my helping hand, tell me, and I'll think about it. I'll do that much anyhow. So long as you don't ask for some more vital part of my anatomy —'

Constance went indoors to prepare for the return of the brave cohort of sportsmen. She heard the faint pip-pip of Clifford's chair.

That evening in the drawing-room Duncan said to her:

'You remember, Constance, when we were at the Villa Real de León?'

'Were you at the Villa Real then?' interrupted Clifford.

'For a very little while,' said Duncan coldly, bored by the interruption. And he still looked at Constance.

'Yes!' she said.

'There was an amusing little musician — I mean a little man who writes music and has no money but still has a valet — do you remember?'

'Yes!' said Constance.

But she was thinking of Clifford's face when he discovered that Duncan had been a guest at the villa near Biarritz. Constance had never mentioned the fact — Duncan had stayed a few days only on his way back from Spain. And now into Clifford's face had come a faint, subtle smile of hatred. The two men suddenly really hated one another for some reason. Previously they had been rather ironical friends, but all this visit they had been on hot bricks with one another. Now she saw the thin smile of real nervous hate on Clifford's face, and on Duncan's the blank of stony indifference: assumed of course, for his nerves were like hot needles.

'Well, he won about half a million francs at Monte Carlo, and the very next day the franc fell from seventy-five to a hundred and ten.'

'Bad luck!' said Constance.

'Yes! But what do you think he did next?'

'Changed into English money, I hope.'

'Not a bit! He gave all the money to the valet, and the sack as well. Yes! He said to the valet: I want to pay you off. Take this! And leave my services at once. — And he gave him the whole half-million francs.'

'Oh but he's mad!'

'I don't think so. But listen to the rest. The valet immediately wired to the man's mother for instructions — yes, he's got an old mother over seventy —'

'Connie, do you mind coming here for a moment!' said Clifford coolly and distinctly.

'Sorry!' icily answered Duncan. 'But I'm just telling her a little incident which I must finish.'

'Really!' said Clifford. 'And I absolutely must have Connie's assistance for a moment —'

She rose and went over to him, to move his leg and ease it of a certain cramp he had sometimes.

When she came back she said:

'And what is the rest of the story?'

'I can't remember. I've got a cramp of the brain. Do you mind hitting me over the head?'

'What for?'

'To make me forget the last two minutes, and take away my brain cramp.'

'Supposing we put on a fox-trot?' said Clifford's cousin, Anne Maitland, with utmost sang froid. And she rose to look at the music-rolls.

The next morning Constance received a letter.

'Dear Lady Chatterley, I thought you might like to know that my case was tried yesterday, and the judge gave me a decree nisi. It will be absolute in six months from yesterday, all being well. Mrs Tewson sends her respects and hopes you are well. She says perhaps you will drop in one day for a talk on socialism if not bolshevism with Mr Tewson. With respects from your obedient servant, O.P.'

She showed this note to Duncan, who read it calmly.

'O.P. 'Op! Is that the nice man's name? 'Ippety 'op!'

'Yes.'

'And will you 'ippety 'op to Mrs Tewson to talk socialism if not bolshevism with Mr Tewson, and meet the discreet Op?'

'I don't know.'

'Better take me along. I should like to look at the father of the heir to Wragby. He might even sit for me — and I'd present the portrait to Clifford when I congratulated him on the child. Portrait of Op, father of all future Chatterleys. — It's a wise child that knows its own father. It's an equally wise father that knows its own child. It's a great pity that with you I always talk so much. I might have been the father of Op's child, instead of Op, if you didn't draw words out of me instead of the seed of man. I suppose you had a child by Op because he hadn't a great deal to say otherwise?'

'I hadn't thought of it. Perhaps it is so. One does tend to talk away all one's —'

'Spunk!' he said. 'Quite! With you all my seed goes in words. Rather a waste, really. Oh, but I don't know! I shouldn't care to be the father of all future Chatterleys. Heaven forbid! No! I shouldn't care to be the father even of my own child. I know it wouldn't be half so clever as the things I say, and one couldn't forget it instantly. No! The infinite fornication of words is more in my line —'

Constance was silent. Though she was smiling involuntarily. It did her good to hear the amusing, scandalous things Duncan said. After all, the world was so full of cant and spurious emotions, the most decent thing one could do was to mock at it all. One must be able to laugh at everything. At the same time, one cannot laugh everything away.

'Do you think I've made a mistake, having Op's child?' she said.

'You haven't got it yet,' he said calmly. 'I suppose you'd have felt you were done out of something if you'd never had a child at all. If you wanted somebody to spill the milk then laugh now it is spilled. Would you rather it were Clifford's child than Op's?'

'It would be easier,' she said. 'I might forget it more instantly.'

'Probably you'd want to if it were a hall-marked little Chatterley. Because the bird's a bastard I suppose you'll feel you've got to be tender about it.'

'Not that exactly.' And suddenly as she spoke, her breath went, and her heart ran hot. The colour swept up in pain into her throat and face. 'I'm afraid I may love it,' she said, gasping a little.

Duncan looked at her wide frightened eyes and laughed. 'If you're afraid you may I'm afraid you will. So the milk's not only spilt, but the fat's in the fire.' He watched her curiously. 'Tell me,' he said. 'Tell me just this, Constance! Would you as leave it were my child as Op's?'

She looked at him with darkening eyes. 'It couldn't be,' she said.

He gazed at her shrewdly and ironically. 'My dear little Constance,' he said, 'do you mean to tell me that you really love Op? I don't mean in love with him. You're half in love with me and a quarter in love with Clifford, and the other quarter, I suppose you're in love with yourself. See how kind I am to you! But love! Do you mean to say you love that Op? I know you're not in love with him. Do you really love him? It can't be! Nobody ever loves anybody nowadays. They're all too busy being in love.'

She gazed at him with wide scared eyes, and her heart went hot and breathless again.

'I know what you mean,' she said. 'No, I'm not in love with him. —But I don't know about the other.'

'You mean about the love?'

'Yes! You see I'm not used to it.'

'No, by Heaven!'

He was smiling with a curious pain in his face, and she was watching him, waiting for his answer. 'You haven't been breaking many eggs about him as far as I have noticed lately,' he said.

'I know,' she said. 'I feel quite free of him: quite clear. And then a sort of fire comes up in me, and it's —'

'What?'

'Parkin.'

'Op?'

'Yes.'

'Hm!'

He mused for a time. 'And how long does this sort of fire last?' he asked.

'I don't know. I never know.'

'And do you like it or don't you?' he asked impatiently.

'I don't know that either. It's so strong. It's just him, as if everything in me was on fire, and the fire was him.'

'Hm! — And do you want to be with him?'

'Terribly.'

'Do you want to be with him now?'

She sighed.

'Yes!' she said.

'Hm! Then I hope the fire will soon die down, for it makes you boring. — How do I throw water on it? — I find people in love a bore, but apparently they're a beauty chorus compared to the genuine article. Ha ha!' He laughed a little theatrically and pushed himself into a corner of the big sofa, sulking.

She sat silent, with her hands in her lap, forgetting her sewing.

'I think a pregnant woman in a blue muse about the man who got her with child is the last word,' he said. 'Why don't you go to your Op if you feel that way about him? Why don't you 'op it with an 'op, skip and a jump?'

'He'll be at work in a steel works,' she said.

'More fool him! Any man's a fool who lets himself be a wage-earning slave, today. Don't waste any more time about him. Helots and hoplites! How much does he earn a week?'

'Fifty-five shillings.'

'Ha ha! Ha ha ha! Fancy the immortal fire hiring itself out at fifty-five shillings a week! Prometheus at tuppence an hour! Op at two dollars a day! 'Op along, sister Mary, 'op along, 'op along! How much have you got, of your own?'

'Five hundred a year, about.'

'Then why don't you buy him out?'

'He won't be bought.'

'He'll be sold, but he won't be bought. — Fire or no fire, I'm afraid Op's a fool, and if I were you I'd drink barley water and get the fire out.'

'He says he's his own sort of fool.'

'Says so, does he! Then he must be an extra one. Fancy priding yourself on being personally a fool! Ha ha! I'm tired of people, Ops, 'oplites and 'elots. Do you know what's the matter with people today — with me, with you, with everybody, including Op?'

'What?'

'Just a sterile and stale egoism that cuts us off from everything. It's not selfishness. Selfishness is still a sort of instinct. It's egoism, small, complete, and self-willed. With a paltry modern egoism, we are like grit between each other's teeth and grains of sand in each other's eyes. Each his own little ego like a grain of sand. It's not only the seed of Abraham that are like the sands of the seashore, it's everybody in the world. A whole Sahara of grains of sand, barren, egoistic little individuals who sing like sand sings, in friction: "Alleluia! Here am I! Wonderful, excellent, marvellous I!" And by pretending to take people at their own value, we keep the ball rolling. — "And the grasshopper shall be a burden, and desire shall fail!" I saw that quotation somewhere. I think it's fine. Not only the grasshopper is a burden, a ladybird is a burden, everything is a burden that is not oneself. Anything that is not myself is a burden to me. And desire has failed, thank God, so the little grain of sand is completely on its own along with all the other grains of sand. Myself! Myself! Myself! And the people who go about talking violets and pouring syrup over us to mix us into a sand-torte, a sand-cake, they are the foulest egoists of all, pouring the slime of their ego over one, like bird-lime.'

Constance sat in silence through this tirade.

'If I believed in a God, I should want him to destroy me. I shouldn't consider myself fit to live in a God-given world.'

'But a God of love would refuse to destroy you,' she said. 'You'd have to destroy yourself or find some other way out.'

'Exactly! That's just what he would do. I'm a grain of sand on the shores of the ocean of love! Ich, armer Tropf! — And don't imagine that you really love Op. It's only your ego. And it'll be his ego even more so. You'll flatter his vanity. The common people are a thousand times more conceited and egoistic than we are. And if that's impossible, then they're more squalid about it. We do at least keep up certain appearances. But they let the mangy dogs of their egos run loose and piss on everybody's doorpost. They're just as egoistic as we are, and more foul in their manners. Op's one of 'em. I could smell it in his letter. "The judge gave me a decree nisi —" as if the judge had presented him with a silver championship cup. He's a little egoist like all the rest. And I'll bet he's a squalid one, he wouldn't be willing to be the father of all future Chatterleys if he weren't. And the divine fire only means your own ego is up to some new little trick. I suppose you think you can put your ego over Op: that he is the simple passionate man who will let you come it over him. That's usually what love means: the fevered and excited attempt of one individual to impose his ego and his will on another individual: though it's usually the woman who is more successful at imposing her will and ego on a man. I suppose that's what you're after with Op! It's no fun any more with Clifford. He's a bony old bird, and his beak and claws are as good as yours any day, so you can only hop round the trouvaille of domestic carrion like a couple of old conjugal crows. But you think Partridge, or whatever his name is, is a more meaty subject for emotion and for subjugation. And if you can't make a complete conquest and annexation, you can at least establish a protectorate in pure benevolence. But if I know anything about miners and steelworkers, you've got about as tough a bit of egoism in front of you as our tough and egoistic post-war world provides. As tough as his own iron, and about as sensitive! He'll make a parade of his little self and get out of you what he wants — and then basta! Goodbye Dolly, I must leave you!'

Constance, who was sewing, sat smiling to herself, though she attended to every word he said. It seemed to her marvellously good, so clever and true. But of course, like all true things when they don't really get you on the raw, so amusing! And it didn't get her on the raw because Duncan was evidently so raw and exacerbated himself.

'Do you remember Voltaire?' she said. 'Modesty has fled from our lips and taken refuge in our hearts! It's my parody to fit my case.'

He twisted like a trapped snake on the sofa.

'It'll find a full house,' he said. 'No accommodation! Your ego is at home in your heart, so there'll be no corner for modesty to creep into.'

'It has wings!' she said. 'It can perch on the bedposts.'

'And drop droppings in your eye! I hope so.'

On the Sunday morning she set off for a drive with Duncan in his little two-seater. Duncan was a clever driver, and he loved speed. They were going for a run in the Peak district.

But as they were passing through Tevershall somebody saluted her. For a moment she did not realise. Then the figure in the navy blue suit and black hat jumped into her consciousness as the car passed on. She looked back. He too was looking back. It was her Op, as Duncan called him.

'Stop a minute! Stop!' she said hastily.

Duncan put on the brakes.

'Something wrong?' he said.

'Only I want to speak to somebody.'

The car stood by the kerb, Constance turning to look round. She waved to Parkin, and he came slowly forward towards the car, lifting the black hat. And in spite of the warmth she felt for him, Constance saw him ridiculous, rather small, rather stiff, with his ragged moustache sticking out and his wary movement. A ridiculous little male, on his guard and wary in his own self-importance! When the sex glamour is in abeyance practically every modern woman sees her man in this light, the light of her contemptuous superiority. It is the sex warmth alone that makes men and women possible to one another. Reduce them to simple individuality, to the assertive personal egoism of the modern individual, and each sees in the other the enemy. The woman, feeling for some reason triumphant in our day, man having yielded most of the weapons into her hands, looks on her masculine partner with ridicule. While the man, knowing he has given up his advantage to the woman and not having strength to get it back, looks on her with intense resentment.

So, Constance leaned out of the car looking at Parkin with her big, innocent blue eyes. And her warm-coloured, attractive face was soft and protectively tender, drawing him near. At the same time she hid her ridicule of him in her heart.

She was feeling triumphant. So! He had had to come to Tevershall, even in spite of the dreaded wife! Constance had not replied to his little note. She felt she had done enough running after him. If anybody was to run he must run this time.

And here he was! No wonder she laughed in her heart in ridicule of him. Her power had been greater than his. He had had to come after all, like a male dog helplessly running after a bitch. And his workman's face was pale and stiff. She gazed towards him with maternal solicitude on her warm face, and with ridicule laughing up its sleeve in her heart.

'How surprising to see you here!' she said. 'When did you come?'

'I com' this morning. I thought I'd see how Albert was getting on, now the gentlemen are shooting.'

'Oh, he's getting on all right. There are five guns this year — had you heard? — including Sir Clifford.'

'Ay. My mother told me.'

'This is Mr Forbes — perhaps you've seen him before. But he doesn't shoot.'

Parkin saluted Duncan, looking at him shrewdly with his hard, contracted red-brown eyes. Constance knew those eyes so well. They did not trust her. And they did not yield to her. When desire made them dilate and flash, then they loved her. But when they contracted again they mistrusted her, they did not love her. And now they were contracted almost to pain. She felt almost a maternal tenderness towards them.

But a maternal tenderness only occupies the breast of a woman. It does not go deep down into the sources of her being. There in the depths only the tenderness of the unknown can penetrate, and the warm gleam of the man, the male she loves. The deeps are dark, and in modern woman they are mostly closed up, closed up so completely and walled up so perfectly that their very existence is unsuspected. Only, from out of the walled-up depth come strange heavings and strange maladies.

With Constance, again, the deeps of her female self were closed up, and the mysterious stream of desire was stopped. She was living from her upper, superficial, maternal female self. She wanted to pity Parkin and be maternally kind to him, keeping her deeper self shut off and the mysterious stream that can flow all the time between man and woman walled back. It is the stream of desire, which should flow all the time, as a rule softly and deeply and unconscious, only at periods surging up into definite passionate desire, and sweeping everything before it. The stream of desire is the stream of life itself. It is that which unites us. It is that, even, which makes a nation a nation: the soft, invisible desire of people making a great swarm like a hive of bees. The clue is some unconscious, living idea which draws multitudes of men in a stream of desire. Such an idea as we have roughly described as Liberty and Democracy was the central clue that kept Englishmen streaming in the living activity of desire for so long. Now the idea seems dead, like a dead queen bee.

With Constance — and she knew it — the great stream of the deep desire was most of the time shut off. Her maternal feeling was much more superficial, more under the control of her ego. Her deeper desire was a flow that jeopardised her whole being. If she let it flow in vain, then all was lost.

Her Parkin! Yes, her desire had flowed towards him. But he, what was he? A limited little individual with no beyond. True, he had more mystery, more 'beyond' than Clifford. But then Clifford never asked for the stream of her deeper desire. He didn't want it. A sisterly comradeship, a maternal solicitude — and for the rest he left her free.

Clifford left her free. Whereas this Op made demands upon the deeper woman in her.

'Won't you come with us?' she said, suddenly opening the door of the small car invitingly. 'There's room for three, easily. You don't mind, Duncan, do you?'

'Not a bit!' said Duncan. 'It's your funeral.'

'I canna get in here!' said Parkin, recoiling and looking round the village.

'Why not? If it was Albert, he'd get in and think no more of it. Neither would anybody else.'

'Nay, I canna get in here,' repeated Parkin decidedly.

'Well, will you walk across the park to Stacks Gate, and we'll wait for you there?' she said.

He looked at her with those hard, contracted eyes. He knew so well she was putting her will over him. Yet he wanted to come. And a certain pain she saw in his eyes made her determined to have him.

'I shouldna! And yo' know it,' he said softly.

'Oh rubbish! You are always afraid. We'll wait for you then.'

'Well! I'll be as quick as I can,' he said with a small smile.

And she gloated in her heart, seeing how much he had wanted to come to her, to be near her.

'Don't hurry too much,' she said, with gentle solicitude.

He turned back to the park gates, and Duncan started the car.

'Op, of course!' he said.

'Yes!' said Constance.

And she sat musing. Her limbs, all her body was full of warm thrills and quivers, because he was going to sit beside her.

'Pity he's got that moustache and that gap in his teeth,' said Duncan. 'Otherwise he's quite a nice man. Quite pleasant to have a child by him, I should say.'

But Constance did not answer. She was now feeling jealous that Duncan should be there at all. She wanted Op to herself.

They waited at the end of the long field-path near Stacks Gate which connected with a gate in the park. At length she saw Parkin coming: and though the striding of the figure in the distance was always a little ridiculous, her heart ran hot at the sight of him. He was coming quickly, with his shoulders thrown back and his hat in his hand, under the September sun.

She held the door open to him invitingly, and he climbed in, squeezing himself as far as possible into a corner. He was panting slightly with the hurry, and Constance felt the warmth of him through her coat.

'You won't be cold?' she said to him. 'You won't be cold with no coat?'

'I'm afraid he will,' said Duncan, who was always warmly wrapped up. 'Here, he'd better take my scarf.'

'I'm all right!' protested Parkin, turning up his coat collar and buttoning his coat.

But Constance insisted on his wrapping the warm scarf round his neck and over his throat.

'Where are we going?' asked Duncan.

They decided to go across Sherwood Forest to Southwell because Duncan had never seen the minster.

Parkin sat very still, and Constance nestled near to him. Secretly she took his hand and held it hidden between them. She felt his fingers close convulsively over her own with the sudden, unconscious, possessive clasp. And she exulted a little in the convulsive nervous clasp. It was really in spite of himself. His hands, his body, betrayed his will. They would not let him resist her. She nestled her hand in his, feeling the hard callouses in the palm. It was a pity! He used to have such warm, quick, live hands before he went to that brutalising work.

'How have you been getting on with your work?' she asked him. 'Do you find it less trying?'

'Ay! I'm about used to it.'

'But you haven't got a driver's job yet?'

'I'm to go with Bill as his man next month. And then in January, when they get a new lorry, I s'll drive his old one.'

'And where does he drive it to?'

'Well, mostly over to Rotherham now, with steel rails.'

She leaned closer to him in the flood of desire which is quite safe because it knows it cannot abandon itself. Oh how voluptuously gratifying he was! She tenderly stroked the callouses in the palm of his hand, with pity. And he closed his fist and drew his hand away instinctively from her pity. So she laid her hand tremulously, tentatively, on his thigh, that seemed to her so strong and full of life. And she quivered with pleasure.

She knew he could make no demands on her. She was with child. She was safe from him. She could enjoy all the voluptuous pleasure of contact without any risk.

But he? How was he taking it? She glanced into his face, trying to make him look into her eyes, though she knew he would not. But she saw his whole body relaxing, and his face changing to that soft, unstrained stillness which made him beautiful. His eyes too were coming open.

Duncan glanced across at him. 'You're sure you're all right?' he asked kindly. 'Not cold?'

'I'm quite all right, thanks,' said Parkin with one of his quick glances at Duncan's long, pale, serious face. How men always sized one another up! thought Constance.

'Mr Forbes is a painter. Will you let him paint your portrait?' Constance said to Parkin.

'Mine? What for?' said the surprised and suspicious Op.

'You'd like to, wouldn't you?' said Constance to Duncan.

Duncan rapidly scrutinised the face of the other man. 'Yes! Very much!' he said, in the brief, detached tone of an artist.

'Will you let him?' asked Constance.

Parkin smiled slowly, in amusement. 'Has he painted yours?' he asked her.

'Mine? Often when I was younger,' Constance said.

'He'd better paint you again,' said Parkin softly.

'What I'd like to do,' said Duncan, who was pure artist now, 'is to paint you together. You'd be such an interesting contrast, and it would be so amusing to try to get the thing that's beween you —something indefinable, yet it's there.'

'Oh, do paint us together!' cried Constance.

'Well!' said Duncan. 'When will you come to my studio in Chelsea?'

'Oh, I'll bring him one day!' cried Constance gaily.

They had a jolly lunch, all three together, at Southwell. Parkin was amusing in a quiet way. Duncan seemed to draw him out. After luncheon Duncan went off alone to inspect the old church, Constance and Parkin walked slowly down the hill. They were warm and happy together, in sympathy.

'I'm so glad your divorce went off all right,' she said. 'Weren't you?'

'Yes! But there's six months yet afore it's final.'

'Ah, that will soon pass. And then what will you do?'

'How do you mean?'

'What shall we do at the end of six months?' she said. 'You and I? We can't stay apart like this for ever, can we?'

'Eh, I don't know!' he said dismally.

'Why don't you know?'

'What can we do?' he said desperately.

'What can't we do? It's quite simple. We can do what we like. We can buy a little farm or a house somewhere, or even we can go abroad. There are lots of things we can do if we think of it.'

'And what about Sir Clifford?'

'He won't mind so terribly. I often feel he hates me, lately — since I've loved you.'

'Why? Does he know anything?'

'Nothing at all. I think he thinks I'm in love with Duncan — Mr Forbes. But of course he never says anything. He wouldn't! Only I know I rub him the wrong way. Mrs Bolton is much better for him, she's so sly and soft and flattering with him. She'd soon console him if I left. No, he wouldn't mind really. It would hurt his vanity and his self-esteem, but he hasn't got a heart really, so it couldn't hurt that.'

Parkin pondered for a while.

'Nay!' he said slowly. 'It'd be a bitter blow to him. Ay! He's sort o' built up on the respect as everybody shows for him. And if you went he'd feel there was nothing left.'

'But why? Me, the woman, he doesn't care about. If he only cares about his wife then that's his affair. I'm not his wife really — as you know very well. If I'm anybody's wife, I'm yours.'

'Ay!' he replied slowly. 'You're not his wife of your own accord. But to him you're his wife. I expect it'd kill him if you left him.'

'Ah!' she cried, quailing. 'Don't you believe it! He's tough enough and knows how to draw into his own shell, and feel virtuous and noble and injured. He wouldn't die! He'd live all the longer if I left him. And I believe he knows it. — Besides, do you care so terribly if he dies or not? You don't like him.'

'No!' he said. 'I don't care if Sir Clifford dies. Maybe better if he did.'

'Well then! When you've got your divorce why shouldn't we live together, you and I, and really make a life? I haven't told Clifford yet about the child — and I shan't tell him. If you and I are going to make a life together, I shall never tell him. I shall go away to Hilda's in Scotland and wait there till the child is born. And then in March, when you're free you will come along and we can have a life of our own. I can get Clifford to divorce me, and we can marry or not as we like. About that I don't care. But live together we ought, and I know it. If we don't, it's a denial of everything in life and of everything I believe in, in life. Don't you feel the same?'

'Ay!' he said slowly. 'It'd suit me right enough. On'y —' and he looked her in the eye. 'I shanna come an' live in your house, on your money. I shanna! Because I canna!'

'But why? Why this mean, paltry spirit about a bit of money? What will you do then?'

'What will I do? This much! I've got to earn my own living an' live on what I earn.'

'But you could do that on a farm. You could make a farm pay,' she cried.

He was silent a while, then he said: 'Ay! If another man can I can. On'y —'

'Only what? Don't you want to?' she cried irritably.

He looked her in the eyes with a sort of pain this time, and he rubbed up his forehead, pushing up his hat.

'Back your life, I want to,' he said harshly. 'You can back your life, I do. I should be my own boss —'cept for you — an' I should be makin' my own way. Do you think a man loves draggin' his guts out all day long for three pounds a week an' niver no forrader, niver no forrader? It's prison, I tell you. It's worse than th' war, for you're doin' it for the money an' for nothing else. I'm glad to be able to earn three pounds a week — ay! But I'm a slave, doomed an' damned, an' I know it: with no hopes nor nothing. 'Cept 'appen the bloody show'll smash up. It would if I could make it! Do you think I don't want to get out? Do you think I don't?'

He gazed at her fiercely, his eyes flashing again with ferocity as they did sometimes with desire.

'Then why don't you?' she said. 'You know I only love you.'

'Ay!' he said harshly. 'Get out on it wi' a woman's money an' live on a woman!' He said it with extreme bitterness.

'But what does it matter, you'd work!' she said.

'Ay! An' t' other chaps? Would they all find women wi' money to pick 'em up an' start 'em on their own? They've got to ding at it till Doomsday, and their children after them, with no more hope in it than if they was dead. — There's Bill, he's a nice chap an' not touchy like I am. But he's got the collar round his neck, and he knows it, and it takes the spunk out of him. — Ay, I should get away on a woman's money! But what about all them chaps as'll niver get away, niver, not till kingdom come an' after? What about them?'

'But what about them? You're not responsible for them. When you were a gamekeeper, you didn't care about them —'

'Right! Right! I didn't! When I was under Sir Clifford, I didn't. I was like a bear with a sore nose, keepin' mysen to mysen. But I shan't do that no more. I'd rather work at Jephson's than be under Sir Clifford or the servant of any man. Ay, or beholden that much to any woman.'

He was trembling with conflicting emotions and pale as death.

'Why do you mind being so much beholden to me — or so little?' she said numbly. 'Are you afraid of me?'

He looked at her in torment. 'I'm not exactly afraid of you,' he said. 'You're a woman as wouldn't let a man down in that way. I'd trust you like I'd trust myself not to punish me for being beholden to you as far as the money went. You're on too high a level for that. Oh ay, I know it! I respect you!'

He stopped suddenly, looking at her.

'But you're afraid of me in some other way?' she said quietly.

'Ay!' he answered softly. 'Ay! I am! So I might as well own up, to mysen as well as to thee. I'm afraid of thee. Ay! That's what it is! I'm afraid o' thee!' He spoke very softly, almost with bitterness.

'But why?' she said, her eyes wide.

'How can I tell?' he said. 'But you're not an easy woman, you know. You'd want your own way. And if I was beholden to you I should have to let you have it, or I should feel myself a rotter.'

And what would it matter if you did let me have my own way?' she said indignantly. 'I should have thought you'd want to.'

'Ay, in a way! But a man likes to feel first in his own house. And it wouldn't be my own house. And I should be second, no helping it.'

'But what a paltry, cowardly way of looking at it! As if I cared who was first or second. Be first if you want to. I don't care if I'm second or seventy-second,' she cried.

'Yi!' he said. 'The very way you say it shows you feel yourself top dog, an' you're going to be top dog no matter who the man is, nor what.'

'But I'm not top dog, even with Clifford.'

'You are as regards yourself. You're top dog as regards yourself. You don't care about him.'

She was breathless with indignation and anger. Her blue eyes blazed with angry contempt.

'Well, if you won't come into my house for fear of being under dog,' she said scathingly, 'what would you do? Would you let me come into your house and me be the under dog, and you be the top dog — live like Bill Tewson and his wife and brats, all in one heap? Would you like me to do that?'

'You'd never do it, so what's the talk?' he said.

'No! I wouldn't! Not for you nor for any other little man who feels he must be God Almighty before he'll let a woman look at him. — But don't trouble, Mr Parkin! I'm running after you no more. We'll say goodbye this time, and finally! — if you're so afraid you're not going to be top dog. In my house, if you please, there is no top dog and no under dog, nor any dogs at all. We are human beings, and we let one another alone, and there is no fight for who shall be top dog. We have the decency to remain free on our own levels in my house. And in my house it shall always be so. I understand nothing of the nasty common business of being top dog and under dog.'

He smiled silently and sourly. 'All right!' he said. 'You asked me.'

'I'm very glad I did! For now I know,' she cried in contempt.

They walked back to the hotel in silence. Constance wanted now to get away. Her nerves were all on edge, and she was very angry. She sent Parkin to find Duncan — whom he found absorbed in some of the old Norman ornament of the church — and in a moment they were away.

'We'll go through Nottingham,' said Constance suddenly.

'Right you are!' said Duncan. And he waited for a corner, to pull the car round. He himself was in a good humour. He had not yet realised the gloom of the other two.

But Constance, sitting between Parkin and Duncan, could not bear herself. She could not stand the close contact of two men's bodies. But especially that of Parkin. She could not be unaware of him. There was his body touching her no matter how he squeezed himself into the corner. And the contact made her feel she could scream. The flow of sympathy was gone. He sat absolutely silent and withheld, hard and tense when the car swerved them against one another. But she could not get herself clear. Violent recoils ran through her nerves, and she felt at moments she could annihilate him.

The car sped along the narrow lanes through the still, fast-asleep villages of South Notts. It was all tall hedges and trees and old houses and cornsticks, the threshing machine standing silent in the stack yard because it was Sunday. A quiet little backwater of England.

But soon they came in sight of the Trent and the smoky heap of Nottingham. Thank God, she could get out soon. She could not sit between these two men any longer.

'Go to the Midland Station, will you?' she said. 'I want to see about a train.'

Duncan drove on towards the dark tower of St Mary's Church.

The town was quiet, with little traffic, and the railway station seemed deserted. But Constance found a porter and discovered that there was a quick train to Uthwaite in ten minutes, if she changed at Trent.

Duncan had come into the station with her, leaving Parkin with the car.

'I'm going home by train,' she said. 'The car upsets me.'

'By train!' he exclaimed in astonishment.

But she had gone to get her ticket.

'Perhaps you might pick me up in Uthwaite,' she said. 'Ask the porter when we shall get there.'

Duncan found that she would be in Uthwaite at 4.30.

'But why?' Duncan said. 'Why?'

'The car upsets me!' she said.

'If you're crowded at all —' he began.

'It's not that!' she flashed, knitting her brows. 'It's the car.'

Duncan lifted his hands. He knew her of old. He took a platform ticket and accompanied her to the train.

'Say goodbye to Parkin for me,' she said. 'Here! Take him my scarf. I don't want it in the train.'

'He can have mine,' said Duncan.

But her inflamed look at him made him take the blue and grey scarf into his hands.

They waited in silence till the train, almost empty, pulled out. He watched her go — her face flushed, her eyes wide and strange. But he knew her. It was useless to attempt anything.

He went up to the car and got in.

'Come on then!' he said to Parkin.

'And Lady Chatterley?'

'She's gone by train. Here, she left you her scarf —' he held it out to Parkin. 'She asked me to say goodbye to you.'

Parkin got in without a word, and they set off.

'She said the car upset her — in her condition —' said Duncan, as he changed gear up the Alfreton Road.

'In her condition?' said Parkin, who was sitting silent, peaked round the nose.

'When a woman is four months gone with child —, said Duncan.

The car sped on in silence. The two men sat in the unspoken sympathy of men who have suffered from the same woman. Duncan and Parkin liked one another instinctively.

'Did she tell you she was four months gone then?' said Parkin.

'Oh, we've known one another since we were kids,' said Duncan. 'My father was the minister where her grandfather was the laird, in the same village. We were engaged to be married once — ten years ago —'

'Ay?' said Parkin dully.

'We were both glad to break it off though. I think we both felt we knew each other too well. — Put the scarf on, won't you? It's none too warm.'

'I'm not cold,' said Parkin.

'You will be though. Put the scarf on.'

'Nay!' said Parkin. 'I'm all right. Let it be.'

After which, Duncan drove on in silence till they had passed Moorgreen.

'How's she going to get out from Uthwaite?' Parkin asked.

'I shall pick her up. The train isn't in till after four. — You'll be going back to Sheffield?'

'Me? Yes! I can look after myself at Uthwaite. There's train and bus.'

There was another long silence. The afternoon was grey and Parkin was cold.

'Here!' said Duncan, pulling off his own scarf and handing it to Parkin. 'Put mine on then! I'll take hers.'

And with one hand he quickly wound her blue and grey scarf round his neck, while Parkin silently pushed the ends of the fawn-coloured scarf deep inside his jacket.

'What went wrong? Anything you can tell me?' Duncan asked.

'I can tell you,' said Parkin. 'She'd tell you, it appears. It's only she offered me for us to live together — on her money — and I can't see my way to it.'

'What's the obstacle?'

'She'd wish she hadn't after a bit. She likes me, in her way. But she's always glad to get away from me. I've noticed it every time. Like today.'

'Perhaps you thwart her. Neither she nor her sister can bear to be thwarted.'

'I don't know as I thwart her. When we've been real nice, mind you, it's always been the same. "I must go now! Goodbye!"'

'To get back to Sir Clifford?'

'Ay, to Wragby.'

'I suppose she had to get back.'

'Yes, she had. But she was always that fligg to say it, I always knowed — "I must go now. Goodbye!" It was as if she was eager to say it to me.'

'And you minded?'

'I suppose I must a' done, else I shouldn't mind now.'

Duncan thought for a time. 'But if she wants you to go and live with her, she can't be so anxious to get away from you,' he said.

'She'd say it. From time to time she'd say it. And she'd go. Just to show as she was free to go: free to come, and free to go. She'd be my-lady just the same.'

'No, you're wrong. It's not my-lady. She was the same as a lassie, before there was any ladyship about it. It's her nature. — Why not let her do it?'

'Why, I don't care! On'y not to me. It's like a slap in the face when you've been that warm with a woman, and you could lie with your arm around her for ever. But she gets up. — "I'm afraid I must go. Goodbye!" You can feel her pining to say it, even before she does get it out. — It's like a kick in the balls to you, when you can't somehow let her go from under your touch.'

Duncan watched the road ahead. 'The thing a woman calls her freedom, it's a devil's instinct in her nowadays,' said Duncan. 'And I suppose you told her what you told me?'

'No! Not that! I didn't let her know that. But I told her I couldn't live in her house and take her money and let her be top dog. That's what sent her off.'

'It would! Letting a paltry thing like money stand between you!' Duncan smiled slyly and ironically. 'I can hear her. Mind you, she'd never begrudge you.'

'I know it! I know it! She'd never be mean,' said Parkin in a hot voice. Then he shook his head. 'But she'd get a man under. She couldn't help it.'

'She'd try to get him all to herself if she was keen on him. That she would do — try to pin him in some corner, all for herself. Would you care, though?'

'God knows!' said Parkin. 'I canna start it, that's all. I canna go into her house an' live on her money. I'd rather the steel fell on me and laid me out.'

Duncan looked at him curiously. 'Feel so strongly about it?' he said. 'I don't think I should mind that part so much.'

'You're different an' you're situated different. You aren't a working man. You're a gentleman of her own class.'

'I? The son of a poor Scotch minister! You'd better not let Sir Clifford hear you. He thinks I'm a long way down the ladder. Not that it matters to me. Nor to her — she's not got that sort of mind. — But why would you hate to go and live on some quiet farm and work it along with her?'

'If I had my own money I might. But I don't know — I'm a working man when everything's said an' done, an' I might as well stick to it. I was brought up wi' working men — why should I try to get up among th' others? I don't like 'em. I don't like gentlemen from what I've seen of 'em. So what should I want to go amongst 'em for?'

'You told me I was a gentleman.'

'Ay! But you're like her — you don't care one road nor another. You're sort of a bit of both. But I'm what I know I am, working class. What's the good of gainsaying it and trying to rise up!'

'You're very much like her, and like me — you don't really care,' said Duncan. 'You're not an ordinary man. You're one of the odd ones that don't fit in any class. I'm another, Constance is another, so is her sister Hilda. Clifford Chatterley's a bird of his class. It's his limitation and makes me want to kick him. — But you're no more the commonplace working man than I am the commonplace gentleman or she the commonplace lady. — We're all of us white blackbirds, when it comes to class limitations.'

Parkin puzzled over this.

'I know,' he said, in a secret voice, 'I'm not what Bill is — nor my mates at Jephson's. But that's because I never was a contented one. My mother always said something ailed me — so I suppose that's it. I was always fretting at something. I suppose summat's amiss wi' me —always has been. I've always felt it since I can remember — as if summat was amiss wi' me, an' I wasn't contented in my inside, like other chaps. Yet the men at Jephson's seems to like me, an' they don't want me to go. Neither do I want to leave them —'

They were already in sight of Uthwaite's twisted spire. It was early: Constance's train would not be in yet. The car ran on swiftly, in silence, till they were down in the knot of a town.

'Shall we go into the Sun and have a cup of tea? Or would you like me to drive you to Tevershall and comeback for her?'

'I shan't go to Tevershall tonight. I s'll go to Sheffield straight from here. If I go to Tevershall she'll be askin' for me, 'appen — and I don't want to face her again today.'

They went into the Sun, the old posting hotel that now is the motor-car hotel. In the lounge was a comfortable fire: and no people but themselves. They were quiet, neither having much to say to the other any more. Parkin glanced at the clock.

'I'll get the four o'clock bus,' he said.

'Will you?'

There was a certain sense of disaster. After all, the connection between Parkin and Constance was a real thing. Parkin was peaked and looked as if he was going to be beheaded. Duncan felt the sense of catastrophe, and his kindness rose again. It was ten minutes to four.

'I'll tell you what,' he said. 'If you'll stay here in Uthwaite till I've taken her to Wragby, I'll come back and fetch you. And we can talk it over: what you and she will do: or what you might possibly do. Perhaps you'll both manage better through me than with one another. What do you think?'

Parkin, who had a peculiarly forlorn look like a stray cat that's got no home, glanced suspiciously.

'Why what could we say more than we have said!' he exclaimed testily.

'God knows! Please yourself. I'll come back for you if you like. If not — you'll have to run for the bus.'

He looked at the clock, and Parkin did the same. But he did not rise. He sat sulkily in his chair till five minutes past four. Then he gave a sort of gasping sigh.

'Ay!' he said. 'I've no right, though, to let you go to a lot of trouble about it. Only what am I to do?' He looked at the other man in dismal, exasperated perplexity.

'I'm not going to advise you,' laughed Duncan. 'Perhaps if you both broke it off now it would be easier for you. The future's bound to be difficult. It's for you to decide.'

To this he got no answer. It was a quarter past four. Both men glanced at the clock, and each caught the other doing it.

'Ay, she's not far off now!' said Parkin grimly, and Duncan broke into a laugh.

'She might be your dreaded wife!' he said.

Parkin shifted jerkily in his chair.

'Ay!' he said shortly. 'A woman's nothing to a man till she's got herself inside him. Then it's worse than that malaria as some chaps got so bad out there in Gallipoli. It comes on in bouts, and all your inside turns over. I can feel her comin' as if somebody was going to stab me.'

'Why stab you?' said Duncan, laughing.

'Eh! It's how it feels. As if somebody was goin' to stick me in th' back o' th' neck.' He ducked his head between his shoulders, wincing away from something behind him.

Duncan laughed and reached for his gloves. 'Well!' he said. 'I'll be back here by six at the latest.'

'You don't want to bother about me!' Parkin persisted. 'Let me go by bus — or th' train.'

'Would you rather?'

Duncan put the question simply and finally. Parkin looked at him as a faltering boy might, uncertain, humiliated, angry, confused, and paralysed.

'I was thinking about you having to come and go,' he said awkwardly.

'Don't bother about me. I shall escape Sunday dinner at Wragby: that's good enough for me. Well! I'll be back here not later than six.'

'Here! You're forgetting the scarf!' Parkin handed him his wrap. Duncan was wearing hers.

'So I am! I'll bring you another.'

He went. Parkin sat down to listen for the train.

The train was almost punctual. Constance seemed very composed.

'I wondered if you'd have got here,' she said.

'Been here nearly an hour.'

'Yes. We had to wait at Trent.'

They went up to the car. She had seen Duncan wearing her scarf. Now she saw his lying on the seat.

'Why have you changed scarves?' she asked.

'Parkin wouldn't have yours. Op for obstinacy! Here!' and he pulled hers from round his neck.

She took it without a word, and they started home. She was calm and dignified.

'He told me you'd had a row,' said Duncan.

'Did he!'

'You've said goodbye for good, I hear!'

'Have we?' she said.

'He seemed to think so.'

'Oh!'

The thing went no further.

'I think it's probably just as well,' said Duncan. 'Incompatibility of station, you might say. Nice man though: much too susceptible to women though: and a bit of a boor, I admit, after Clifford. Clifford's every inch a gentleman — even to the half of his little finger that the bullet blew away. It must be somewhere, a speck of dust. It'll be a speck of gentlemanly dust wherever it is, refusing to mingle with the common clay.'

'Why not!' said Constance.

'Why not indeed?'

The car ran rapidly forward.

'Sunday tea-time!' said Duncan. 'I always think of the kirk. There's only three things a Scotchman can believe in: God, money, or women: and you can only believe in one at a time — or else in nothing. Connie?'

'What?'

'You're half-English. What do you believe in? Just yourself?'

'Probably.'

'Ay! as Op says. 'Appen so!'

But she was not going to be drawn.

'Do you know, Lady Chatterley, what I've promised to do?'

'How should I?'

'I have promised to go back to Op when I've deposited you, and take him your last word and convey him to Sheffield.'

He could feel the anger glow in her.

'You'll have to invent it then,' she said.

'What?'

'The last word.'

'Oh, that's no effort to me.'

He took off the gear as they came to the top of Tevershall hill. 'Surely the son of a Scotch minister can invent the last word of a woman like you!' he said as they ran smoothly down the long incline of the village. In a few moments he was tooting at Wragby lodge gates: they ran up through the dense coppice that screened the park, and to the house.

Constance got out. 'You're coming in?' she said.

'Didn't I tell you I was coming back?'

'But you'll have tea first?'

'Didn't I tell you we waited an hour at Uthwaite and had tea at the Sun?'

'But what are you going to say?'

'Didn't I tell you I'd invent it? I'm an improvvisatore, I can only do it on the spot. A rivederci! I shan't be back to dinner, so don't let them lay for me.'

And with a smile and a bow, he set the car in motion and swept into sudden speed round the oval sweep of the drive in front of the old house. He was angry. Constance could feel it in the very motion of his car. Well! she too was angry.

Duncan drove back very rapidly to Uthwaite. Parkin was not at the hotel. But in a few moments he came sauntering down the street. He hurried forward in some surprise.

'You've been quick!' he said.

'Quite! Get in!'

In another moment they were buzzing along the Sheffield road. Neither said anything. Duncan was too busy driving. And the miles dropped away. Nevertheless, lights were all on before they came to the town. It was dark.

'Have dinner with me,' said Duncan.

'Nay! I'll get home!'

'I've got to have dinner somewhere — too late to get back. I don't want to have it alone. So come and have dinner with me.'

Parkin could do no other than obey. They went to the Victoria. Duncan, being angry, was short and peremptory with the waiters. There was only a sprinkling of people in the dining-room.

'What'll you drink?'

'What are you drinking?'

'I'm having whiskey and soda.'

'I'll have the same then.'

Quick, nervous, and angry, Duncan began the meal. He drank up his whiskey and ordered another — also for Parkin. And during the meal he said nothing. After dinner he went to the lounge and drank a neat whiskey with his coffee. Parkin did the same. Duncan ordered more whiskey — and took only a dash of soda. Parkin did the same.

Duncan remained perfectly sober, only he grew intense. On his pale cheeks the pallor deepened. Parkin, being naturally fresh-coloured, became flushed, and his eyes grew very bright.

'Want to talk?' asked Duncan peremptorily.

'Ay — if you do,' said Parkin, his bright eyes growing brighter. Duncan had not yet uttered a syllable about her.

'I don't — particularly,' rapped Duncan. 'But I will, for your sake. She refused to send any message. She refused even to mention you.'

'She did?'

'Yes.'

Duncan sipped his whiskey.

'Wha' d' you feel about her?' he barked. 'Can you let her go out of your life — forget her — blot it out?' He spoke like an actor and made vehement gestures.

'I — I shan't die of love — I should think — if that's what you mean.'

'It's not what I mean. No man would die of love for a really modern woman, such as she is. But could you marry some other nice woman, a bit younger than yourself, and cut her out — cut her out?'

'I don't know as why I need marry anybody,' said Parkin, his bright eyes shining.

'Ha! You! If some woman didn't attract you you'd attract her. You're that sort. — How are you getting on in your lodgings with Mr and Mrs What's-their-name?'

'I'm all right. Tewson's their name.'

'And isn't Mrs Tewson in love with you yet?'

'In love with me? I don't know about in love. She likes me.'

'Thrilled by you?'

'Ay! 'Appen she is.'

'You thrilled by her?'

'I like her, but I'm not thrilled by her.'

'Husband mind?'

'No! I don't think so.'

'Do they ask any of their young lady friends in in the evening?'

'Ay! There's Bill's sister comes in most nights.'

'How old?'

'I've not asked her.'

'Thirty?'

'Maybe twenty-seven or eight.'

'Do you like her?'

'Ay! She's a nice lass as iver was.'

'Would you marry her?'

'Me? Marry her?'

Parkin's eyes were very bright and amused under this fire of questions. But at the last something like fear sprung into them.

'I've no idea of marrying her,' he said gravely. 'Nor of marrying anybody.'

But Duncan had seen enough in the recoil and gravity of the other man's eyes to know all he wanted.

'If Sir Clifford died — would you marry Constance?' came the next quick question.

There was a long pause.

'Ay, 'appen I should if she wanted me — if she wanted me — which I doubt. — And I don't wish Sir Clifford all that harm, mind you.'

'Of course not! And if you married her — would you go and live on a farm or in some pleasant house with her — in some place of her choosing?'

'I don't know! I don't know! What do I know? If I get a driver's job — we might live a bit out of Sheffield, in a nice house for her — and I could come in to my job.'

'Why do you care about your job? It's not worth caring about, I should have thought. Have some more whiskey. I'm having some.'

He pressed the bell for more drinks, then repeated: 'Why do you care about your job?'

'That's another thing!' said Parkin, lowering his voice. 'I'm secretary for our men, at our works, of the Communist league. That's another thing I don't want to drop.'

'Really! Does she know?'

'I've not told her.'

'Why not?'

'We don't brag about it a lot. — An' she's Lady Chatterley, mind you, be she what else she may.'

'So you're a Communist.'

Parkin glanced round the lounge.

'Yes! But we don't go round telling folks.'

'Really! And you want Soviets like in Russia?'

'Yes! Workin' men mustn't sell their work, it comes to selling your soul if you have to. We'll do our share of the work to keep everything alive. But we won't sell our work to make profits for other people.'

'You want to be like Russia? You want to kill off all the upper classes, for example?'

'No! There's no need to kill 'em — except maybe a few. But they can climb down an' be like other folks, can't they?'

'I don't know. A monkey can climb down a tree. But when he's down he's neither a dog nor a human being, he's still a monkey.'

'Monkey or no monkey, he's going to climb down,' said Parkin grimly.

'You think you can make him?'

The two men eyed one another narrowly.

'Ay!' said Parkin. 'An' goin' to.'

'Oh well!' said Duncan. 'That's all there is in it, really. — And do you think the lady in question would live with you if she knew this?'

'I don't know.'

'Why haven't you told her?'

'She never asked me. She's only told me her plans. She'd never think of mine. Do you think she'd live with me, at that?'

'Knowing you were secretary for the Communist league? I doubt it. She'd have to be a Communist herself. Which she isn't, not by any means.'

'She's not far off.' There was a wistful note in his voice.

'You think not? Well, I've not sounded her.'

'What's your own opinions, might I ask?'

'Mine? I haven't any. I should be a Communist if I were a working man. As I'm one of the privileged classes — at least I enjoy some of the privileges — I'm nothing.'

Parkin, bright eyed, watched him steadily.

'No!' he said.

'Then there's this!' said Duncan. 'Supposing she did feel herself in sympathy with your Communist thing — really in sympathy — and would come and live with you somewhere just outside Sheffield — you never know what a woman night do — would you be glad?'

Parkin's eyes shone with alarming brightness.

'Do yer think as 'appen she might?' he asked.

'I wouldn't answer for her for a second. She might, and just as easily, she mightn't. But if she did it would please you?'

'Ay, it would please me,' said Parkin, pushing his moustache from his mouth with a curious motion. 'If I could have times again with her like in the cottage — an' if I thought she'd back me up i' th' t'other — eh! Eh lad! eh!'

His face flickered with an unconscious smile, and from his eyes came the flashes only Constance had seen before.

'Do you think she might?' he asked with sudden gravity.

'Live with you — and back you up as a Communist? She wouldn't just at the moment. But in the future she might.'

"Appen a man, no matter how lucky he is, never gets but half of what he wants,' said Parkin. 'An' I've had my half — this spring. Eh, but I shouldn't like to think as I shall never have her again! I'd give my life to stroke her and feel her open out to me — stroke her at the sides of the belly — ' His eyes opened in a wide flash, then darkened in a kind of swoon.

Duncan emptied his glass again. 'Yet you won't go and live with her on her own terms?' he said.

'Eh! She'd niver open to me proper — niver the last bit. If I gave in to her she'd hold the last bit back. She couldn't help it.'

Duncan rang violently for more whiskey.

'And you don't mind if Clifford gets this child?' he said, changing the subject.

Parkin frowned.

'If she doesn't. It's her business —' he said impatiently.

He too drank his whiskey. Flushed, with eyes dilated, he was handsome, and there came forth from him a sort of power: a glow of soft, human power which made Duncan suddenly see democracy in a new light, men kindled to this glow of human beauty and awareness, opened glowing to another sort of contact.

'Why don't you get those two teeth put in?' he said.

'Eh?' The dilated eyes flashed with resentment and as instantly changed again. 'Ay, I will one day,' he said. 'Bill's wife is always at me about it.'

'Well!' said Duncan. 'There's nothing to be done at present.'

'No!' said Parkin.

'Leave her alone for a time — till she gives you some sign — or till you feel you need to see her. Then tell her about this Communist thing. It does matter to you, I suppose?'

'What? Our Communist club? Ay! It's something as I've laid hold of, an' I can't let go — like an electric thing. Ay, it's a sure thing.'

'Then tell her about it, some time in the future — and about the house outside Sheffield — and just see.'

'Ay! That's what I s'll have to do. — It's not so bad waitin' a bit, while she's havin' a child. Though mind yer, if I had her and could sleep with her held up to me, inside my arm — Eh well, 'appen I should only forget other things, an' do what she wanted an' repent it later. — I'll wait! I'll wait! I know it's best.'

His bright, dilated eyes seemed full of strange, unborn things. Duncan looked at him and rose, a little unsteadily.

'Shall we be going — before they shout "Time"?'

'Ay!' Parkin rose, squaring his shoulders against the hostile atmosphere of the hotel. It was not his own element. The peculiar physical glow of his presence made him conspicuous among the many men there drinking, and the hostility of the place was evident in him. Duncan laughed. He had long learned to be almost unaware of strangers in hotels.

Duncan insisted on driving the other man to his door, but would not go in.

'Goodbye!' he said. 'I'll see you again one day.'

'Ay! I hope so. And thank yer, yer know.'

'Right!'

Duncan drove away, feeling peculiarly lonely, as if some fire had gone out in him.

'If she feels like this she'll never let him go,' he said to himself as he drove out of the town and into the lurid night of the furnaces. The clouds were low, with a red glare. What did it matter! What did anything matter! Let the world end if it liked to end!

But Duncan enjoyed this sort of reckless, surging despair. It was so much more passionate and alive than his usual nervous tension. He rushed through the industrial night like Lucifer, smelling the sulphur far out in the country under the low sky.

And he enjoyed slipping to his room at Wragby without seeing anybody. When he had shut and locked his bedroom door he looked round in an exultation of triumph. He was alone! No one could come at him! This room was his own small inviolate world.

He left a few days later without having had any serious talk with Constance. He only teased her.

'Do you remember, Constance, when we were such warm socialists — or were we the last rose of the Fabian summer?'

'It was fun,' said she.

'Oh, fun for a time: till it became a bit too Webby. Do you feel anything that way now?'

'I?' she looked up at him. 'I suppose I feel very much the same. I'm a socialist as far as the County are concerned — especially after they've called on me — or on

Clifford rather — and been sweet. I'm a sea-green Robespierre for an hour or two. Then it fades. I'm afraid politics don't interest me any longer.'

'They aren't interesting. — And how about Communism and the "downright bolshies" as people call them?'

'Well! They aren't inspiring, are they?'

'Not to me. Yet perhaps they've got a sense of genuine injustice. And for an unsubmissive people that's a very real thing.'

'Yes! Yes! Only somehow I can't bother very much about big vague injustices that don't hit me personally. Life is always unjust. It is unjust for Clifford to be paralysed — and unjust for me as his wife. Fate and injustice seem very much the same thing. Everybody must bear their own injustice.'

'But what if they feel they can shake it off?'

'Then they'll have to do it, I suppose.'

He pondered for a time.

'You're frightened of Communism?' he asked.

She looked up, and pondered herself.

'Yes!' she admitted slowly. 'I suppose I am. I'm afraid of anything which is materialism — wages and state ownership — and nothing else.'

'What is it but materialism today?'

'I know. But today it leaves a margin for everybody not to be materialistic if they don't want to be. Clifford and I needn't be materialists just because a certain amount of material ease is assured us. It seems to me the only way not to have materialism.'

'And you and Clifford aren't materialists?'

'I don't think so. Are we?'

'Not far off, I should say.'

She paused, thinking something over. 'Anyhow,' she said, nettled. 'We aren't even then as materialistic, atavistically materialistic, as we should be if we were in Russia today. — Or do you believe in Russia?'

'No, I'm afraid I don't. Not that I know anything about it. But I feel it is atavistic materialism, just as America is progressive materialism. I'm perfectly willing to be shown otherwise though.'

'Quite,' she said. 'But one has a sinking of the soul at the thought of the Russia there is now. And in the same way, one has a sinking of the soul at the thought of Communism.'

'One does,' he said. 'I do myself. Yet I can see, the working people will have to do something about it sooner or later. And after all, England isn't Russia. A Tevershall collier isn't a Russian moujik. I can't see English working men battering your brains out just because you live in Wragby Hall. Can you?'

'No,' she said. 'I can't. And I don't think they would. They're much too human.'

'Quite! But they're becoming less human every year, it seems to me. Hopeless! I get an awful feeling of hopelessness, of death, in your part of the country here. — Do you know what I think the English really want?'

'What?'

'Contact! Some sort of passionate human contact among themselves. And perhaps if the Communists did smash the famous "system" there might emerge a new relationship between men: really not caring about money, really caring for life, and the life-flow with one another.'

There was a silence. Constance stitched slowly.

'It might be,' she said. 'Only I don't see how it's going to come out of socialism — or Communism. Why don't we start it now?'

'Because we know perfectly well we're all being carried around by the "system". We're all of us on a bus, or a merry-go-round, or a tram, or a train, or a pit-trolley, or in a private car, being conveyed around by the mechanisms of a materialist system. We never meet because we've only just got off some sort of conveyance, and we're going to get on another in half an hour. And so on, till it's the hearse. — It's the system. I believe the English, a sufficient quantity of them, are weary of materialism and weary of hardening their hearts to keep it going. — No, I've hated democracy since the war. But now I see I'm wrong calling for an aristocracy. What we want is a flow of life from one to another — to release some natural flow in us that urges to be released. Only we're all afraid we're going to be run over by the bus, so we hop on it and are carried away —'

Constance was not sorry when he hopped on his little automobile and let it carry him away to London. She felt he was trying to force her in some way. Ever since their broken-off engagement he had been trying to compel her to give up something in herself which she did not intend to give up. She said goodbye to him with relief.

Already October was coming in, in full yellow leaf. And she didn't want to bother about anything or anybody. A deep, voluptuous, almost lascivious indolence and contentment had come over her, a strange female contentment that had something vindictive in it. She was with child, and she felt well. She felt exceedingly sleepy and full of life, like a cat that has been out for a long night and now drowsily, lasciviously licks its own fur before the fire. Let no one disturb her! Particularly let no man try to disturb her or lay his thoughts on her. She felt she could tear him open with one stroke of her paw if he tried. Parkin or Duncan — à la bonne heure! Let them keep out of her way. It was her own hour now, absolutely her own womb-filled female hour.

Clifford left her alone. And this which made her hate him when she needed life and response made her appreciate him coldly now. He wanted nothing of her except certain appearances and certain housekeeping activities. She ran his house carefully and well. He was comfortable. He could go his own weird way unthwarted. And she wanted nobody. Let him turn on his radio and get Madrid or get heaven itself, she did not care. She was a good deal alone in her own room, with sewing and books, silks and writing materials. And she wanted nobody.

One Sunday evening when the radio did not interest him he asked her to stay down and sing something to him.

'Do sing something, Connie! It's so long since I've heard you.'

'It's so long since you've wanted to,' she said.

'Well, never mind that,' he said deprecatingly. 'I feel you're too much away in that room up two flights of stairs. Do sing — and I'll try to join in. Shall I?'

'Very well!' she said. And she went over to the piano.

She had a rather small but pleasant voice that tended to go flat. She tried their old favorites from Brahms, Schubert, Schumann — but they all seemed so sloppy now. She liked the more ordinary songs better. 'Oh can ye sew cushions, and can ye sew sheets!' Suddenly that became full of feeling for her. And suddenly even the 'Keel Row' was real to her.

> 'Oh wha is like my Johnny
> So leish so blithe so bonny
> He's foremost 'mangst the mony
> Keel lads o' coaly Tyne —'

There she was, lilting away, and never realising it was cruel to Clifford. 'And well may the keel row —' It delighted her. She rocked herself liltingly at the piano.

'I think blithe is such a nice word,' she said, not looking round.

'Connie!' he said.

She turned from the piano. And to her amazement there were tears in his eyes.

'Why?' she asked, astonished.

'It's not much of a gay life for you, is it, with me!' he said. 'I don't wonder you keep away from me as much as you do.'

She realised she had been unconsciously cruel, and her heart contracted. But she felt also the monotony of his self-centred thought. He was thinking of his own misfortune.

'Oh, but I'm perfectly all right,' she said. 'My life is what I want it to be.'

'Really! I'm so afraid you're moping — up there in your room.'

'Oh no — quite the contrary,' she said.

He looked at her strangely.

'I've not told you I think I'm going to have a child,' she said, suffocating a little in her throat.

There was dead silence. He looked down at his hands.

'I wondered if that might be the case,' he said quietly.

It was her turn now to be silent.

'When do you expect it?' he said in a strained, distant voice.

'Well! In the spring. March, I think.'

She sat on the piano seat, retired into her own pregnant self. He sat in his chair, his head dropped.

'I wondered if that might be the case,' he repeated in a musing voice in which she could read nothing.

'Aren't you pleased?' she said.

He looked up with an ironical smile. 'Vicariously, I suppose,' he said. 'I hope the man was at least —, His eyes flickered on her face.

She did not answer.

'It's not Duncan Forbes' child, is it?' he said.

'It's horrid of you to ask questions,' she said, retiring on to her dignity of maternity. 'Why must you?'

'That one popped out,' he said. 'It's such an obvious one —' And he smiled satirically.

'No, it's not Duncan's child,' she said calmly. 'If you ask any more I must go away.'

'One more mild one, dear! — At least it will have an English father—?'

'English! Yes!'

She rose.

'No! Don't go! I won't ask anything further. I take what's given. Gather ye rosebuds while ye may — And you? You're feeling rather bucked about it, aren't you?'

'Rather.'

'You look blooming. Curzon was saying what a beautiful womanly bloom you have. — Tell me this, Con. It's not really a question. Did you — did you do it for my sake, at all? I know it sounds egoistic. But if I felt you had just a bit of desire to do it for my sake —'

'I hoped it would make you happy,' she said swiftly, the blood dyeing her throat and face.

His eyes shone curiously, and he smiled with emotion.

'How beautiful you are!' he said. 'You are a virgin mother. A Madonna like a rose instead of like a lily. By God, I hope the child will be worthy of you. I'll get my paints out and try to paint you: the modern Madonna! — and I the Joseph! I shall fall into mariolatry —Mary-worship! What a wonderful woman you are! Give me your hand a moment, will you?'

She rose and gave him her hand. He kissed it and pressed it to his face. Then he kissed her wedding-ring. And she, as she stood, was thinking to herself: 'What a scene! What a scene! How one loathes being called a wonderful woman. But I suppose it's part of the divine justice that I must hear it from Clifford.'

Then he said to her: 'I hope it'll be a boy, don't you?'

'Yes! But we mustn't be disappointed if it's a girl.'

'Disappointed! My darling, wonderful woman, if it's a girl I can worship it as I worship you.'

Constance felt her skin going goose-flesh at this. 'Don't worship!' she said. 'It puts me in such a false position. Let us be sensible, whatever else we are. I'm awfully glad if you're pleased. But don't let us make a thing out of it. Let's be quiet about it. It's so lovely being quite quiet and letting Nature flow in one like a full river.'

'You're right! You're absolutely right!'

Constance went upstairs to her room as soon as possible after this scene. She had always an excuse now to be as selfish as she wished. And Clifford could not get up two flights of stairs without a great fuss of men to carry him. Indeed he never went upstairs.

Constance felt curiously sick, sick in her stomach, after the little scene with him. A deadly inward nausea came up in her. She could not bear him and his behaviour. No, she could not bear him to kiss her hand and her wedding-ring in that ghastly semi-insane manner. He was semi-insane. And of all diseases, insanity was most horrifying and repulsive to her. It seemed to her to proceed from evil: the soul being evil, the mind went mad. It went mad in order to fit the evil of the soul. For the first time in her life she wished he would die. She had never wished it before. And even now she shrank from herself. But yes, out of the remote depths of herself she felt a voiceless desire emanating. It was the wish, now, for his death.

This frightened her too. But tonight she was frightened with a drear, grey fear; the fear a woman has of baboons: the world seemed grey and baboon-like. And it seemed as if a doom was imminent, coming in like a slow, slow tide. Grey, slow, nauseous doom, she felt its oncoming dankness like a mildew on the walls of her room. And she could not bear it.

She had loved her room. It had delicate pinky-grey walls, and on the floor Italian rush matting that smelled sweetly of rushes, and a few thin Persian rugs on the matting, pale blues and old pink. And there was a spinet and a delicate rosewood writing table, and chairs in chintz with tulips, and a beautiful piece of toile de Jouy behind the sofa-bed. She had a delicate little fireplace of yellowed marble, and a bright fire of logs. And there were two big jars of pinky button chrysanthemums.

Tonight it was all dead. She saw her own effort after a beautiful interior like powder on the face of an old hag. Nor the fire nor the lamp could take away her nausea, nor remove her dread, as she felt the mildew of slow doom settling on the chintz chairs and the walls. And she herself, sitting alone in a soft chair by the marble hearth, was an old hag, immeasurably old. A hidden obscenity was creeping out of everything, and with it a terrible cold fear in her belly. How was it possible? Was the child inside her turning to a corpse? The thought filled her with unspeakable fear. Was she already a graveyard in her body? Why did she feel this cold, dread fear in her inside?

It came out of everything: not only out of the semi-insane Clifford, but out of the dank park and the sulphur smell of the pits, out of Tevershall beyond the trees. A grey, mildewy horror that would be the end of the world.

The mildew of corruption and immorality. There was a strange immorality in Clifford. Life was a thing he turned into a grisly phantasm. Just to suit himself, his own selfish egoism, she had now become a stainless mother, a virgin big with still another virgin birth. How horrible! A virgin birth in itself was an obscenity when she felt the warmth of the man inside her. The child was the life of the man inside her. How insulting to charge her with a virgin birth!

But so it was! Clifford had always hated sex: hated anything that was beyond his own egoistic control. And she herself had been nearly as bad. She recognised her sin with him: how they had thought, he and she, they could use sex between them and increase the ego that was in each of them. Each had wanted the triumph of the ego, she of her own, he of his own. And now he, stricken but persistent, was growing conventionally insane, his egoism was becoming lunatic. As for herself, she had half-gone over to something else, and half she resisted.

She thought again of Parkin. He too had some demon in possession of him, something that frightened her and that she must keep away from. But it was an alive demon, not an obscenity. It was a pale, deadly sort of anger which walked in his soul like a ghost. She felt the inevitability of it. She must wait, she must wait. She felt the anger pacing back and forth, back and forth in his soul, like a pale caged leopard that was determined to get out and spring in the face of the captors. Well, it would have to be so! She would have to wait.

But if the other thing, the tender, rosy thing that was between them, died! What if it died? She felt it had suffered a death tonight. She had betrayed it, and it had died.

What? What? The contact, the infinitely subtle living contact between her and him. The relationship. Duncan was right: it was the new contact that was the clue to life. She knew it now, now that it had suddenly broken off, and she felt herself like a dead limb cut off from the body of life. Till now it had flowed so warmly and surely with his child in her, she had never realised it existed. She had thought it was all just herself, her own superb health.

And now, tonight, with the world gone grey and baboon-like, and a cold, gnawing unease in her belly, she realised her mistake. There had been a holy thing, a living, flowing, intangible contact between her and the man. And tonight she, with her stupid arrogant will, and Clifford, with his baboon lips, had broken it.

Oh, how dared she trifle with it like that! It was life to her. Not the man himself, personally: but the contact she had with him. That was life to her. It was the only life-contact she had. She realised now that, broken off from this contact, she was only another grey baboon, pinky grey baboon like Clifford and like so many people.

And her heart surged against the baboon. They ought to die. They only lived in order to make everything baboon-horrible. They were as relentless as decay. They could know no change — only an increase in decay. They were that, and nothing else.

She slid to her knees and buried her head in the chair, and prayed helplessly: 'Save me from it! Oh save me from it! Save me from seeing it all horrible! Don't let it break between me and him. Keep him for me, keep him for me, and keep me for him! Don't let me betray anything. Oh, don't let me betray it. Show me what to do! What shall I do, what shall I do, not to betray? I don't want to betray. Oh, don't let me betray! Don't let me betray! For the child's sake, I mustn't betray. I must bring it into life, not into death in life! I want it to have life. Oh, I want it to live and have life. I want it to be born into life, my child! It's all I want for it —'

Her whole soul rose in a passion of prayer, as she kneeled with her face in the cushions of the chair. And she pressed the cushions to her breast, and gradually passed into a sort of stillness like a sleep, a peace, the coldness and the horror departing again. Her soul was coming warm again. The contact was coming back: she seemed to be going softly, warmly to sleep.

She started in a shock of fear and horror. There was a noise outside. Yes! There was a knock! Had he come upstairs? Horror of horrors, it had begun, the baboon persecution.

The knock was repeated. It needed all her strength and social drill to carry her to the door. Feeling herself turn to stone, she opened. It was Mrs Bolton.

'Sir Clifford asked me to come up and see if you were safely in bed, and if I could bring you anything,' the woman said in a soft, insidious, caressive voice.

'Oh! It isn't late, is it?'

'About a quarter to eleven.'

'Oh! I'm just going to bed.'

'And won't you have a glass of hot milk — or a cup of bovril and a sandwich? Do now! I'll bring it you when you're in bed. You'll need to take all the nourishment you can.'

'Why?' asked Constance.

'Sir Clifford told me!' said the woman with infinite confidential softness and secrecy. 'And I'm sure it's the best bit of news I've heard since I don't know when. Only of course we shall have to think of your ladyship now as well as of Sir Clifford. I tell him he'll have to take second place now. But he's very good, he'll be only too pleased.'

Constance stood in the doorway and listened to all this in a sort of swoon. The pale face of the other woman was soft and secretly exultant, and her eyes searched Constance's figure with peculiar eagerness.

'Oh!' said Constance. 'No! I don't want anything, thanks.'

'Are you sure now? You'd feel better. And can you take stout? I'm a great believer in Guinness myself, for those that can take it.'

'Yes! I rather like it.'

'Well!' It was an exclamation of delight. 'Then I'll order a couple of dozen tomorrow, and that'll be something. You expect it in March, Sir Clifford told me?' This last she spoke in a voice of utter secrecy and thrill.

'Yes. I think so.'

'That's five months we shall have to be thinking of you. May I ask a question: has your ladyship seen a doctor?'

'Yes! I saw Dr Theale the other day.'

'Dr Theale! Oh, that's good! He's safe, anyhow. And did he say anything?'

'He said I was perfectly all right — and he guessed it would be about the beginning of March.'

'Oh but fancy! I'm sure I'm that pleased!' and she gave a queer, hysterical little giggle. Then she looked at Constance with blazing eyes, full of knowing, as if she knew her secret and congratulated her in it. 'And your ladyship is pleased too, I should think?'

'Yes! I'm glad!'

'I'm sure you are. I'm sure you are! It's a woman's life. — And the lucky one is Sir Clifford, my word!' She gave another knowing look from her flashing eyes.

'Yes! I think I'll go down to bed now. Will you see that the fire is safe? I shan't want anything. I don't like eating at bedtime. So don't disturb me! Good night.'

'Good night, my lady! I'll see to the fire and put everything to rights here—'

Constance went down to her bedroom on the first floor, and locked her door. So! It had begun. The baboon-grimacing had begun.

Well, she must go away. Fool, fool, fool that she had been to think she could stay and let that ghoulish Clifford have the child. The child! The child! As if it had no say in the matter! Her living child, hers and Parkin's! Fool that she had been to tell Clifford! Fool that she had been to trifle with her very life, and the whole life of the child. She might as well have tried to break the great blood-vessel that fed the child in her body, and let herself bleed to death, and the child be a clod of clay. For the child's sake even, how could she think of that death-in-life, dooming it to Wragby!

She must go away, quietly, on the pretext of a short visit to Hilda. And then she must tell Clifford she would never come back, and ask him to divorce her. If he would not divorce her, she must find some way of saving the child from him. If she must change her name and go somewhere far away, she must do it.

It was strange, once her soul roused itself, how she hated Clifford: the deadness and fixity that had turned to obscenity in him: the morality that was so ghoulish. Never a breath of fresh life, never, never. Always that soft, putrescent tolerance, a tolerance that consisted in turning a false light on everything, to make everything, everything, even her very technical adultery, an event flattering to himself. Always subtly flattering his own vanity: like some highly bred, cunning ape, like a young-gentleman baboon! No, she hated him, and her pity for him was an evil thing, a cunning sort of selfishness of her own. Let him die! Let the tidal wave sweep him and all his sort away for ever.

Meanwhile she must go quietly, stealthily, as one would slip out of a baboon's den. And she must not trouble Parkin. She must send him a kind word as soon as she had got away. Then she must wait for him, till he had got his divorce, and she had got her child.

She must go to Hilda. And she must get her father's lawyer to act for her. She must get clear of Wragby for ever. She must wipe away all the slime it had put on her, all the slime of her ladyship, which she now loathed like a disease. My God, how good it would be to be merely Mrs Parkin! She would feel honest again. She had always, always felt dishonest as Lady Chatterley. She had always felt a sneak, somewhere, when they said 'your ladyship!' to her: though of course, also, her vanity had loved it.

But now, to get away from the whole leprous contamination of it: to be just Mrs Parkin if she could; or else take back her own maiden name: to live in an ordinary house in some suburb! What bliss! To be out in the cold air of life, not stifled in the lifelessness of Wragby.

No, she needn't go into a workman's dwelling! But some farm-house, or some suburban villa with nine or ten rooms — she didn't care! Anything, to be in contact with life. And if she could possibly be in contact with the working people, well and good. It would be nonsense to try to pretend to be one of them.

She breathed deeply and clenched her fists. Ah, she felt happy! To be going, to be going for ever! To be going away from this! How she hated Wragby, the great deadhouse that it was. How she hated the very conceit that was built into its walls. Generations of superiority, centuries of conceit! The very walls were rotten, the very mortar that held the stones together was crumbling in a deathly dry rot, rotted with inane, inert conceit of superiority long since evaporated. She wished she could burn the place down before she left. What a tomb! What a tomb! And she had never known it. In spite of all her free life and experiences in the artistic world, she had accepted Wragby as as good as she could get.

Till she had loved Parkin — her Op. Yes, she loved him. He was a man, if he wasn't a gentleman. Anyhow there came a breath of fresh air with him, and a breath of fresh life. My lady's fucker, as he called himself so savagely! How he had hated her for not taking him fully seriously in his manly fucking! Ah well! The future was still to hand!

THE END

Other titles from the Blackthorn Press include:

D H Lawrence: Complete Short Stories, Complete Travel Writing, Complete Plays, Complete Essays, Complete Novellas, Complete Poetry and all the novels. Wilfred Owen Complete Poems, William Wordsworth Selected Poems, Brontë Sisters Selected Poems, Winifred Holtby Truth is Not Sober, Trollope Complete Short Stories and many other titles available as paperback or ebook.

All these and other titles are available from our website www.blackthornpress.com or from the Amazon website.

Printed in Great Britain
by Amazon